MENACE FROM THE OCEAN'S FLOOR

On a bleak little island in the West Indies, Griff Gunston faced many baffling questions. Why were so many small island cruisers adrift and abandoned? Why was the sea disease that Griff's scientist father was investigating radioactive? Why were the colonies of octopi growing larger and becoming so strangely organized and daring?

Before the answers could be found, civilization blanked out beyond the isolated island. Atomic attack had left the little group isolated, alone in a world gone silent, in a world about to endure the terrors of atomic fallout and total devastation.

But before Griff was to find the answers to the manmade terror he learned that still another danger had come—the danger from the ocean floor where a new and competing type of intelligence was prepared to seize the world for itself.

Turn this book over for
second complete novel

SEA SIEGE

by

ANDRE NORTON

ACE BOOKS, INC.
1120 Avenue of the Americas
New York 36, N.Y.

Project Sea Serpent

I

ONE DUPEE—BEACHED

"PERFECT OPPORTUNITY—chance of a lifetime!" Griffith Gunston exploded to the empty reaches of the wide blue sky. "I don't think!" he added forcibly.

He was standing defiantly, his hands on his hips, breasting the trade wind. It was blowing steadily, pushing the booming surf against reef and rock, sounding an organ's deep notes, bending the bushes and trees with the flail of its invisible current. Griff knew that down on the beach one could hear another song, the tuneful whisper of sand on the move, as restless under the push of the wind as he now was under the lash of his personal frustration.

There were few real heights on San Isadore. It was an island born of the sea, not of volcanic eruption. But the coral block building, once part of the old saltworks, which his father had turned into a combined laboratory and home, was on the cliffs. And from this vantage point of headland Griff could now survey not only the sleepy indifference of dying Carterstown but look across the wide sweep of Frigate Bay to the waves smashing on the barrier reef—that division which separated the shallows he had explored, during his exile of the past few weeks, from the depths into which a skin diver dared not venture.

5

Below him, the *Island Queen,* swung at her moorings, her spars bare to the pull of the wind. And beyond her the rich aquamarine of the water was split by a wedge of silver flying fish. It was a world of color—the sea. But, on the other hand, the island hues were muted, ghostly. Here was none of the gaudy luxuriance of the tropics that one might find elsewhere in the West Indies.

San Isadore was truly a sea island—encased, encrusted in salt. Gray-white crystals gathered not only in the beds of the old saltworks but about the trunks of the trees, at the roots of shrubs, and lay in crusts on the thin soil. The vegetation was largely silver-gray, some leaves glinting metallically in the sun. Among the plants were the pointed, brittle fingers of cacti and the menace of skeleton thorn trees, with only the darker sheen of lignum vitae and sea lavender to break the salty sweep. Men had their gardens on San Isadore, but they were planted and reaped in defiance of nature, not with her cooperation.

Griff strode into the full drive of the wind. He wanted to fight something. His impatience, repressed for days, had come to a head with his father this morning—disastrously. He had advanced his plea to be allowed to return to the States, advanced it, as he thought, with reasonable restraint. And what had happened? Griff's fists clenched until his nails bit into the palms of his hands.

He wasn't ten years old and he was not going to be treated as if he were. To be spoken to like that with Hughes sitting there on the other side of the table! The perfect assistant, Hughes, Dr. Ramsey Gunston's shadow and alter ego. The calm good sense of all the answers Griff's father had marshalled had only added to the humiliation and disappointment of that scene—every one of Griff's own points demolished without any real understanding of how he felt, what he wanted to do!

Run away little boy and play—find some way to amuse yourself—that was about the sum and substance of Dr. Gunston's reply. But Griff wanted his own life—to follow the plans he had been making for years. Did his father believe that he had existed in a sort of vacuum, growing no older, doing no thinking for himself for the past five years? True, his father did not know him well—how could he? Ramsey Gunston had been out in the East Indies chasing fish all over the place, writing scientific papers that might be in an obtuse code as far as his son was concerned. What did Griff care about the diseases of fish—Fish! He couldn't be less interested!

His father had turned up again just after Griff had graduated from Emmsly, swept him off to this West Indies salt pot, as if his son had no right to a life of his own at all, and settled in for another season of prying into stinking messes of seaweed, of analyzing scum.

Oh, he supposed it was important—at least some of the magazines and papers back home had said that it was—this study of the Red Plague, of the strange new death in southern waters that had appeared without warning a season ago and was making great inroads in the profits of the fishing industry, sending the dead bodies of fish floating ashore by the millions along the lower coast of the United States and among the West Indies. Dad's job was backed by both the American and the British governments. He'd been brought halfway around the world to do it. But there wasn't one small piece of it his son could help with. And Dr. Gunston had the perfect Hughes always at his elbow, making Griff's first fumbling but honest attempts to help seem so childish that the younger Gunston soon stopped trying.

So—why should he be chained here, on an island even tourists did not visit, so far off the shipping lanes that the *Island Queen* was their only link with civilization when she made her biweekly trip to Santa Maria. And what was Santa Maria, in spite of its government house and port for freighters, but a dirty flyspeck on some out-of-date charts? Let him go home and try out for the Academy. For a moment Griff saw not the blue sea—but the blue sky. Jets—those were the future—not fish! He didn't know one fish from another and had no desire to be formally introduced either.

But there Griff was belittling his own curiosity, a curiosity that he had no intention of admitting to either of the two men now at work in the building behind him. His diving adventures along the reef during the past few weeks, his companionship with Christopher Waite, the mate of the *Queen*, had taught him more than he realized about the finned and shelled inhabitants of the bay—including some lore that might have surprised Dr. Gunston. But Griff took a perverse and childish delight in keeping to himself the results of his own underwater explorations. After all, both Dad and Hughes must have forgotten more than he would ever know. Why babble about such kindergarten stuff to them?

He wanted to get away. If he didn't, he had a vague fear that he might fall under the same spell that doomed Carterstown, that inertia that had sapped the energy of the islanders since the closing of the saltworks. They fished; they planted a few grains of corn, melon seeds, some garden truck in those tiny potholes of real soil to be found at such intervals that a small garden patch might cover several acres; they caught conch and dried them to sell in Santa Maria for the only cash they ever saw. But no one worked regularly or cared much about the future.

Griff, some of his hot resentment cooled by the press of the wind against his sun-browned body, considered languidly his own plans for the day. He could take out the underwater camera and try for some shots along the reef. He could strike inland to the plate-shallow salt lake and study the flamingos. He could try to find the bat cave Le Marr said was back in the desert strip. Or, he could again tackle the books he had flung aside last night with a petulance more suitable to someone half his age. He ought to sweat out that course sometime, in case he could ever take the Air Force Academy exam—if Dr. Gunston would even consider allowing him to try it!

Once more that stab of irritation. Lord, he didn't *like* fish, he never would! Moodily he stared down at the *Island Queen* without really seeing her at all.

There was a stir of life on her deck. A figure wearing only

ragged dungarees pattered barefooted on the snowy-clean boards. That would be Rob Fletcher, his white-blond hair identifying him even at this distance. The islanders were an oddly mixed lot. Some "red-legs," rebel-convicts of the eighteenth century political wars, Scottish clansmen after '45, or the Monmouth rebels, had been sent here by their planter-masters to start the first of the salt beds. Then the pirates of the cays had added men from time to time, marooned freebooters or shipwrecked buccaneers. There were Negro slaves and a few Indians—and now the islanders were a mixture of races, colors, heritages—Saxon names wedded to black skins, blue eyes beneath thick fuzz, startling blond locks now and then. And among them was a very small core of families who had not altogether slipped back to the semisavage existence of the rest, a core that produced from time to time an island leader or a man able to better his condition and try for some degree of civilized living.

Angus Murdock, the captain of the *Queen*; Fletcher; and Chris Waite, his mate; Dobrey Le Marr; Braxton Wells who managed the one store in Carterstown—you could count their number on the fingers of one hand. But they were there, distinct from their fellows, with a measure of energy, a degree of curiosity and of solid belief in themselves, and some ambition for the future.

Griff made his decision about the day's employment. He'd join the crew of the *Queen*, give them a hand as he had so often done before. Chris had just come above deck, his darker bulk looming over that of his slighter companion. The date of their scheduled trip to Santa Maria was still two days away, but there was something in that sudden appearance of Chris that suggested action, and Griff hurried down the winding cliff path.

He followed the rutted path, which could not be termed a road, between the tumble-down ruins of Carterstown. From one house in five he caught the sound of life. The rest were left now to the lizards and the spiders. As he trotted into the main street, he almost ran into Angus Murdock.

"Slow you down." White teeth showed in a wide friendly

9

grin, and a rich slur of voice somehow soothed the sting left from the curt interview in the lab house.

Griff grinned back happily. "Care to sign on a new hand today, Cap'n?"

"You aimin' to go worryin' them fish 'long the reef?" was Murdock's counter question. His well-muscled shoulders moved easily under his loose and very clean white shirt. The officer's cap, its captain's insignia carefully rubbed into winking brightness, was cocked over one eye in a way that gave his square-jawed face a rather rakish cast. Murdock traced his lineage back to another captain, one whose reputation at the time had been far from savory but over which modern romance cast a softening glow. There are few modern sea-rovers who can state with truth that their great-great-great-great-grandfathers were highly successful pirates.

"Not unless you do—" Griff returned, matching his stride to the other's rolling gait. "Is something up?"

"Up? What you mean, mon?" Murdock was at the dingy, preparing to launch out to the *Queen*. "We ain't sailin' today—"

But an impatient hail from the ship interrupted him. Chris was waving from the deck, his arm a whirlwind of summoning, and Murdock, with Griff, pushed off, to swing through the water at an oar speed much greater than usual. It was clear that something had happened, something actually drastic enough to excit the usually placid Waite.

"They's found the *S'Jawn*, Cap'n!" Chris blew out his news in a mighty blast almost before his superior officer clambered over the rail.

Murdock paused, pushing back his cap. Then, with a frown cutting a deep line between his brows, he confronted Waite as if he were accusing the islander of being personally responsible for bad news.

"Where they find her?"

"Driftin'—" Chris waved an arm to indicate the vast expanse beyond the reef. "She was driftin'—without no mon 'board her. Jus' like the *Neptune* an' *Flyin' Fish!*"

"On the wireless you heard dis?" Murdock asked.

"Aye, Cap'n. They say it from San' Maria. She was found this mornin' by the Dutch freighter. No mon 'board her—driftin'—"

Rob Fletcher had a single comment, which he made with the sullen persistence of one who had said the same thing before and did not expect to be attended to any more this time than he had been the last.

"Dupee—"

Murdock rounded on him, and the frown became even deeper. "A dupee? A ghost thing from the sea, eh? That's what you say, mon? Me, I don't believe in no ghost dupee thing without I see it with these two eyes—"

Rob shrugged. "So you don't believe, Cap'n? Then tell me true—what takes the mons from those ships an' leave them sailin' without no mon on board? Tell me that? No storm, no fire, no thing bad, jus' ship sailin' without no mon on her—that dupee work, that is!

"No mon knows what things be in the deep sea." He expanded his argument. "There's this red death what be killin' off the fish, ain't there? And Buzzy Defere, he saw that debble thing a-swimmin' off the reef in the moonshine—"

"All right," Murdock countered. "So there be things in the sea what be strange. But they're no ghostes— They're things a mon can see—like barracuda or shark. I don' believe in dupees—no ghost thing is gonna climb on the *Queen* an' push us off!"

It seemed to Griff that Rob did not look at all convinced. But he had a question of his own.

"What do you think *does* happen, Cap'n?"

Murdock was staring at the distant reef, to the deeper blue of the wave-ruffled water beyond.

"I think—subs!"

All the rumors of the past months, the tall tales that had passed from island to island, that had been mentioned on broadcasts from the States, were summed up in that one word—for not only had the red scum come to plague the sea but also this other lurking menace.

11

Several years before, similar tales had come from the far islands of the Pacific. There, too, small craft had cleared port with full crews and passengers for short runs between one landfall and the next—only to be entirely lost in a calm sea or to be found drifting days or weeks later, deserted by any living thing, with no evidence of any disaster such as fire or storm. And there had been rumors then of a new type of shark prowling the lanes, a sub that struck, killed, and struck again for no gain anyone could fathom.

Because the tension between the Eastern bloc of nations and the West had been building, so that they were on the brink of a holocaust, which both sides knew might put an end not only to the actively warring nations but to perhaps the whole world, the story of an underseas scout, a lurking, unnamed enemy, had been readily accepted and believed. And only because the mysterious attacks had suddenly ceased had real conflict been averted then.

Now within the circle of the Caribbean and the Gulf, the same game was being played once more. Three small island ships, the *Neptune*, the *Flying Fish*, and now the *St. John*, had been plundered of life and left to drift after the familiar pattern. And the affair of the *St. John* struck close to home with the men of San Isadore. She was a small vessel with the usual crew of three—twin to the *Island Queen*—and her home port was Santa Maria.

"Cap'n Luis, an' Sim, an' Marco." Chris was reciting the roll of the missing.

"An' Florrie, Sim's woman," Rob added. "She be 'long this time—do cookin'. Dupee done caught hisself big mouth-ful!"

"Them Reds." Murdock's voice lost much of its warmth. "They's gonna find out that they's got some real mons on their tail this time! We ain't gonna be gobbled up like the hound fish gobble up their dinner 'long the reef. We gits us some teeth like a shark an' then we goes 'til we can use them right!"

There was a menace in that last, though Griff wondered how Murdock proposed to face up to a modern sub, probably atomically powered and armed, with only three diver's knives, a shark gun, and the automatic that was the captain's own prized possession, those being the total sum of all armament he had ever seen aboard the *Queen.*

"They's give out a warnin' "—Chris's slower drawl was a cushion to the captain's heat—"do any ship see something, they say it by the wireless. Government boat, it be all ready steam out an' help—"

Rob shook his head. His long face was all solemn disagreement. "No government boat ain't gonna find no dupee. Get Papa-loi make a gris-gris charm—That's the only thing send dupee back where he belong. I speak Le Marr—he make gris-gris for the *Queen*—"

Murdock shrugged. "Gris-gris—an' guns! We git them both. Then we see who bigger—this thing in the sea or we."

"Ahhhh—" The hail echoed over the waters of the bay, and the four on the deck of the *Queen* turned to look at the dilapidated boat that was approaching under oar power from around the point. Its two man crew was putting on a better burst of speed than Griff had yet seen any of the islanders produce, and their excitement was manifest. Had the mysterious jungle "telegraph" that operated on San Isadore spread the news of the *St. John's* discovery this soon—or was it something else?

"Mosely Peeks." Chris identified one of the oarsmen without much concern, Mosely being on the bottom rung of the island's social ladder and of little consequence to the more solid citizens now represented in the gathering on the *Queen.* "Whyfor that mon make all this noise?"

"Got him a conch pearl an' think he be rich for all days," suggested Rob. "He talk, talk pearl all the time since Josie find that one last month."

Murdock walked to the rail. "Mosely!" His hail held the ring of command. "Whyfor you yell your throat sore that way? What big thing you have to say, mon?"

"Dupee—!" The word echoed over the water, rising above the boom of the surf. "Done found dupee lyin' out there!"

Rob spat disgustedly into the water. "Done got sun in

the head," was his verdict. "Dupee don't go 'round lettin' hisself be foun'—"

"Sub!" Griff and Murdock snapped the word out almost together. And when the captain swung down into the dinghy, Griff was only seconds behind, his heart beating fast. Could a sub actually be in these waters after all?

Murdock sent the dingy toward the wallowing, weed-hampered boat of the two conch fishermen. He put out a strong brown arm and anchored them to its side, looking into the excited faces before him.

"Where this dupee?"

"On beach—Daid Sailormon's Point. The birds, they's peckin' it. That dupee's sure daid, sure is—"

"Whale." Griff lost his keen interest of the moment before. No birds would be pecking at a sub, even if the underseas vessel had grounded. But at his explanation both of the fishermen shook their heads vigorously.

"Ain't no whale, nosuh," they chorused. "Ain't never seen this thing. It be dupee for sure—for sure—"

Murdock, after a careful study of their expressions, settled back at his oars, and under his stroking the light craft swung into a course that would bring the dingy and its passengers to Dead Sailorman's Point, where the outer reef ended and a jumbled mass of coral boulders stuck out into the raging surf of unchecked waves.

"Surely it's a whale," Griff repeated, suprised at his companion's action.

Murdock was frowning again. "Mosely—that mon, he be mostly no-'count. But he know daid whale. He say this ain't no whale, it ain't. An' I want to see this dupee for my ownself."

There was certainly something grounded on the rocky point, something dead, a loadstone for all the winged scavengers on the island. During all his months on San Isadore, Griff had never seen such a large gathering of screaming birds. And, as the dingy neared the place where they must land to advance on foot, avoiding the smashing surf rolling in from the open sea, he was aware of something else, the sickly stench of rotting flesh. Yes, whatever had beached here was very dead.

He struggled after Murdock across the sharp ridges of broken coral, feeling the bite of the razor-edged stuff through his sneakers—though the captain's bare and callused feet took the same path with apparent ease. They pulled up to the cliff top together and looked down into a small cove where something lay half buried in the sand.

Not only birds had been drawn to the beast, but a multitude of crabs, so that the beach itself crawled with snapping life. But it was what was being torn by those busy beaks and claws that brought an exclamation out of Griff. In those few seconds his lifelong belief in the omniscience of science was rudely shaken—he was seeing legend clothed in sloughing flesh.

Mosely's dupee—the vicious ghost of voodoo folklore—was a creature out of the fairy tales of Griff's own heritage. The fanged and grinning head, turned up by some freak so that the empty eyepits stared at the two men above, bore a photographic resemblance to the dragons of his childhood reading!

II

OCTOPI REEF

HALF THE population of Carterstown was assembled to beat the feasters off their maladorous banquet as Dr. Gunston and Hughes took photographs feverishly, measured, dug to free the carcass from the sand. They had something new right enough—or old enough if one wanted to recall the very ancient legends and later accounts of "sea serpents." An unclassified sea animal some twenty feet long, a snake's supple neck planted on a barrel body equipped with propelling flippers, a toothed alligator-like head. The stench of the rotting, rubbery flesh did not appear to bother the fascinated ichthyologists, but Griff, at last, climbed to the headlands once more to gulp in cleaner air.

"That thing"—Chris Waite dropped down beside him—"be a bottom thing."

"Bottom thing?"

Chris waved a big hand seaward. "Bottom—far down bottom out there. That thing come up from the bottom—"

"Why, do you suppose?"

"Maybeso something chase he."

Griff surveyed the length of the beached thing. Something from which that monster had fled would indeed be formidable. Shark? But if so—an oversize in sharks.

"Did you ever see anything like it before, Chris?"

The islander shook his head. "Never no time. But some things in the big bottom—no mon ever see them! An' Defere, he see something swimmin' two-three weeks ago. Might be this here—"

"Wonder what killed it?" Griff mused.

Chris shrugged. "Birds, fish, crabs, they nibble, nibble 'til a mon can't tell that. But the doctor, he be pleased!"

"I wonder how old that thing is—or was?" Another thought had struck Griff. Memories of fantastic stories spurred his imagination—the "lost world" where prehistoric monsters still lived, waiting to be discovered. Did that lump of decaying matter down there come from such a place? Did it represent a species that had inhabited the swamps of an earlier continent? He had browsed enough in the laboratory library to know that odd discoveries had been made of survivals from the unreckoned past. There was the Latimeria, the monstrous armored fish caught in the net of a trawler off the tip of South Africa back in 1938, a fish that rightly should have been dead a hundred and thirty million years like its carefully preserved fossils of the Devonian period.

However, this time they had photographs, measurements, careful observations to back up their report—proofs the unfortunate ships' officers and earlier travelers could not offer in testimony when they had tried to explain what they had seen, and so suffered the ignominy of complete disbelief.

Later that night the Americans learned another fact—one which was almost as great a shock as the original discovery had been. Hughes burst out of the laboratory, his tousled hair glued to his sweating forehead, his eyes wide with excitement. And the very impetus of his entrance brought him a full audience at once.

"That thing was 'hot'!" he exploded.

For a bemused second or two neither Griff nor his father understood. Then it was the younger Gunston who answered, "Radioactive!"

"Certain?" Dr. Gunston asked with schooled detachment.

"The counter says yes. It's about double that of the last batch of scum, too. I'd say that thing caught a good blast—maybe enough to kill it!"

Griff followed the others back to the laboratory workroom, hovering near the dissection table, listening to the fatal clicking of the Geiger counter. But he knew better by now than to ask for an explanation. The creature had somewhere, somehow absorbed enough radiation to make its carcass "hot."

"We must report in tonight—"

Hughes shifted his weight from one foot to the other. Griff believed that he wanted to protest that decision.

Then Dr. Gunston added, "I don't think it is necessary to go into too much detail as yet. Just say that we found a new marine life form, a large one, dead on the shore and that it registered exposure to radiation."

"Yes, sir!" There was plain relief in that prompt reply. "I'll code it and sent it short wave to Dr. Langley's office at Key West—"

Griff waited until Hughes had gone. "D'you suppose this thing"—he indicated the remains on the table—"came out of the depths—what Chris calls the big deeps?"

Dr. Gunston looked tired. He ran both hands through his stiff brush of gray-brown hair. "Well, it certainly wasn't hatched, born, or spawned on that beach. And we haven't been able to get our claws on its like before. There'll be a regular consultation over it when the news gets out."

"And 'hot' too—"

His father stiffened. "That you'll keep quiet, Griff." He was no longer speaking equal to equal, but giving an order. And hearing that tone, Griff's old resentment awoke. Stubbornly he voiced another question.

"So the plague scum is radioactive, too?"

"Hughes had better keep his mouth shut!" Dr. Gunston exploded and then added, "That's another point to forget, Griff."

The younger Gunston leaned back against the row of shelves with their jars of bottled specimens. "Is somebody experimenting with atomic stuff out in the Atlantic, Dad?"

Dr. Gunston stood very still, his mouth thinned into a grim, straight line. His eyes were bleak. Griff had a second of something close to panic under that keen scrutiny.

The doctor's hand shot out. His fingers closed with a pinching and compelling grasp on his son's upper arm, and he propelled the young man before him down the short corridor to his office. There he released his captive and went to the desk. From his pocket he brought a cluster of keys fastened to his belt by a length of chain. Selecting one, he unlocked a drawer. He did not open any of the folders that lay within, merely shuffled through them, glancing at the notation on the front of each as if making sure that they were in some special order. Then he relocked the drawer and turned to his son.

"So that was just a good guess, Griff?"

Griff's Indian-brown face was impassive, but his hands locked together in a tight clasp behind his back. So, his father dared to think that—that he had been—spying!

"It would seem so, sir." He was proud of his control.

Dr. Gunston did not appear to notice any change in his son's attitude. "You've been around with Murdock, with these other islanders. You heard them say anything?"

"Nothing about atomics—" But his father was not going to let him off that easily.

"Maybe nothing about atomic experiments—but you have heard something that made you think?"

"Murdock believes the 'mystery sub' story about the trouble with the ships. Well, there're atomic subs, aren't there? And I don't think one of ours could have turned pirate. So if there *is* one patrolling, or observing about here, there's a reason for it—"

Dr. Gunston sat down in the desk chair, fumbled with the pipe he picked up, and sucked at it unlighted. "Logical deduction, Griff. But such bright ideas are not to be peddled outside of here, understand?"

"Yes, sir." Mentally Griff shrugged. Three warnings in three minutes or so—did his father think that he habitually ran off at the mouth?

Hughes appeared in the doorway. "Report through and acknowledged."

The doctor put his hands over his eyes and then pushed them upward through his hair. Under the garish light he suddenly looked very tired. "Good enough. Time we locked up for the night, Frank. That'll be all, Griff."

So dismissed, the younger Gunston went on to the room that housed his cot and foot locker. But he did not make any move toward going to bed. Tiny brown lizards, which could have curled comfortably inside his class ring, flashed across the ceiling and walls in the glare of the unshielded light bulb dangling from an electric cord. And outside, the nightly chorus of hermit crabs, their claws clicking on the rocks, their stolen shell houses clanking as they scuttled, was an undernote to the high squealing bray of one of the wild donkeys come down to raid garden patches in the town.

Griff pushed aside the netting and lay down on the cot, his fingers laced behind his head. The constant roar of the surf under the rising wind beat in his ears as a low boom. But he was trying to forget one thing, that his father had been willing to believe that he had rifled that desk drawer. Had everyone working for the government become so "security" conscious that now they suspected everyone else? Or—

Five years was a long time, and even before Dr. Gunston

19

had left the States on his first trip, they hadn't been together very much. Griff had lived with his Aunt Regina after
his mother's death—until he went to school. His relationship, with his father had always been on a visitor basis. So
maybe it was natural that Dad could believe him capable of
a trick such as that. But— Resolutely Griff tried to think of
something else.

So the red plague scum was "hot"? That was an interest-
ing fact. Atomic experimentation of some kind under the
surface of the Atlantic? Near enough to the West Indies
so that traces of such activity could be detected there?
What kind of experimentation and who was doing it? Somehow Griff was sure that it was not his countrymen, nor
their allies, unless the various "security" precautions, which
were growing more and more irksome, had taken to concealing one government project from another, leaving it that
one finger could no longer learn what the other was dab-
bling in.

And if that atomic research was *not* the concern of
friends—then what? It was hard to lie in the dank heat of
this island night, listening to the vociferous life outside in the
dark, a life that had nothing to do with the concerns of
bipeds such as himself, and think of the cold, thin fear
that had lain on the horizon of his world as long as he
could remember.

Griff got up. There was an adventure he had in mind—
perhaps this was the night to try it. He stripped and pulled
on swimming trunks. The rest of his equipment was in the
second locker. He strapped on the watch protected against
moisture, the wrist depth gauge, and buckled about his
waist the weighted diving belt, fastening his knife in place.
The aqualung, the mask, a rubber-encased flashlight—he
gathered them all up and a few moments later was going
down the cliff path. Chris would be willing to take him out
to the reef. This was a plan they had discussed for some time.

Here and there lamplight shone warmly yellow from un-
shuttered windows in the dying town. But there were few

other signs of life. And then the steady beat of a drum, to be heard above the surf, told him why.

Le Marr—Dobrey Le Marr—was drumming up the spirits. Nominally the islanders were Christian. There was a church they attended on Sunday, a vicar who came over from Santa Maria twice a month to hold services.

But underneath that shell of the civilized world there had always lurked something else. And in late years—perhaps because of the world-wide unrest—it had bobbed once more to the surface. Dobrey Le Marr was no witch doctor of the jungle, but he claimed some of their ancient powers. His knowledge of herbs had confounded Dr. Gunston, and his psychological understanding of his fellows, shrewdly used, had made him the most powerful man on the island, though he made no open display of his power. Luckily, Le Marr was a benevolent despot. And the Gunstons believed that he had a better education in the field of civilized learning than he now admitted. He was a racial mixture, as were all the islanders, but when he had been ten, he had gone off island, not to return until he was a man in his thirties. From then on he lived quietly among his fellows, saying little for five years or more, until he began to practice medicine as the men of San Isadore knew it, with potions and spells. But he refused utterly to use his skill to kill. A gris-gris fashioned by Dobrey Le Marr was always for a man's protection, not his neighbor's damnation.

He had held aloof from the Gunston laboratory when the Americans had arrived and started their work. But Dr. Gunston had deliberately sought him out. And when Le Marr discovered that the scientist from the north was willing to listen without impatience to his theories and explanations, he had fallen into the habit of coming in once in a while in the evening, sitting for long silent moments turning the American cigarettes they gave him in his long, artist's fingers, his thin hawk face—with the features of an Andalusian grandee—composed, until at last he told some fantastic tale that they could accept as true. Le Marr always used the idiomatic speech of the island, but he did it with the precision of one who speaks a foreign tongue, and Griff suspected that he could have spoken as an off-islander of education had he so desired.

For a minute Griff hesitated on the path. He longed to watch Le Marr at his business—see a voodoo gathering. But he sensed that that was one place where he would not be welcome. And his presence there might undo all the friendliness of past relations. The Gunstons were interlopers here, and there were parts of island life that could never be open to them. Anyway he was sure he would not find Chris in that audience. Though Rob Fletcher was a devoted follower of Le Marr, Captain Murdock and Waite held aloof from the calling drums and the dark belief born in an older and hotter jungle land.

Griff's feet, clad in rubber-soled sneakers, made no sound on the road. He came to the three-room coral block house set in a garden patch and turned in.

"Who's there?" A dark shadow detached itself from the doorway and moved out, to be outlined against the cream-white of the wall.

"Griff Gunston. That you, Chris?"

"This me. Ha—" The other had a cat's eyes in the gloom. "You gonna dive now?"

"Can you take me out, Chris?"

"Sure. But you mighty teched in the head, mon. The fishes, they eat your skin offen you some day, you do this fool thing."

"You ought to try it, Chris."

The other chuckled. "Me, I ain't gone in the head yet, mon. I'll pull the crazy one out—afore the crabs eat him to little pieces—"

Inside the reef the water was calm, not the blue-green of the day, but a purple-blue. And Griff, looking down into it, began to wonder about the wisdom of his plan. But he knew that the world below him, in which man could only be an intruder for short spaces of time, had two separate lives—that the activity that filled it by night was not the activity that it knew by day. And he had long wanted to observe he difference for himself.

As they rowed out along the reef, Chris was full of news.

"The wireless, it go war, war all evenin'," he remarked. "Big talks here, there. They talk bomb, bomb all the time. Say, 'You do what I say, mon, or I blow you up.' Think that they do that, Griff—blow us up?"

"They've been talking that way ever since I can remember," Griff remarked somewhat absently, his attention more on the water into which he was going. He kicked off his sneakers and adjusted swimming flippers.

"Sometimes"—Chris's powerful oarswing shot them forward—"I think that maybe this world's gonna get powerful tired of mons. Spit us out like we ain't no 'count no ways. There's things on this world mon ain't never seen, no matter how big he talk with the mouth. Your father, he know many things, but he ain't never seen that there dupee afore, had he?"

"No," Griff admitted as he adjusted his tank between his shoulders.

"New things comin' outta the sea. Maybe new things comin' other places, too. Mon, he mess 'round, start things comin'. But what if they don't stop? Back there"—in the light of the lantern his chin pointed to the land behind them—"they ask voodoo for gris-gris. Me, I think better ask for good wits in mon's head—so he learn he maybe ain't top cap'n afore it be too late!"

Some of that sunk into Griff's mind, past his preoccupations of the moment. But now he made ready to dive and slipped over into the weird world, the existence of which he had suspected, but the reality of which completely bewitched him.

He was familiar with the fairy tale seascapes that confronted the daytime diver—the rich color of live coral and sea fans, the butterfly tints of the small fish, the dusty patches of sunlight that filtered down through the waves to dazzle the diver and upset his judgement of distance.

But this—this was very different. His finger moved on

the torch button beneath its rubber coating. A beam of light cut through purple murk, struck coral into life, brought into its cone furious fish, their colors all altered so that Griff had to reidentify them. Then the light caught and centered on what he had come to find—that crevice in the rock wall with its telltale pile of shells beneath it.

The octopi clan had long furnished a boogy man for the ocean. Since the days of the legendary Great Kraken—said to arise from the depths to wreath its arms about the mast of a ship and draw it down into darkness—there had been horror stories of the cephalopods and their cold-blooded enmity to his kind. Yet most of those tales were sheer fantasy. When man faced octopus, he was facing a creature that, had native conditions varied only the slightest degree, might have been this planet's ruler in man's place. They were the keenest witted creatures in the ocean for the same reason that man had been forced to develop a brain in order to survive on land. If they possessed thumbs and fingers instead of tentacles armed with suckers, the whole history of the world might be different.

Organic evolution had left them, as it had puny man, without adequate physical protection against the dangers of their world. What were man's teeth and nails against the talons and fangs of the creatures he faced—until he lengthened and strengthened his arm with a stick and a rock and learned to build fires in the night? And the cephalopods, mollusks that had lost their shells in the dim past, became streamlined in action, used a smoke screen of ink to mask their escapes, and lived in houses of their own contriving.

That pile of shells outside the door was in itself remarkable, testifying to the fact that the owner of the dwelling was unlike other water creatures. They were not all empty shells—a goodly portion were still living, stored in anticipation of a hungry morrow.

Griff had located this largest inhabitant of the reef some days earlier when he had been about to steady himself with one hand against a coral boulder, only to see two black eyes regarding him bleakly. Then the rock had separated, and the larger portion had oozed away into the crevice, from which at last only the point of a single tentacle trailed as if to wave him good-by.

Now he picked up those eyes again. The octopus was enthroned on the same rocky vantage point, its stare into the flare of his torch unchanging. Would it change color? He watched for the livid white shade, which he knew meant that it was alarmed. But that alteration did not come. Instead Griff felt a queer sensation—as if hundreds of tiny wet and clammy hands pulled at the skin on his thigh. He looked down. A tiny edition of the large mollusk clung there, spread star-fashion, less than eight inches across.

In that moment Griff lost his taste for night exploration. There was something about those unblinking eyes—that touch from which his flesh shrank. He tore at the infant on his leg. It slipped across his skin, but he could not pry any one of those arms loose from their sucker clutch. It was as if the small mollusk was determined to go into the air with him!

Then the large octopus moved. With the lightning speed usual to its kind, it swam away out of the light, leaving Griff staring at the rock where it had been only a second or two earlier. He had decided now about calling an end to this adventure. He wanted above all to lose the baby thing that clung so persistently to him. With a practised flip he swam up toward the dark shadow of the boat and the waiting Chris.

III

BASE HUSH-HUSH

GRIFF SAT cross-legged in the scrap of shade thrown by a single wind-warped palm tree, regarding intently the drama in his own private pool jungle. It was on the top of the cliff, a depression hollowed out by the beat of falling spray through the centuries, filled drop by drop by that same moisture, kept heated by the sun to blood temperature.

Without any clue as to how they had made the journey up the cliff from the sea below, hundreds of small rainbow-colored fish flashed their vivid blues and golds, their gleaming silver, their flamboyant purples and reds, their black and yellow stripes, as they wheeled and sped or hung suspended on quivering fins. Shrimp and prawn, which might have been ghosts of themselves, so transparent that one could see their lunch being digested inside their frankly revealed interiors, scuttled across the sandy bottom.

Amid all these was the newcomer introduced by Griff in the early hours of the morning. A strangely streaked rock gave resting place to the baby octopus that had clung to him, refusing to be parted even when he had climbed into the boat. And true to its nature, the lurking cephalopod was now the same shade as that rock, only visible to Griff because he had seen it anchor itself on that point. In the light of day it was quiescent. But two tiny crab shells, emptied of their lawful contents, marked activity in the last hours before dawn. And if it allowed a rainbow fish to brush a tentacle with a careless fin, it was because that was its period for rest.

Griff thought of what he had seen the night before—at least ten of the shell-heaped crevice doors along the reef—an octopi town. And Chris admitted that at the other end of San Isadore there was an even larger colony of the creatures. The law of the sea, supply and demand of food—Griff frowned at his small specimen in the spray pool. Why so many of them about here now? Was hunting so rich hereabouts that the cephalopod population was going up? Were more of the young surviving than was usual? An octopus was a noted mother, protecting her eggs as they lay concealed in some carefully selected crevice, sending the water moving in currents over them by sweeps of her arms so that algae and other tiny plants and animals could not root on them, refusing to leave them even to hunt for food. But, with the prodigious wastefulness of sea life, for every one that hatched and reached adulthood, perhaps hundreds of others died. Conditions must be unusually favorable to bring such large colonies to settle about the island at this time.

A shadow fell across the pool startling the fish, which fled in rainbow bands. Griff glanced up.

"Dobrey Le Marr—"

In the freshness of the morning it was hard to connect this thin tall man, possessing the air and features of high-born Spain, with the drumming of the night before, with Le Marr's acknowledged—could you term it?—profession?

"The reef—how it be at night?" Le Marr asked abruptly. As usual he spaced his words as if he spoke in a foreign tongue.

"I didn't stay long." Griff wanted to explain that sensation he had had of menace, of being cut off from his own world, which had sent him out of the water and back into the boat last night, but somehow the words were missing.

"You bring something from the reef?"

"Baby octopus—" Griff pointed to the new occupant of the pool.

Le Marr leaned over, his odd yellowish eyes finding the small mollusk quickly.

"It came to you, you did not hunt it?" There was a new note in his precise voice.

"It clung to my leg—"

"It came to you. Now it stay—an' watch—" Le Marr's head lifted, and he looked down out over the sea. "Other things come soon. Life change—mons change too maybeso—"

"You mean—the sea monster—?"

Le Marr shook his head. "First come mon. Then—" He brought his slender hands together in a smacking slap, which sounded almost like a shot. "Then—all the trouble in the wide world!" His gaze flickered to Griff and became more human as the seer faded into the man. "We go inland—see things—"

Griff was ready to agree. Since the incident of the night before, he fought shy of his father. And anyway both the elder Gunston and Hughes had been shut up in the laboratory almost since dawn. Also, Le Marr was none too generous with invitations to explore the wasteland that was the interior of San Isadore, and this might just be the time when he would reveal the site of the bat caves.

"Thanks!" The American went in to gather up a canteen, a pair of shoes suited to scrambling over coral rock, and a broad-brimmed hat to keep off the sun.

He joined Le Marr, who had a donkey on a rope, on the faint path leading inland. No islander ever showed any interest in the passing of time, an hour more or less made little difference to their plans. But there was something in Le Marr's attitude that suggested he was eager to be on his way.

The heat increased, and Griff did not relish the thought of emerging from the shade to the open country about the shallow salt lake, where the flamingos fished and water birds were thick. Their trail wound through the type of jungle peculiar to San Isadore, a matted growth of tangled thorn trees and stunted bush. Now and again Le Marr paused with an unerring sense to scrape loam and brown leaf mould out of hollows, allowing the murky liquid to gather so that the donkey could suck at it noisily, easing the tongue that lolled, foam-flecked, from his mouth.

They came out at last on what Griff considered was one of the weirdest of all the island features—a hard floor of gray rock. The hoofs of the donkey, the tread of his own heavy shoes, even of Le Marr's hide sandals, caused low booming sounds. San Isadore was in reality a vast stone sponge, eaten into, channeled under, by the sea. This flooring was hollow, probably covering some vast cave or series of caves in which the sea washed. Loose slabs were piled here and there, and these, Griff knew from earlier experiments, gave off the sound of bells. To cross the strip was to tread from key to key on some giant piano.

And always, the drift of salt, the soil that was 90 per cent shells and the remainders of sea life. Above them wheeled flamingos in formation. A wild clatter of sound heralded the retreat of some wild donkeys across the hollow rock.

Le Marr plodded on around the edge of one of the sea pools, deep, blue, leading down to unplumbed depths with some outlet to the ocean. Such wells rose and fell with the tides, and Griff saw anemones and scarlet sponges growing along its sides. Doubtless other marine life lurked in the underwater, but it was also a good place to meet a moray eel.

The islander paused. This was one of the big wells, a good sixty feet in diameter. Le Marr stared into it with the same measuring intentness with which he had regarded the surf pool on the cliff. After a long moment of silence he asked a question.

"Could you dive down there? Like you do by the reef?"

"I suppose so. But it might be dangerous—"

"Some day—maybe you have to," was the reply. Le Marr went on, across a dried-up lake, where the bodies of tiny fish, desiccated because of the high salt contents, now made a silver carpet of scales. They did not proceed to the flamingo lake but cut over to come out on San Isadore's nearest approach to a real headland.

Beneath them was a knife-sharp valley, which might have been on another planet. Some hurricane of the past had scoured brain coral, massive chunks of it, free from the sea floor, the surf tossing it high enough against the outer cliff for it to be seized by the wind and brought over that obstruction to lie here, a weird monument to the horrors of wind and water unleashed.

The mass of boulders and coral were embedded in sand, and that sand was patterned by the tracks of countless wild pigs. This appeared to be one of their favorite hiding places. But Le Marr was interested in neither the evidence of the forgotten storm nor the prospects of good hunting. Instead he pointed seaward, as if he sighted there something he had been waiting to see.

And Griff was completely surprised when his gaze followed the line indicated by the other's brown finger.

The *Island Queen* linked them with Santa Maria. There was also a Dutch freighter, which called at widely spaced intervals. But this ship, coming to anchorage now beyond the ruffle of the reef, was neither island sloop nor small freighter.

"Mons come—" Le Marr's voice held a hint of satisfaction as if some prophecy of his own was about to be fulfilled.

"But who—why? And why not come to Carterstown? There's no landing point here."

"These mons—they make their own landin' place. They think they can move the world. Maybe so—maybe no."

Griff watched the amazing activity beyond the reef with a faint feeling that somewhere he had seen its like before. Surely that wasn't a boat they were slinging over the side of the ship—Yet when it hit the water, it did not sink, and the men aboard it, hardly distinguishable dots at this distance, flung off the slings and started the queer craft. It made straight for the reef, and then, turtle-like, it actually crawled through the pounding surf, up over the exposed coral ridge, and slid into the quieter waters of the lagoon, heading for the shore as if those who piloted it did, indeed, have no fears of their mastery over both water and land. And reading the insignia painted on the crawler, Griff understood a little of their confidence. They had built and wrecked around the globe in their time and done it well. But what were Seabees—American Seabees—doing on San Isadore?

Within three days the first foundations of the mysterious buildings of Base Hush-Hush were being erected. The men from the north with their wealth of machines and supplies worked feverishly around the clock, in the daytime under the torrid sun, at night under floodlights. But as far as the islanders were concerned, what they slaved to create remained a puzzle. The commander had come armed with papers for the resident commissioner, and guards patrolled the area the newcomers had selected, keeping all sight-seers away.

Naturally wild rumors circulated. Griff, lounging on the deck of the *Island Queen*, heard a collection of the choicest from Rob Fletcher. As usual the islander's long face mirrored a worried expression, and his hand fondled the small bag hanging on a cord against his bare chest.

"They done bring the bomb—the big bomb. An' they's gonna bust it right here."

Griff shook his head. "They're working too hard to build whatever it is to smash it with an atom bomb."

Chris came along the deck and dropped down beside the other two. He lighted one of the coarse island cigarettes, and the blue smoke floated lazily on the air. Rob turned to him.

"They's gonna bust the big bomb right here!"

But Chris also disagreed with that. "No bomb, I think. Maybeso make place to hide sub—"

Griff sat up. Now that made sense. A sub base! But why all the hurry? Those Seabees were putting to it as if they had a time limit imposed.

He caught sight of the dinghy, with Angus Murdock aboard, headed for the *Queen*. And when the captain came over the rail, his good-humored face was very serious.

"Chris, you been harkin' to the wireless?"

Waite got up. "Bad news, Cap'n?"

Murdock took off his peaked uniform cap and rubbed the back of his hand across his forehead.

"They's another ship amissin'—the *Rufus G.*—down at Nassau. They got the government cutter out cruisin' 'round. She had the governor's aide 'board her."

"So?" Chris moved toward the radio cubby. "I done listened to all the talk 'bout the big no-war meetin'. Seems like every time they talk like that things gets worser. But they didn't say nothin' 'bout the *Rufus G.*"

"Just come on the wireless at the Government House ashore." Murdock waved an explanatory hand. "Do you think these here Navy mons are buildin' a place for subs?" he asked Griff. "They gonna send out subs to hunt down this thing what gits the mons on the ships?"

"I don't know any more about that than you do, Cap'n," Griff was forced to admit.

"They's sure in a hurry 'bout whatever they do," Murdock

commented. "An' they's not lettin' any mon see what they do— They warned Mosely to git outta there when he went out for the conch."

Rob roused at that. "How come they think they can say where a mon do fish? The best conch, they lie 'long there. They ain't *own* this here water!"

"They's got 'em a paper from the government—say they do what they want. They don't care water good for the conch. Why, they cut right through the reef—change all that part of island. Ain't never seen nothin' like that before—" Murdock gazed toward the scene of activity now hidden from the *Island Queen* by miles of curving and recurving shore line, for the site of Base Hush-Hush was the northern tip of San Isadore.

So far, save for the bafflement and irritation of some conch fishermen and the unrewarded curiosity of the islanders at large, a wonderment at the energy of the northerners and speculations concerning their purpose on San Isadore were the substance of the comments Griff overheard. Le Marr, after his initial sight of the task force, had withdrawn to some hidey hole of his own and had not been seen. And the Gunston project had had no reason to contact the Naval party, the doctor and Hughes being intent on the problem of the "sea serpent" as represented by the bones and remains over which they labored in the laboratory.

The *Island Queen* cleared for her scheduled run to Santa Maria with the mystery still unsolved. And it was that evening that Project Sea Serpent had its first brush with the Navy. It was time for the sample testing along the reef, and Hughes went out in the small motor launch, Griff ready with diving equipment. They took four or five samples at selected sites, and then Hughes pointed the course farther north to a section where the reef broke, near the promontory where the carcass of the monster had lodged.

Griff shrugged on the tank, made sure of the easily released clasp of his weight belt, the presence of his wrist depth gauge and watch.

"Get a sea fan," Hughes told him, "and water samples.

Three or four small plants ought to be enough. Then we'll take another about a mile or so to the north—"

But as Griff started to descend the small diving ladder, they were both startled by the ear-piercing shriek of a siren. On a course headed straight for them was a needle-slim cutter, slicing through the waves at a dazzling speed. With masterly seamanship it pulled up in a circle about the project launch while one of the three men on board called across, "This is closed territory. Do your fishing down-reef!"

Hughes stood up, and there was a snap to his voice as he answered, "No closed territory for our work. We're from the Gunston laboratory—Project 914-5. Now get out before you stir up the stuff we're collecting—"

"Don't know anything about your project," the other replied brusquely. "You get out and stay out—this is a security order. Can't you get that through your thick heads? We have to run you blasted fishermen off the lot every time we turn around—"

"We represent Project 914-5," Hughes repeated. "Our orders are to prospect this reef. We'll take this up with your superiors—"

"Do!" The other sounded as if he hoped that they would. "We have *our* orders—they're to keep all unauthorized persons out of this area. Now get going, and make it snappy!"

Griff climbed back in the outboard and took off the air tank. Hughes raised their anchor line. And the Navy launch continued to circle them, escorting them out of the disputed area of lagoon. Hughes headed back to the lab anchorage, making no comment to Griff, but every line of his stiff shoulders, his set mouth, suggested his inward seething. In Hughes's estimation the project was second to nothing in importance, and Griff guessed that he now lived to make that clear to the interlopers from the base.

He left Griff to gather the equipment and headed up the cliff path at a pace which seemed excessive in that heat. Griff wondered what his father's reaction would be. But he was not to learn then. Both his elders remained in the laboratory, and he ate alone, turning his attention to the collection of shells he had been driven by boredom into assembling.

Afterwards he wandered out to the surf pool. A carpet of empty crab shells in one corner testified to the skill and appetite of the newest settlers therein. And he watched the octopus feast now, marveling at the neatness and dispatch with which the cephalopod acted. A crab snared in the tentacles was turned bottom-side-up as one might hold a soup plate, while the miniature parrot beak of the captor pierced the soft lower shell and the file tongue inside that beak rasped out the contents.

The patch of bitter aloe blossoms by the path had attracted a flock of humming birds, and they sipped and hung fearlessly almost within Griff's grasp. It was close to sunset, and the sun was a vivid cherry-red.

There was a flurry in the pool as the octopus made another kill. But it seemed to the spectator that those black beads of eyes were now staring up over the body of its victim, straight at him—as if the new master of the pool had some plan of its own—some plan into which it was fitting the man who could crush it in one hand. As that fantasy crossed Griff's mind, he shivered. The spray borne inland by the wind, flicking his shirt and salty on his lips, was for the moment icy cold.

"Hello there!"

Griff got to his feet. There was a tall man on the cliff path, a man now outlined by the odd flash of greenish light that was the island phenomenon at the setting of each sun. His white shirt and slacks were vivid, but his face under the shadow of an officer's cap was partly concealed.

"Dr. Gunston here?"

"He's in the lab."

"Tell him Breck Murray's here—Commander Breck Murray. I'm from the base—"

"So you finally got here, did you?" That was Hughes. He was standing belligerently on the path leading to the building. "What's your explanation for this afternoon?"

"Dr. Gunston—?"

"I'm Hughes, his assistant. Dr. Gunston is occupied."

The commander made as if to turn. "When he's free, he can find me at the base—" His retort was pointed.

"Who's there?" Dr. Gunston called through the dusk. The sky above them was now gray, deepening to the purple of the quick-falling tropical twilight. "Commander Murray? Your people said you would get in touch with me. Come in, sir—"

Hughes stepped aside, and Griff knew he was not pleased. But both of them followed the other two men inside.

IV

COOPERATION—ENFORCED

THE HARSH LIGHT of electricity, which always seemed alien to the houses of San Isadore, drew lines in Dr. Gunston's face, pointed up Hughes's irritated twist of mouth, highlighted the creases about the outer corners of Commander Murray's eyes. His peaked cap had been thrown on the small table; his long legs were stretched out before him. He should have been at ease, but he wasn't as he turned his tall glass with nervous little jerks. However, as he looked at the doctor, his expression was faintly amused.

"I assure you, Dr. Gunston, that we were not landed here just to provide difficulties for Project 914-5. In fact, three months ago I was peacefully engaged in erasing a few hills preparatory to building a dam out in Arizona. Then they grabbed me back by my reserve commission, gave me a briefing, and sent me down here to do my worst. You don't argue with top brass—" For a second his amusement flickered out, and a hint of other emotion took its place. "Understand that you haven't spent much time back in the States recently, Doctor." He took a sip from his glass.

In contrast to the commander's controlled tension, Dr. Gunston appeared as relaxed as one of the islanders.

"I've been in the East Indies for the past five years. And

35

I gather that while we were not informed about you, you know a great deal about us—?"

"Security can probably tell you right now how many grains of sand lie down on the beach!" That exploded from Murray with a force that appeared to have nothing to do with the subject. "Well, Doctor, while you were back of beyond, a lot of things have changed stateside. The race is nearing the finish line." He stared ahead of him at the wall, and the muscles about his mouth tightened visibly. "We're running it too fine, much too fine—"

"War?" It was Hughes who asked that. Dr. Gunston frowned and shifted uneasily in his chair.

"We can pray not. But it's getting close—too close!"

"They're meeting in Geneva tomorrow—the Peace Conference—" Dr. Gunston's protest was eager.

Murray laughed, and there was no amusement in that sound. "How many peace conferences have they had in the past twenty years? And has any one of them led to as much as laying down a single gun? Though guns are outmoded now!"

"This base—you seem to be working against time here—"

Murray put down his glass, and the click of the crystal against the wood of the table was unduly loud.

"I think our time is running out fast, gentlemen, very fast. But there is nothing we here can do to alter that. We have our own problems." He achieved the light touch once more. "As you have pointed out, it is necessary to your work that you have samples from along the reef, even in the now restricted area. Gentlemen, as far as I am concerned you can cart off the whole blasted reef piece by piece if you wish. But"—he was openly smiling now—"very unfortunately I do not have the final word on the subject!"

Hughes bristled. "I understood that you commanded here—"

"One would think so, wouldn't one?" the question was sardonic. "But in the new setup, we have our little problems, too. And a major one is Lieutenant Charles Holmes—our security officer. Security has declared Base Hush-Hush to be strictly that, and I can do nothing about it. You've already protested to *your* high brass—" He paused and glanced at Dr. Gunston, who nodded. "Well, now it depends upon just how much weight they can throw about in certain circles stateside. I'll send in my report, but I must be frank with you. My word against Holmes's orders doesn't weigh at all. However, there is one thing I can do—ask you to give Mr. Holmes a demonstration—"

"Demonstration?" Hughes was wary.

"Who does most of your diving?"

Dr. Gunston answered that. "Griff does the ordinary work. Hughes and I take over if we have to see something for ourselves."

"Suppose I detail Holmes and Bert Casey—he's one of my own men, an underwater demolition expert I brought on this job—to go out with you tomorrow and watch how you do your stuff? Then Holmes will see for himself that you are working on a project, that you are experts. I'll make him file a report of all this to his department. It may help—you can never tell."

Surprisingly Hughes laughed. "And it gets Holmes out of *your* hair for a while—"

Murray grinned. "I won't answer that. But is it a deal?"

Dr. Gunston answered. "We're merely doing some routine sampling; it may be dull. And your men aren't to dive unless we say so—indiscriminate exploration might upset our observations—"

"I don't think you could get Holmes under water. And Casey'll abide by your orders. Shall I send them around? Believe me, Dr. Gunston, if you want to make a stiff protest through channels, I'll not be upset. This is not my decree. By the way—" he got to his feet and picked up his cap, but still lingered— "know anything about the country inland? I have the official charts and the material the briefing crowd assembled, and if what they say is true, this place is a weirdie. Any of the native sons willing to help us explore?"

"You'd better contact Dobrey Le Marr on that. If there

is anything to know about the interior, he has it filed away in his brain."

"Native?"

Hughes snorted. "Very much so. He's the local witch doctor!"

A shade of annoyance shadowed Dr. Gunston's face. "Le Marr is an unusual man. Yes, he's a native and practices what the islanders recognize as medicine—of a sort. But if you can establish a friendly relationship with him, you might discover it to be to your advantage, Commander."

When Murray had gone, Dr. Gunston continued to sit, sucking at his empty pipe. Hughes broke the silence first.

"So we put on a show for the Navy?"

The doctor smiled wryly. "Murray's laid his cards on the table. I don't think he likes his orders any better than we do. Yes, we'll give a demonstration for the Navy. But not just our usual job. How about it, Griff?" For the first time he spoke to his son. "You've been haunting the reef. Where can we really show them something of interest?"

"According to Chris there's a stretch of reef to the northeast where there's an octopi town—big collection of them. I was going to take a look at it anyway. Think that might be impressive enough?"

"Octopi—" Dr. Gunston considered the point. "You haven't dived there before?"

"I haven't. Chris did—straight skin diving without a lung. Take it with a lung and we might get some good camera shots—"

"All right. Make it this octopi paradise and do just that —take the movie camera—"

They made ready in the early morning of the next day, taking diving apparatus enough for three in case their guests decided to share in the exploration. And the Navy cutter was on time, coming smartly in to drop two passengers. The shorter of the two cast a knowing eye over the equipment Griff was carefully stowing in place and, without a word, stepped down into the motorboat to help him with the ease of long familiarity with such gear.

"Bert Casey," he introduced himself casually. "You've got some good stuff here." He handled the tanks with open approval.

"All the latest. I'm Griff Gunston."

"Pleased to meet you, kid. You the regular diver?"

"I do a lot of it. My father's the real expert, though."

"Don't see any harpoon or spear gun—"

"We don't hunt," Griff returned a little shortly. He liked to stalk with a camera only.

"Nothing you have to worry about? No sharks?"

Griff laughed. "That shark boogie has been pretty well exploded. As long as you aren't killing fish and there's no blood in the water, you're safe nine times out of ten. Barracuda's worse. But if you really want to make trouble for yourself, plant a foot on a sea urchin—or get tangled up with a Portuguese man-of-war! For the rest—" he patted the knife in its sheath, its cork hilt in easy reach of his hand—"moray's bad, but you have to tickle them up before they jump you—keep an eye out for their heads sticking out of rock crevices—"

Hughes came down the wharf carrying the underseas camera, paused at the sight of the other officer standing there, and then nodded stiffly.

"Lieutenant Holmes," the other introduced himself. "You are in charge?"

A smothered noise came from Casey. It sounded suspiciously like a snort. The lieutenant, it was very apparent, desired neither to win friends nor to influence people.

As abruptly, Hughes replied, "I'm Frank Hughes, assistant to Dr. Gunston. This is his son, Griffith."

The lieutenant favored Griff with a disapproving stare, and he realized that in his trunks and burned brown by the sun, Holmes had taken him to be an islander and so not worthy of notice.

"All ready, Griff." Hughes passed the officer to hand down the camera, and his voice was far more cordial than usual. In face of a common enemy Hughes was closing ranks. He took his place at the motor, leaving Holmes to get aboard by himself, and they headed out into the bay without another word.

Casey looked about him with frank curiosity. "Lots of color," he commented to Griff.

"You've dived here?"

"Not yet." Casey pushed the cap with its Lieutenant, J.G., insignia to the back of his bullet head. "I've been down mostly in the north. During World War II I was a demolition man. That's how I met the skipper—he was running a show in Alaska. But that was frogman stuff, and we wore suits—"

"I understand that your project is connected with the collection of marine specimens." Holmes cut across Casey's reminiscences.

"Collecting and observation." Hughes was curt. "What bearings, Griff?"

Griff squinted back at the curve of the shore. "Clear around the bay, Frank. It's near Finger Cay—opposite the mangrove swamp—from what Chris said."

White water boiled in their wake. A line of flamingos etched across the sky, and they passed one of the weed-grown conch boats wallowing along, exchanging hails with the island fisherman.

"What do they get out here?" Casey wanted to know.

"Conch. Sometimes a pearl or two," Griff answered.

"No kidding! I didn't know that they did pearl-diving here—"

"Conch pearls. They're supposed to be turned in to the commissioner when they're found. But precious few are. There's not much market for them—they're colored, apricot, lavender, rose, and mostly baroque. But they are pretty. And conch meat, dried, sells over at Santa Maria. It's used to make fertilizer, I believe."

"Deep water out there?" Casey pointed to the darker hue beyond the reef.

"Dips to two thousand fathoms or more." Hughes answered that. "We haven't tried there; our kind of diving doesn't reach such distances."

"There's Finger!" Griff hailed their landmark. The tiny island, hardly above sea level, was unique. There were three wind-worn palms on one end, but the major portion of the land mass supported a single tree—only, what a tree! A mangrove that had several hundred separate trunks, stemming from some thousands of kneed roots on a platform well above the wash of intruding waves. And, above, the branches and leaves had entangled in a canopy of dark green leaves, covering well over an acre. Bobbing in the water at the shore line were drifting coconuts and another spear-pointed mangrove seed trying for a rooting, to increase the holding of land over sea.

Hughes sent them between the island and the mainland and brought them to anchor behind the reef, while Griff got into his diving kit. He turned to ask Holmes politely: "Care to go down, Lieutenant?"

"Perhaps later." Holmes was making a point of non-interest, preserving the attitude of one carrying out boring orders.

"You, Mr. Casey?"

"Yes, sir!" The other was already stripping off his shirt. Holmes looked as if he might protest, but he remained silent on that point if not on another.

"What is your research here?" He spoke to Hughes, who was rigging the overside glass through which those in the boat could watch activity below.

"Octopi settlement—or an alleged octopi settlement."

Casey paused in the process of shucking his slacks. "Octopi?"

Griff laughed. "Not dangerous at all—and these are small ones. Most of the stories about them are in the same class with shark tales—only more so. They're intelligent after their own fashion and don't go around picking fights. You let them alone, and they won't even give you the ink treatment."

He slipped his mask into place, made sure of his air, and climbed down the short diving ladder, shivering a little as the chill of the sea hit his sun-warmed skin. Then, instantly, he was in another world. Above him was the bottom of the boat, festooned with feathery green stuff. Golden spears of sun struck down to be swallowed up by endless blue. The distance became hazy, overspread with an almost pearl luster. For perhaps a little more than fifty feet he could see clearly, the fantastic forest of yellow coral trees into which he was descending standing out with the sharp relief of a silhouette. Sea fans, brilliant blood-colored sponges, and then the dark caves in between. And always the flights of gemmed fish in brilliant array of every shade and color. He judged his distance and took off in one of the slow-motion bounds, which cleared a hedge of purple sea plumes. The flooring, which, from above, had looked so smooth and flat, was in reality a hillside, jagged and torn with crevices and outcrops, pitted with hidey holes and caves, each of which, Griff knew from his past experience, housed a varied collection of inhabitants. He jerked his hand back from a careless grip on a pinnacle of smooth, brownish coral, which stung hotly.

Drifting, he made a feather-soft landing some twenty feet from the point where he had taken off. But in doing so, he dislodged a growth of anemone, and within seconds he was the core of a whirling pool of fish, all feeding or attempting to feed on the crushed and dying flower-animals. A flounder crawled on a patch of white sand and dug in, its eyes rising on stalks above its chosen ambush.

As usual Griff had to drag his attention back to the job on hand. He progressed along the line of sea fans, watching for the telltale piles of shells, which marked octopi dwellings. And with mounting excitement he saw that Chris had been right—this section of reef housed more of the cephalopods than he had ever seen gathered together before. He jerked the signal line for the camera to be lowered.

A weird shadowy form moved toward him with deceptive slowness, and the sea-monster head turned so that he recognized Casey. He reached out to draw the other down beside him and indicated the crevices. Whether the other understood or not, he could not tell. But the Navy diver helped him steer the camera around to face that stretch of wall. Now if he could just get one or more of the creatures out of their holes to put on a real show—

He caught the sign of an octopus at home, the end of a tentacle issuing from a crevice, a slit in the porous rock, which seemed too narrow to house a creature of the size he knew lurked there. Would a current of water set up by waving hands entice the things out of hiding? He flipped tentatively in the direction of the nearest, and the result was spectacular.

Accustomed to octopi that were retiring, who fled from man rather than courted him, Griff was not prepared for the sudden eruption of some five of the species, who oozed out of their homes and appeared to be intelligently waiting for him to declare his intentions. Advancing with their arms pointing to the bottom, the ends curved slightly, their head-bodies erect, they presented the curious aspect of walking on tiptoe. And that concentrated move was so unlike the habits of their kind that he gaped at them for a long moment while Casey withdrew with a quick flip of his fins.

A five-foot, sucker-adorned arm curled lazily through the water as if its owner wished to drag to it this outland monster for a closer inspection. Griff, alert to an opportunity he had never had before, was busy with the camera. Five—no, six—seven—he counted as he watched a new big-eyed dome crawl across an outcrop of brain coral, shooing before it a wave of parrot fish.

An azure Beau-Gregory, jealous of its homestead rights as always, flashed down to defend its chosen section, but, baffled by the cephalopod, merely darted about the bulbous head, which was also body, as a bee might dart about a bear. Griff worked feverishly, intent upon filming the scene. But when a hand fell on his shoulder, urging him back, he became aware of something else, that he now floated in a ring of solemn mollusks, the center of attention for a whole circle of dark, expressionless eyes. And for the first time, his belief in the relative harmlessness of octopi was shaken. In all his observation, in all his reading, he had never seen nor heard of any such move on the part of their species. It was as if some strange being from another planet had landed on San Isadore and the natives had ringed the new arrival around, not menacingly—as yet—but curiously, intent on discovering just what the thing was and why it had come to disurb their peace.

Casey was tugging at his weight belt, signaling with exaggerated jerks of his arm for a quick retreat. But Griff, though uneasy, was intrigued. He knew that an octopus could move fast, but he was also sure that it was possible to escape that steadily narrowing circle when he wished to. He was still busy with the camera, getting what he hoped was a clear and detailed shot of the scene.

A sharp warning tug on his signal cord broke his absorption at last. No diver dared ignore such a summons. He was being paged from above. Those three stiff pulls meant to surface. Casey was already spiraling up, the splashing of his flippers stirring the floating plumes. Reluctantly Griff released the camera and followed. Holding onto the lowest rung of the boarding ladder, he waited for Casey to precede him out of the water.

"What is it—?" he pushed up his face mask and demanded in annoyance. Then he heard the beat of a motor. Around the mangrove-covered cay and straight for their anchored launched came the Navy cutter. It couldn't be another warn-off. They weren't in the disputed territory. And what was his father doing in that cutter?

"Hughes, Griff." As the Navy craft came alongside Dr. Gunston called to them. "Take a tow—we're needed!"

They retrieved the camera, stowed their gear temporarily, and took up anchor to accept a towline.

"What's the matter, sir?" Hughes asked for them all.

"Diver in trouble at the base. I don't know the particulars, but apparently Murray believes we can help. And it's a rush job."

It was Lieutenant Holmes who protested. "That's restricted territory, Doctor. You haven't been cleared to enter it—"

Dr. Gunston favored him with a grim stare. "I gather that there's a life in danger, Lieutenant. Your commanding officer has asked for our assistance, and he's going to get it."

Holmes did not answer as they trailed along behind the cutter. But Griff had an idea that he would not accept the rebuff so easily and was planning to take steps of his own. In the meantime, since diving would probably be required, Griff knelt to check his apparatus carefully.

V

DEPTH SCOUT

THE MUDDLE of clashing machinery and visibly rising foundations, which marked the site of Base Hush-Hush, meant little or nothing to Griff. There was activity unleashed over a wide section of territory where the cliff wall had been graded down, where the whole face of San Isadore was in the process of being drastically altered. And not for the better was Griff's secret thought.

However, the cutter did not point in toward this anthill of action but swept on farther north, coming in to a waste-land Griff had never explored and which even the islanders avoided, there being nothing to draw them to the desert of curdled rock and salty sand.

Here, at some time in the past, a large slice of cliff had broken loose, to fall outward, forming a roughly surfaced natural wharf, over the lip of which spray was flung in rainbow bubbles. It was probably almost beneath the surface at high tide, Griff judged by the lengths of vivid yellow sea moss that clung to it in ragged patches.

Breck Murray was easy to note among the three men who stood there awaiting the cutter and its tow. His khaki shirt was plastered to him by the spray, and his stance suggested impatience. Griff remained in the laboratory launch, content to await developments, but Casey and Holmes went ashore.

Hughes stared down into the water at the edge of the rocks.

"Not too good a place for a dive—"

Griff chose to believe that was addressed to him. "Have to take it easy," he agreed. "This surf could smash you before you got under."

Hughes leaned back, studying the broken cliffs with narrowed eyes. The rock was pitted and creviced all the way along. There could be innumerable caves and crannies below as well as above. A diver swept into one of those by some freak of current might well find himself in dangerous difficulties. This was no place to dive alone, nor without all the safety precautions possible.

"What are they trying to do, anyway?" Hughes mused. "They couldn't have picked out a nastier place to work."

"Frank—Griff—" They both turned at Dr. Gunston's call and scrambled over the greasy footing of slimy waterweed to the rocky platform.

"What about it?" The doctor motioned along the edge of the surf.

Hughes was scowling. "No place to play the fool. Not a place to dive unless you are pushed into it." He gave his verdict frankly. "Most of it is an out-and-out death trap—"

Now Murray was frowning, too. "All right. We understand that. Only there's a job to be done here. Jim Lasalles, my expert, is down under there somewhere and"—he looked at his watch—"time's about run out for him. Those cylinders hold just so much air, remember? How can we work to get him out?"

Dr. Gunston paced closely along the edge of the natural wharf, studying the boil of the waves. "You know where he went in—but he may be half a mile from this point now. We can at least take a closer look." His fingers were busy with the buttons on his shirt as he spoke.

"Chief—let me go down!" Hughes was at his side, while Griff simply slid back into the launch and reached for a tank harness.

But the doctor shook his head firmly. "I'll do it, Frank. After all, I've had the most experience—and I've had time to learn my way around down there. You'll keep a line on me, I promise that!"

Griff, silently rebelling, was forced to accept that ruling. He strapped on his father's weight belt, made sure that watch and depth gauge were safely in place, testing each fastening. But when he turned to pick up the tank, he discovered that Casey, too, was making preparations to enter the water. And almost side by side, the two used the same trick of an expert diver, catching the exact moment to slide into an advancing comber. Frank was crouched over the water glass, watching their descent, while Griff stood with Murray, paying out the lifelines, feeling the pull with sensitive fingers, the pull that meant all was right below.

Seconds seemed hours long during that period of waiting. Griff would gladly have surrendered his hope of returning to the States to be making that dive himself. It was easier to battle the actual dangers lurking along the broken shore line than to sweat it out up here.

"Sharks—" He caught the mumble from one of the attendant Seabees.

There was little to fear from sharks here. But morays—this was just the type of coast line to attract the deadly eels. And barracudas had been sighted in island waters from time to time. Resolutely Griff tried to curb his imagination. He had dived without fear for himself, but now he discovered it was very easy to know anxiety for another.

"Can't see him!" Frank's head lifted from his glass watch. Griff's grasp on the signal line tightened. He must have given it a noticeable twitch, for a reassuring tug was telegraphed back.

"He signals 'all right'!"

"Where's Casey?" Murray demanded.

"Working his way around the point, sir." The Seabee pointed north. "Must be rugged down there, he's taking it mighty easy—"

Disaster struck so suddenly that for a moment they did not really understand what had happened. A low swell of water, which did not seem alarming from their viewpoint,

47

hit the rocks, dashing up with a volume of spray that betrayed its force. And in that moment the line spun between Griff's fingers, burning flesh. Instinctively his grasp on it tightened, but he had followed it almost knee-high into the water by then.

"Hughes!" He cried the warning. What was happening down there? His father must have been swept away. Griff pulled the cord, praying for the return signal. But the line was now stiff, as if it were hooked upon some projection of rock. And he dared not exert any more pull for fear it would snap.

A nightmare span of time followed. Casey was recalled to trace Dr. Gunston's line as Hughes made ready to dive. And then came the paralyzing answer. The cord was fouled, right enough, about a sharp spur of coral even as Griff had dreaded. And beyond drifted a frayed end. His father might have been sucked into any one of half a hundred cracks and caves, caught there unable to win free again.

Griff fought panic. The island was a porous sponge, carved out below sea level. And a cave big enough to admit the body of a diver might run back for some distance. There were the sea wells dotting the interior—they were fed through such breaks in the cliff wall. Here the combers would endanger a diver, give him a limited chance for search. But if a man might go down one of those pools—

"The wells!" He must have said that aloud, for Murray had spun to face him. But Griff was staring inland, trying to remember all he knew of the sea pools.

"You have an idea?" Murray pushed.

"The sea pools, inland—they have their outlets." He didn't want to explain too much, and he stopped before he had a chance to even try.

Murray was startled and then thoughtful. "There's a large one, about a quarter of a mile due west—"

Before he could elaborate, the head of a diver broke water, and Hughes climbed up the weedy verge. He shoved up his mask and squatted, panting, a pinched look about his nostrils.

"I think maybe I've got it—" But there was little exultation in his voice. It was plain he did not consider his news good. "Traced in from where the cord fouled. There's a cave there—reaches pretty far back. The chief may have been jammed in by that wave. I need a lamp—"

"We've got that." One of the Seabees produced an underwater lamp of the latest design. As he rigged it under Hughes's direction, Murray spoke again to Griff.

"About that pool—"

Griff leaned over the busy pair before him. "Frank, in which direction does that cave run?"

Hughes sat back on his heels, glancing from the surging waters to the cliff front. "From about there"—he indicated a point some hundred yards to the south—"west. It's pretty long, that's why I have to have the lamp—goes straight in."

Murray was obviously thinking. "Could be—just could be—" was his verdict.

Griff was willing to accept that. He waited until Hughes submerged once more, and then he assembled his own equipment from the lab launch. He'd probably need extra weight on his belt. With care he tested its latch, making sure it would release at a touch. Too many divers had been drowned because of faulty belts, and what he proposed to do was the trickiest bit of underwater work he had ever attempted.

"You've dived the inland pools?" Murray asked the question Griff dared not answer with the truth. As far as he knew, no one had ever invaded the mysterious depths of one of the sea wells, but that fact was not going to stop him now. He nodded, rather than spoke.

The blistering heat of the sun dried the last remaining drops of sea spray from Griff's half-naked body during that trek across the upper reaches of the cliff. One of the Seabees helped him with his equipment. They crossed a stretch of heated rock, found a gully running back in the general direction, and dropped thankfully into the thick white sand that drifted there. The well, when they finally came to its lip was no different from the others Griff had seen. The deep blue surface, the scarlet sponges growing along its walls, seemed to add to the secret, closed-in quality, a quality the waters along the reef never had. To slide over into that and to allow oneself to spiral down through the liquid that appeared from above to be thicker, less like salt water, was going to be an ordeal.

And the reasoning behind Griff's recklessness was so flimsy a guess. Griff could not have explained it—had no wish to put into words his feeling that there *was* a connection between this deep sapphire well inland and the cave on the coast. He was going by hunch now, and a kind of inner stubbornness kept him to his decision. It was good that Murray believed he had done this before—no use asking for complications.

Griff inspected his equipment with the care of a veteran diver who knew only too well that a single slip or rash lack of examination might mean his life. The depth gauge was his special protection now. If the blue hole before him was too deep, he would have warning and be able to drop his weight belt and pull out in time.

But, even as one part of his mind thought that, he was looking about for a piece of coral of the right size to add to the weight about his middle. Holmes had followed carrying an underwater lamp, and Commander Murray dropped from his shoulder a coil of lifeline.

Griff slipped his feet into his flippers, made them fast. He shrugged into the tank straps, felt the weight of that precious supply of air settle into place like a knapsack, wriggling muscles until he was sure of the right balance. He wouldn't try a straight dive here; instead, he used the lifeline to lower himself slowly into the water. The surface, warmed by the sun, was at blood temperature, but as the water closed over his head there came a chill.

He made the descent, using the line as a check. Someone with a good sense of timing was lowering the lamp at a speed almost equal to his own. And, as the mark around him deepened, he flashed it on. Fish swam here, came to gather in the beam, goggling in stupid bewilderment.

Another object came dangling down, and Griff identified a light fish spear. He used it to fend away from the broken surface of the wall, keeping a watch for a crevice or hole from which the flat, evil head of a moray might project.

Down, down—now he was in a twilight, which might have been more disturbing had he not had that experience of diving after nightfall. The ray of the lamp gave him an excellent picture of his surroundings, and it might keep at a distance the larger creatures of the deep.

A sea urchin clung to a ledge, its poisonous spines thrown into high relief by the light. Anemones, crabs, other life flowed, swam, crawled about him as he kicked his way down. Time ceased to have meaning as it always did under water. He would have said that he had been a half hour in the leisurely descent, when his water-protected watch registered only minutes.

Then he saw what he was searching for, what the hunch had told him did exist. But as he clung to the line, drifting, he swallowed, and a prickling chill, which was not born of the water, ran along his spine. Opposite him was a black hole, a hole into which the full light of the lamp beamed to show no inner wall. If this wasn't the entrance of the sea passage, it was more than just a cave.

Now he must enter that hole, swing along into the dark unknown, where he could be trapped, where a lifeline fouled about a rock, as his father's fouled in the sea, would not help him. But this was what he had come to find—and inwardly Griff knew that there was no returning.

He fastened the spear in his belt loop. Then he gave the agreed signal on the line. Unhooking the lamp from its cord, he flipped his way into the hole.

Ragged rock, sea things— He flinched from stinging coral, trying to watch for any unpleasant surprises, animal or vegetable, which might lurk there. The passage sloped downward, to Griff another proof that this was what he sought—it must drop to below coast level. He kept his attention on what lay ahead, tried not to remember that he was making his way down an enclosed vein in the rock. Now and again he gave a tug to the line. It was free, untrapped by the rocks.

Just as it was difficult to judge time under water, so did distance cease to register properly. Perspective under the surface was warped, and Griff could have been inches from what he saw ahead—or feet. But the steady, unfailing beam of the light showed him what obstructions to avoid. It was a journey that could not have been made in darkness—too many projections, and once a turn, which he negotiated with care.

Then, all at once, the walls of the tunnel fell away, and Griff swam out into open space. The sea? But it couldn't be! Beyond the path of the lamp was darkness. He flapped up until his head broke surface. Where in the world was this?

Treading water, he pulled up the lamp and swept it around. He was in a vast pool, and to the left were rocks with their tops above water. Griff made for these and clung there, one arm across a slimy surface in support. The lamp displayed a ledge a little above, and he pulled himself up on that.

Gingerly he pushed up his mask. There was air—but it bore an odd and disagreeable musky taint. The walls were glistening with weed to a point well above his head—they must be covered at high tide. He turned the light out over the survace. It centered on a rock some distance away.

"Helloooo—"

Griff started, almost lost his grip on the slippery ledge and went back into the water. That hail, distorted by the echoes that magnified and dehumanized it, was the last thing he had expected. Bracing himself against the wall, having taken the precaution of snapping down his mask again against an involuntary descent into the flood, he got to his feet and flashed the ray of the lamp in a slow crawl along the opposite wall of the cavern.

Then the light picked up and held a waving arm, found the head and shoulders of a weird, masked monster, who apparently could not move but lay on water-washed rocks.

Griff went into the water and swam, the light beam before him pinpointing that figure. Then he fetched up against the tiny rock island, and a hand closed with convulsive tightness about the wrist he lifted for a hold.

"Snap off that light!" Griff knew his father's voice, hoarse, low, and hurried, as if they were in some danger that could be drawn by that core of hard yellow radiance.

Griff pulled up on the islet and levered up his mask. They were crowded together in the dark, and he heard the click of metal against metal as his air tank struck against some part of Dr. Gunston's equipment. His father was breathing heavily, as if half-winded from some exertion.

"How did you get in?" The question came with queer pauses between words. "It's waiting out there in the other cave. If it hadn't had that poor devil to amuse it. *I* wouldn't have escaped—"

Griff felt a shudder pass through the body so close to his. He drew a deep breath of the tainted air. His father didn't sound hysterical, but there was an odd note in his voice.

"I took a chance on one of the inland pools. Just followed a hunch—"

"The wells!" Dr. Gunston was honestly surprised. "A back door. Then there *is* another way out of here! We don't have to pass it—"

"Pass what, sir?"

"The monster—the thing, whatever it is, that's laired up in the outer sea cave here. I was swept in by a wave. It was—busy—" his father's voice again slid up scale a tone or two—"with the Navy diver when I caught it in my lamp. Then the light drew it. I dived, dropped the lamp to the bottom to interest it, and came up in here. The Lord only knows where 'here' is! But there's no going back with that thing doing sentry—"

"A dupee—?" Griff used the only term he knew for the dead monster of the beach.

"I didn't get a good look at it. But it's something which

has no right to be alive in this day and age! One of Le Marr's voodoo nightmares!"

"We can make it back to the pool," Griff said confidently. "The passage is fairly easy."

But to his surprise his father did not agree at once. There was a lengthy pause, and then Dr. Gunston spoke.

"I've a game leg—gave it a scrape on something when I dived to get away from the thing's rush."

Whether it was wise or not, Griff used the lamp, training the lowest wattage beam on his father. Across his thigh was a line of red dots, and about them the flesh was already puffing into ugly swelling. Griff could guess the agony of pain that must be knotting muscle and flesh. And that must be seen to at once! It could be the mark of any kind of wound from a coral scrape to breaks left by the poisonous spines of some fish.

"We'll get out!" From somewhere he found that confidence—making his voice sound firm even in his own unbelieving ears.

A length of the snapped life cord was still at his father's belt. With that linking them together, he should be able to win back up the vent to the well and safety. At least that was their only chance now.

VI

TOO LITTLE, MUCH TOO LATE

YEARS AFTERWARDS nightmare memories of that journey back up to the inland pool awoke Griff bathed in a cold sweat. Dr. Gunston, with iron endurance, had held on to consciousness. But for much of the trip back Griff was supporting a limp body. He dropped his own weighted belt, the spear, every bit of extra equipment he dared abandon.

A coral graze on his shoulder set blood to staining the water and brought a dryness to his mouth. What if that summoned the mysterious nightmare from which his father had fled—or any of the other carnivora that might lurk in the circle of day beyond the lamp? He could only force himself to swim at that steady pace which would mean their eventual salvation.

The tunnel walls opened out—he was in the well. And someone above had sense enough to rig a ladder over the lip of the rim. He clung with one hand to the rungs, supporting Dr. Gunston's weight with an arm that felt as if it were being pulled from its socket. A splash of water in his face—then the weight was gone. Hands, locked in his armpits, pulled him up. But it wasn't until he lay on a blanket on the sand, his face free from the mask, tank and flippers stripped from him, that Griff realized he had made it.

He sat up. "Dad?"

A Seabee grinned at him. "They're carting him down to the base—where Doc can get to work on him. He's got a bad leg—"

Griff pulled himself up. He knew just how bad that leg could be! And there was Hughes and Casey. If his father's story were true, any seaside diver might be in trouble. He had to get moving. But he was plowing heavy-footed through the sand as if weights were on each foot. A hand slipped under his arm.

"Go small, mon—" The soft slur of island speech brought his head up.

"Le Marr!"

There was something reassuring about the voodoo man. Griff had a queer feeling that alone of those around him now Le Marr could believe in that weird world beneath them, take at face value his father's report of the menace that had killed the Navy diver.

"Debble thing—" It was as if Le Marr read his mind. "Mon go in debble thing's house-hole—come out. You have the gris-gris in here." His long ivory finger tapped Griff lightly on the breast.

"There *is* something in there?"

Le Marr nodded, his face serious. "Debble thing."

"Has it been there long?"

The other answered in the negative. "Come lately. Sign—bad sign—"

They had crossed the sandy desert and were following a line of tracks back to the base.

"What kind of sign?"

Le Marr did not answer that. Instead he spoke over his shoulder to the Seabees trailing them with Griff's diving apparatus.

"Tell mons that dive—debble thing down there—"

"Sure, pop." The cheerful American voice rang loudly over the softer speech of San Isadore. "The commander's already passed the word to stop."

The glare of the sun and his own fatigue blurred his surroundings for Griff. He had a vague idea that he had been half-carried over the last section into the base, and only when pain pricked his upper arm did he come around. He was lying on an examination table while a medical corpsman cleaned and treated the coral graze.

"—you'll fly him out then?" Murray's deep voice came from the hall.

"It's a matter of time, Commander. Yes, I'd say his only chance was the mainland. Hooker can take a stretcher in the cabin, and I'll make the trip with him. Frankly—I've never seen anything like it. Some kind of poison and a very virulent one. It's amazing he's lasted this long. We've got to learn what it is before we have another case on our hands."

"All right. I'll alert Hooker. You want to leave at once?"

"As soon as it is humanly possible."

Who were they going to fly out? As the corpsman walked to the supply cupboard, Griff sat up.

"Hey, fella—"

The man turned, but Griff was already on his way to the door. He reached that vantage point just in time to see a stretcher being borne past. And his father's face, flushed and swollen, puffed eyes half-open but unseeing, his father's voice muttering in a thick, senseless whisper flashed before him. The corpsman had caught up with Griff and could not be shaken off when the younger Gunston tried to follow the stretcher down the corridor.

"Take it easy, kid. Doc's flying your old man up to the States—they'll be able to fix him up. We aren't equipped to handle it here. They'll have him under treatment in three—four hours. Lieutenant Hooker's a hot pilot and knows how to get speed out of that bus of his—"

So Griff had to watch the seaplane off; blinking as it disappeared into the bright blue of the afternoon sky. Hughes reached the landing stage just as the plane lifted.

"How is it with the chief?" Beneath his tan, his face was greenish white and drawn. There was a moment of silence, and it was Griff who replied, steadily enough:

"He got some scratches—"

"Poisoned?" Hughes demanded sharply, almost as if Griff had been responsible.

"Something new—at least Doc can't diagnose it," Murray cut in. "That's why he's flying him north. He needs an expert opinion."

"Something new," Hughes repeated savagely. "Yes—we're up against something new all right, Commander. Your man is gone, you know—"

Breck Murray's mouth set grimly. "So we pieced out from some things Dr. Gunston said. What did he tell you?" He rounded on Griff. "Or what did you see down there?"

Griff described the underground cave but added that all he knew about the menace that guarded the sea entrance was what his father had told him—that some unknown sea dweller had killed the Navy diver and that Dr. Gunston had only escaped from it by chance.

"And what did *you* see?" Murray swung now to Hughes.

"I got in far enough to spot the torch the chief dropped. Then it was caught up by something. I didn't get a good look at it—"

"Shark?" Murray hazarded.

Hughes replied to that with a firm negative. "I'd take my oath it's nothing we know. You heard of the thing that was found on the beach before your arrival?"

"Some garbled stuff about a sea serpent." Murray looked perplexed.

"Not a sea serpent in the snake sense," Hughes corrected. "But it was an aquatic mammal, large, unknown, and we are still trying to classify it—"

"Man-eater?"

"It was a flesh-eater, yes," Hughes admitted. "And it bears resemblance to the most recent reports of the so-called 'sea serpents' that have been sighted from ships."

"And now we've another of the things roosting down there in that cave!" the commander burst out. "It's liable to make things hot for any diver?"

"How can I tell what it will do?" Hughes shouted back. "We don't know anything about it. But it did get your diver this morning, and it attacked Dr. Gunston, I'd say you'd better get rid of it if you want to feel safe under water here. It may hunt only at night, keep under cover during the day. But we can't be sure of that—"

"What we need, skipper,"—Casey, looking as tired and drawn as Hughes, had come up to join them—"is a bomb planted down there."

"Maybe you're right. Look over our stuff, Casey, and see what we have which will be a good answer to a sea serpent—" Murray rubbed his hand wearily across his sweating face.

Griff sat down in the half-finished mess hall. The food, which had just been placed before him, was good—it smelled like home. But, though he hadn't eaten since early that morning, he did not pick up his fork. There was something wrong. The same hunch that had led him to venture into the inland pool was working. He could agree that they had no way of enticing the mysterious monster out of its cave, nor could they be sure that it *would* come out. There were sea dwellers content enough to remain in self-chosen prisons from which they never emerged, allowing the water currents to supply them at random with food. Perhaps Casey's suggestion was the only possible answer, and he was a demolition expert, used to such tricks under water.

Only Griff could not rid himself of a feeling of foreboding, a feeling that was not born of the worry connected with the plane beating its way north. They had had two radio reports in flight. Dr. Gunston was still holding his own, and as long as life remained they had hope.

"I will speak with the commander now—" The voice was soft over a core of iron. Griff glanced up to see Le Marr.

The islander was at ease, a man with a mission, and he manifestly was in no way influenced by Holmes's scowl and refusal.

"This is restricted territory. You'll be given an escort to the edge of the zone and then—you'll beat it!" But in spite of the authority of those words, there was uncertainty below them. Holmes had been briefed in the routine of his job, was zealous in its duties. But there were no regulations to cover the happenings of the past few hours. Nothing in security files taught a man to stand up to an unknown carnivore at the bottom of the sea, nor did it prepare one for tactfully handling a voodoo priest, the unofficial ruler of the island. Griff cut in.

"I think Commander Murray wants to see Le Marr."

"And that is the truth!" As if the mention of his name had been a conjure spell to summon him, Breck Murray materialized just within the doorway. "Glad to meet you, Le Marr." He held out his hand. "Yes, I know, Mr. Holmes, he hasn't been cleared by security. Le Marr, I'm told you know a lot about this island and what makes it tick. There's some sort of a wild thing down in that sea coast hole. It's taken my diver, and now Dr. Gunston's out of the picture, too. Have you any idea of what it is or how we can get it out of there?"

Dobrey Le Marr's ivory hands fluttered in a quick gesture. "This debble thing be new to the island, sir. It comes up from the deeps—"

"Why?" Murray demanded flatly.

"Who knows? Maybeso trouble there—I think that. But I know it not fo' true. Debble thing run from trouble; it 'fraid, it hungry. It find hidey hole an' wait. Pretty soon maybe it forget—it not like mon." He tapped his own chest. "Then maybeso it go—"

"Well," Murray shrugged. "We can't afford to sit it out. But you haven't hunted these things then?"

Le Marr shook his head.

"What killed that one found on the shore?" Holmes asked the question as though trying to force Le Marr into some damaging admission. Again Griff struck into the conversation. The circumstances, he thought, released him from the promise he had given his father.

"The Geiger said it was 'hot.' Maybe radiation got it."

He was amazed at the result of his perfectly truthful statement. Both of the officers froze, almost as if the thing they discussed had appeared in the center of the floor. Holmes opened his mouth and then closed it tightly. But Murray strode to the table and glared down at Griff.

"That the truth?"

"Ask Hughes. He discovered it during dissection. It was 'hot'—so's that plague scum—"

Murray ran both hands through his thick brush of hair and then glanced over his shoulder at Holmes. "D'you know that?"

"I have nothing to say," snapped the younger officer in return.

The commander bit off a forceful word. "That answers me." He was curbing his temper with a visible effort. "Maybe someday they'll give a man all the facts before—" He swallowed. "So this menace may be radioactive along with all the rest! That's pleasant. I guess Casey's answer is the only one."

"Bomb it out?" Griff's earlier uneasiness awoke as he saw Le Marr give a start.

"You put bomb down there, sir? That be bad thing— very bad thing!"

"Why?"

"Sea run under the land—far, far." Le Marr's hands moved in graphic motions. "You break that—land fall—into the sea."

"You've got a point. But we can't lie around here waiting

for that thing to move out. We've got to get it out and fast!
We're working against time—"

Out of the tail of his eye Griff saw Holmes make a warning
gesture in a vain attempt to stop Breck Murray's explanation. But Griff, remembering a problem of his own and
how he and Chris Waite had solved it, dared to interrupt
once more.

"Look here, sir—could you rig some sort of small ex-
plosive which could be planted in bait. If we could get that
thing to eat it—"

"Hmmm—" The commander stopped pacing. Even Le
Marr looked thoughtful. "You tried something like that
before?"

"Chris Waite, he's the mate of the *Island Queen,* and I
got rid of a big moray in that way. We baited a hook and
pulled the eel out of its hole—though we had to use a block
and tackle to do it. We couldn't hope to drag *this* out of
hiding, not if it is the size of the dead one we found on the
beach. But supposing it was eating and a small charge
blew up in its face—that ought to kill it."

They held a conference, Hughes, Casey, the commander,
another demolition man, and Griff. A party went inland
with rifles and returned before the hour was up with the
rangy carcass of a wild pig. The scrawny frame now occupied the position of honor in the center of the table while
Hughes examined the bristly corpse and asked questions of
Casey and his second-in-command.

"We may be able to do it," was Hughes's verdict, "as-
summing that the thing doesn't like its dinner alive and
kicking when it gets it and assuming that you can measure
out a charge which will answer the purpose." He glanced
out of the window to where evening shadows were purple-
black and thick. "A lot of the big ones feed at sunset—"

Griff, remembering octopi activity, nodded at that. Now
that they had made up their collective minds, he was eager
to get into action. Anything was better than to sit in this
half-finished building listening to the clatter of work without,

waiting for the arrival of a messenger with a new radio report—

But there proved to be little that he could do except watch the evisceration of the corpse and the rigging therein of some complicated wiring and grenades dreamed up by the demolition people. Casey straightened up at last from the gory table with a tired ghost of a grin.

"That ought to do it, skipper." He spoke across the smelly board to Murray. "Just let the whatsis get its back teeth into that and whamo!"

They could not depend upon the sea to deliver their prize package. It must be introduced by hand into the ominous cave opening. And it was Casey who overrode all the others in his demand to be the one for that job.

Armed with a harpoon gun-spear, a lifeline fast to his harness, his face very sober behind his mask, he entered the combers and hung, one hand anchoring him to a rock, as his assistant gingerly lowered the bait into his reach.

With the pig bomb in hand he went under water. And those above had to depend upon the reports from Hughes and Murray, crouched by the water glass, as to his movements. Almost immediately he was beyond their point of vision, and they could only stand on the natural jetty, the spray soaking through their clothing as the dusk with its odd greenish glow gathered fast.

Griff's fingers were on the lifeline. He caught the signal and he shouted. "He's in the cave!"

The commander's hand fell heavily on his shoulder. Griff nursed the line, now taut, waiting for the second pull, which would mark Casey's escape. It was far too long in coming.

"What's Bert doing!" That was his superior officer, tossing away a half-smoked cigarette in order to light another with hands that shook a little. "Shoving its dinner right into the thing's teeth?"

"Now!" Griff caught the "mission accomplished" twitch.

Casey had better make it fast. If he had waited to see the bait seized, he might have waited far too long—for, in spite of all their care, the charge might be too strong and would bring the cliff down as Le Marr had warned. Yet the islander did not appear to heed his own warning. He was teetering back and forth on the wet rocks as intent upon seeing the end of the game as the rest of them.

Casey's head broke water. He swam for the rocks and found a reception committee scrambling down to lift him in. But before he made land, he thrust out his spear, a weird armored captive still wriggling upon it. Hughes automatically grabbed at that. Casey snapped up his mask and drew a deep breath.

"Did it take the bait?" demanded Murray.

Casey's usual lightheartedness was gone. "Something which was mighty hungry did. I didn't see it close—I didn't want to!"

Murray was watching his wrist watch, and now he counted aloud: "—five—six—seven—eight—nine—"

But he never reached "ten." Griff could not have told afterwards whether it was sound, or vibration, or both. There was a tremor, a muffled noise—

"That's it." Casey broke the hush.

"Look out!"

Holmes's shout brought them about to face the cliff wall. A section split off, crashed down into the swirling water. A wave licked knee-high about the men on the rocks. They waited for more. But nothing came, and then Murray gave an order.

"Get into the cutter—we'll take the sea route back."

Griff was crowded against Hughes. The other had out a pocket flash, examining the fish impaled on Casey's spear. It was a new variety to Griff, with a warty, thorned skin, an odd pugged face.

"What is it?"

Hughes replied with more than a little amazement coloring his tone. "Something which does not belong here. Scorpion fish—from the Barrier Reef. If this is what got the chief—" He stopped almost in mid-word. "Maybe we're too late. We're doing much too little, too late. Half-way around the world from where it belongs! Lord, who's mixing us up— or what is happening?"

VII

THE *ISLAND QUEEN* DOES NOT REPLY

"You say it's a *what?*" Commander Murray regarded the ugly, spined body of Casey's capture with obvious distaste.

"It's a stonefish—a scorpion fish—We saw enough of them on the Pacific—Banda Sea project. They range from Polynesia to the Red Sea—"

"But not here?" Murray caught him up on that.

"Not known to be here," Hughes corrected cautiously. "But how can we make any definite statements? In 1954 they brought in a live Latimeria Chalumnae near the Comore Islands. And by rights the thing should have been dead more than a million years ago. It was a living fossil. In 1949 fish scales, as large as those from a tarpon, but from a totally unknown fish, were sold to a souvenir dealer in Tampa, Florida. And none of the experts in Washington could identify them. So there might be a whole colony of stonefish cruising about here—"

"They're deadly?" Casey surveyed his catch with open curiosity. "It made a run at the pig, that's why I speared it. Then I forgot about it—I was too interested in the other thing."

Commander Murray leaned back in his chair. "Which, luckily, we don't have to worry about now!"

Casey nodded confirmation. An hour after his exploit Hughes had insisted on making a night dive. He returned with the information that the entrance to the monster cave had been sealed by the landslip they had witnessed and that, living or dead, they need worry no more about attack from the unknown.

Griff stared at the stonefish dully. He knew that the

poison from its spines was as vicious as cobra venom. If this was what had struck his father, he could only marvel that Dr. Gunston had survived. But Hughes had an answer to that also. Using a pencil he prodded the warty skin.

"This will be proof for Gongware—"

"Dr. Gongware?" Casey alone recognized the name. Hughes shot him a surprised glance.

"Yes. He's been working on anti-poison serums for divers on the pearl banks. The chief volunteered to play guinea pig. If he was attacked by this, it must have been Gongware's stuff which kept him alive—though it's been over a year since he was inoculated. You sent news about this to the States, Commander? It may give the doctors a lead in treatment."

Murray nodded and then yawned. Griff looked at his watch. It was close to midnight. But he didn't want to leave until they had some word. Holmes came in, blinking at the bright light.

"There's a row going on down island, sir," he announced.

Murray had echoed the word "row" when Griff stepped past the security officer to the door and out into the night. The flood lamps made a harsh white day for a little circle, and there was the clatter of machines to fill it. But some trick of the wind brought another sound, faint enough, but in its very faintness depressing. Griff had heard it before—but never in such volume.

"What is it?" Murray had followed him out.

"The voodoo drums, sir." Griff could feel that beat eating under his own skin. He knew that there were certain rhythms of those ritual drums that were not for the hearing of his race, that would twist and turn emotions to a pitch a paler-skinned northerner could not stand. And this was fast approaching that point. A Seabee near him halted a bulldozer to listen.

"I don't like it!" Breck Murray snapped. "Voodoo, eh?"

"The island brand. But I've never heard it like that before. Not since old Kristina died the week after I came here. She was the Mama-loi, the priestess, a kind of witch, I think.

Most of the islanders were afraid of her. She cursed more than she cured—different from Le Marr. And they were drumming out her spirit so she wouldn't haunt them."

"What are they drumming out now?"

"It might be the cave monster, Commander. They consider that to be a dupee—a voodoo devil. Or—"

"It might be us? Le Marr hinted at something of that sort before he faded away this evening."

"Well, the islanders are a close-knit lot. A few of them—Le Marr, Captain Murdock of the *Queen* and his crew, the shopkeeper—have been off island and know more about the world. The rest of them—they are apt to be suspicious of any new thing. It's in their history. They came here as slaves, rebel-convicts, or pirates—fugitives from the law—and they have an instinctive distrust for our brand of civilization. I'd listen to Le Marr, sir; he has more real power than the commissioner, though there're still some who follow the spirit of old Kristina and would like to return—"

"To the ways of the bad old days? Such as this for example?" Murray produced a tiny bag of brilliant scarlet calico. In the light of the working lamps it lay a dollop of blood in the hollow of his palm. "What is it?"

Griff did not touch it. "That's a gris-gris, and not a good one, I'd say, though I'm not a student of voodoo. A gris-gris—amulet—can work either for good or evil. A good one you carry as a luck charm for protection. And an evil one you plant on an enemy. Where did you find that, Commander?"

"Lying just within the door of my office."

"Take it back, put it down in the same place, and then get Le Marr to remove it for you," advised Griff.

"Using the right formula?" One of Murray's expressive eyebrows slid up.

"You lost a diver today. Every bit of bad luck you have from now on will be credited to voodoo, and the reputation of the one who made that gris-gris will grow accordingly. It could add up to bad trouble. Listen!"

The beat of those drums was steady, pulsing in time

with one's blood, or pulling the blood into rhythm with it. Griff was breathing faster; he found it difficult to stand still. He wanted to be out of this place of light and machines—to run into the quiet dark where he could crouch and cover his ears in blissful silence. And yet that windborne sound pulled at him, as if to draw him across the island to its unknown source.

"We don't depend on native labor," Murray pointed out. "Our supplies are brought in from our own ships. I don't see that we have to worry about any trouble with the islanders."

Griff leaned back against a coral slab wall. Maybe the base didn't have to worry about ill will of the men of San Isadore. But he was sure that voodoo or no voodoo, if he were in trouble he would want Le Marr on his side of the barricade. Maybe the islander had no supernatural powers but he had something—something that even the scientist in Dr. Gunston had been forced to acknowledge. And Griff respected Dobrey Le Marr as a man of authority.

"Griff!" Hughes bore down upon him. His eyes were shining and his hands dropped on Griff's shoulders, whirling the slighter and younger man around with him in a circling that had nothing to do with the distant drum, an outburst as foreign to the assistant's usually staid control as Apache war paint.

"They've got it under control! The chief'll pull through! We just heard it by radio. It was the serum that kept him going until they could get the proper antidote."

Griff could never remember afterwards how he got back to the lab. Drugged with fatigue, he made his way up the path from the cutter to his cot at the lab. And then even the beat of the drums, now loud and steady, could not keep him awake any longer.

He did not quite sleep the clock around, but by the slant of the sun across the floor, it was well into afternoon when he rolled over and blinked blearily at the scuttling lizards on the ceiling. Wind rustled in a dry clatter through palm fronds, and beneath that hummed the eternal pound of the surf. He sat up, aware of an aching void in his middle.

The house was quiet. He went down the hall to the shower and saw that the lab door was shut. When he knocked, there was no answer. Hughes must have gone out. Showering was a luxury, dressing a lazy process. He raided the food safe. It was so very peaceful that he decided to visit his spray pool.

But as he stood in the thrust of the wind and looked out over the bay he knew again that vague uneasiness. Something was missing—Carterstown was a deserted town, but that was usual at this hour. Two fishing boats rocked at anchor in the bay. Boats—!

Griff knew now what had bothered him. The *Island Queen* was not at her accustomed berth below. Yet she had been gone three days—and she should have returned that morning. In all the months he had been on San Isadore, he had learned that Angus Murdock, unlike the majority of his compatriots, ran his communication service between the islands with the regularity of a clock. The *Island Queen* had been due to drop her anchor before noon today—yet there was no *Island Queen* to be seen.

Clapping on his palm straw hat, Griff went down to the town. And it was as he threaded his way along the ruts of a side lane that he noticed the second mystery. About one house in three or four was still inhabited. But usually there were signs of life about those. Now—

In spite of the blaze of the sun Griff shivered. Closed shutters, no scrawny chickens scratching half-heartedly in the littered doorways—a brooding quiet. He might be walking through a town waiting for an attack.

The Union Jack hung limp from the pole in front of the Government House, its folds sun-bleached from scarlet to rose. Griff hesitated for a moment and then climbed the three broad steps that set the building on a more imposing level than its neighbors. The wide inner hall was deserted, but echoing loudly through the general silence came the click of an inexpertly pounded typewriter. Someone was busy during the siesta period, and Griff went in search of the worker.

In the second office he found his quarry, a young man of his own age hunched in concentration over the keyboard of an old and battered machine, pecking out some composition letter by painful, two-finger style.

"Henry Grimes!" Griff approached the desk.

The other looked up, startled, but not with the welcome Griff expected from Angus Murdock's nephew. Grimes was due to leave the island in two weeks time on a scholarship the governor at Santa Maria had helped to arrange. But now Henry's square young face, a less tough edition of the pirate Murdock visage, was very sober, and his eyes were both cold and wary. Griff asked the question that had brought him there.

"What's the news from the *Queen?* Didn't she come in on schedule?"

"Did you see her in—the—bay, mon?" Henry counter-questioned, changing in midsentence to the precise diction he tried so hard to use.

"What happened?"

"Ask—the—Navy mons—men— Trouble comes with them. The *Queen*, she don't answer the wireless!" As his agitation grew, Henry lapsed into the island idiom. "The commissioner, he speak to San' Maria. They say *Queen* sail on time, same as always. But she no come—"

Griff stiffened. Those other stories of the mystery ships, the drifting derelicts—he had listened to them, speculated concerning their fate with Chris and Murdock himself. But those reports had never seemed true. They were just something that happened beyond the horizon to strangers, nothing that touched his own world. Only now—what if the *Island Queen* was caught up in that ugly web?

"They've tried to reach her by radio?"

"The commissioner, he expect something important comin' by my uncle's hand—to him from the governor. When the *Queen* do not come, he worry, so he call San' Maria—'cause there be no storm, no thing to keep her back. San' Maria say *Queen* sail like always—calm sea, no winds, no thing bad. But the *Queen*, she do not come. So there *is* something bad!"

"And her own radio?"

Henry's shoulders hunched as he leaned farther over the typewriter. "They call—they are still callin'. She do not answer."

Griff started for the radio room, the islanders' one link with the outside world. There was the shuffle of hide sandals behind him as Henry followed.

The room was hot and dark, the shutters having been pulled to against the straight glare of the afternoon sun. Commissioner Burrows had shed the white coat he wore in public, but he had made no other concession to the heat. He glanced up as Griff hovered in the doorway, gave a nod, which was both greeting and invitation to enter, and waved to a chair. But he did not remove the earphones clamped across his crisp black hair, nor did he relax his listening attitude.

Henry coughed, and the shuffle of his sandals was unnecessarily loud. The commissioner sighed, slipped up one earphone, and reached for one of the strong island cigarettes lying in a box on the table.

"No news, sir?" Henry asked.

"No news for us."

"And you can't raise the *Queen* at all, sir?"

Burrows shook his head. "Santa Maria has sent out the cutter." His clipped English with its overseas accent still carried a trace of the Indies drawl. "So far—nothing!"

He watched the smoke curl lazily from the tube between his fingers and then added abruptly, "Would you be willing to do something for me, Mr. Gunston?"

"Of course—"

"It may be necessary for me to see Commander Murray at the base—but I don't want to make too much of our meeting. I understand very well the necessity for declaring the installation being erected there restricted territory, but you have a legitimate reason for visiting the base. The plane that flew your father to tht States returned this morning. You will desire to have news—"

Griff was already on his feet. Probably Hughes had already gone to the base for just that reason. He knew a twinge of resentment because the other had not wakened him for that trip.

"Present my regards to Commander Murray"—the commissioner's tone became more formal—"and ask him when it will be possible to meet with me to discuss an important matter. Henry will run you up in our launch—"

As Griff went out into the late afternoon with Henry, it was into a still deserted town. A pig sleeping in the rut of a side road, the ever-present hummingbirds flitting from one flowering spike of aloe to the next, were apparently the only living things in Carterstown.

"Where is everyone?" Griff ventured to ask.

"They wait—"

"Wait? For what?"

"For what comes!" Henry's hand went to the breast of his shirt, in that movement Griff had seen Rob make so many times. So Henry, too, had his gris-gris, his protection against the unseen.

The American spoke boldly. "The drums sounded last night. Le Marr—"

Henry's broad face was impassive; it was as shuttered as the windows of those houses back in town. For all his scholarship, his off-island plans, Henry was of San Isadore. But he did volunteer one strange statement—something that startled Griff.

"Dobrey Le Marr—that mon be not so big-big—" The words trailed off into a mutter as Henry realized that he had made that remark to an off-islander.

Dissension in the island ranks? Griff wondered about that as he cast off the mooring lines of the small boat that was the commissioner's official "launch." Had a segment of the die-hards who had followed the dark beliefs of old Kristina begun to re-establish their brand of the ancient worship?

71

Was that the explanation for the new drumming of the night before?

They headed straight for the Naval settlement. But to Griff's surprise they were warned off long before they reached their destination by the cutter, which had run the laboratory boat from its work two days before. Griff signaled vigorously and shouted across the water that he had a message for Commander Murray from the commissioner. But in the end he had to transfer to the Navy craft and let Henry return alone to Carterstown.

A guard, armed, marched him at a quick trot through the section where construction was in the same frenzied progress to a core of buildings that had sprouted rooms overnight, like cells in a wasps' nest. Once there he ran into Hughes in earnest conversation with the doctor, and Griff broke from his escort to join them.

"He's more than holding his own," the doctor assured Griff. "That serum stemmed the poison until they could pump an antidote into him. But if he hadn't had that—" He shook his head. "Nasty beggars, those stonefish. I'll take one apart scale by scale and see if I can discover what makes them tick. In the meantime, I had them wire Gongware for some more serum. If he has a supply on hand, they'll fly it out to us. Better to be prepared—"

"Two more stonefish brought in this morning," Hughes told Griff. "I want the commander to offer a reward and see if we can get the islanders to hunt them. But how they got here in the first place—halfway around the world from where we thought they belonged—!"

It was a puzzle all right, thought Griff—but no more of a puzzle than a lot of other things which focused on San Isadore at the moment. He saw over Hughes's shoulder the plane bobbing on the water by the improvised landing, and in that moment an idea occurred to him. Visibility from the air was wide. The *Island Queen* could not have drifted so far off her course since she had left Santa Maria that she could not be sighted by a search plane. Could the commander order the machine out to aid in the hunt? No longer attending to Hughes's talk about stonefish, Griff turned to the guard.

"I'd like to see Commander Murray as soon as possible—"

"You've been the one holding up the procession, fella—"

"What's up?" Hughes gathered that there was something else in the world beside fish.

"The *Island Queen* is late—and she doesn't answer radio signals," Griff flung over his shoulder as he trotted after his guide.

VIII

HOUR OF ULTIMATUM

BUT GRIFF WAS to have no satisfaction from Commander Murray. Scant attention was paid either to the message from the commissioner or to his own idea of using the seaplane in the search for the *Queen*. The atmosphere of the base had always been one of hurry and tension, but now it was building to a kind of controlled frenzy. If the Seabees had been working against time from the start of the project, they now raced with disaster. And Murray had no moments to spare.

Shunted to one side, not knowing how he was going to return to Carterstown, since an overland trek at night was a risky business and Murray had made no offer of a trip in the cutter, Griff watched the scene in bewildered amazement. The lamps flashed on as night closed down.

More lights tonight—this time at sea beyond the broken reef. Then landing craft, a rugged fleet, coming ashore in a steady procession to land quantities of bales and boxes on the beach. Tractors towing flat trucks toiled down to that point, where robots loaded with a speed and efficiency that made Griff tired to watch. He did not understand a tenth of what he saw—he had never known that such machines existed. Most of the labor was apparently done by push-button control over new unmanned cranes and trucks.

The train of goods waddled by, passing the now almost completed administration building to some hidden interior destination. A second tractor with its tow was already pulled up beside the mountain of material on the strand. About him the handful of men were directing only, most of the work was robot. Griff was ignorant of construction work, but surely this precision and remote control was new, though any dullard could have guessed that government brass never published all it knew, nor displayed openly all that it might accomplish in times of stress. Atomic power for machinery had been commonly discussed, and there had been a few timid and costly excursions into that in the civilian field. But Griff guessed now that he was probably surrounded at the present by machines running on atomic power. Perhaps the atomic breakdown also supplied the light under which those various pieces of apparatus went their efficient way.

What was the purpose of the base anyway? He could make a rough guess at a storage depot. The mound of goods moving in a steady and unending stream to an inland pool could not be just for the use of the fifty or so men now stationed here—unless they were only the fore-runners of a large garrison.

But the low, heavy-walled building that served as head-quarters, barracks, mess hall, and hospital was still the only erection in sight, and there was no indication of another being planned. A sub base? Griff was trying to fit that idea into the general scheme of things when Hughes and the Navy doctor came out. The doctor halted to light a cigarette. In the glare of the working lights his eyes were red and puffy, and he inhaled the smoke with the sigh of a tired man. But Hughes was alert, alive, his fingers drumming on his belt, then moving to ram into the pockets of his slacks.

"Mutant—" Hughes said.

"If you think so. It's your field rather than mine. And I don't remember ever dissecting a fish before. Mutant—? But it wasn't 'hot.'"

"Not this generation—"

The doctor's lips shaped a soundless whistle. "So that's

your theory. Well—maybe so." But he didn't look convinced. "Twenty-five years since Hiroshima, and we haven't seen what the horror merchants dreamed up would follow that— no superbrains or monster-men—"

"Not quite a full generation," Hughes pointed out. "And maybe man reacts more slowly to radiation than—"

"Than your fish? You think that thing you found on the beach, and whatever it was in the cave, were mutant forms also? Mutants of what—whales—seals—?"

"There have always been reports of strange things seen at sea, even weird remains washed ashore," Hughes countered. "Dr. Gunston's theory was that unexplained radiation suggested some experimentation in the depths—"

"Which drove Fido up here?" The doctor grinned. "You may have something there. Or maybe the Reds have turned a gimmick loose—just to foul up the picture generally for you brain boys—"

"We could accept that, too, if one of our undercover men hadn't gotten the tip out to us that they're also worried— having trouble with the same red scum off China. They're making their own investigations."

"Which could be a blind—"

Hughes shrugged. "Sure enough. Only we do have it on *our* hands. And sooner or later we'll get to the bottom of it."

"It had better be sooner." The doctor's levity vanished. "There may not be a later—"

"War? But power's too evenly balanced. They know what the retaliation would be if they dared to jump us—"

"They also know what revolution would mean—to them. And there's always the hope that you can move faster than the other fellow—if you jump him without warning. Their grain crop was a failure last season, and they have other internal troubles. They would like to focus their peoples' anger elsewhere than on their own policies. I know—cold war for twenty or so years. We've heard all the rumors and alarms until they don't mean much any more. But that doesn't mean that a spark at the right place at the right time won't set off the blaze!"

Hughes shook his head slowly. "They're not idiots. No one wins an atomic war. Oh, I wouldn't deny that they may be trying some fancy tricks under cover. And maybe we're doing some crowding, too, where it doesn't come out into the light of day. But an out-and-out war—that's suicide!"

The doctor tossed away his half-smoked cigarette. "Let's hope that you're right and we're heading into a half century or so of hot peace. Now I'm going to call it a day—" He yawned widely, but Griff cut in.

"Have you had any more news of my father, sir?"

The doctor blinked at him. "You here, too? Yes, there was a report about an hour ago. He's got a long pull ahead, but he ought to be back poking into your smelly fish in a month or two. Sooner if the bright boys at the lab there can get that poison broken down." He turned to Hughes. "We'll ship your specimens up in the morning. If Dr. Gunston can identify them as the thing which attacked him, we'll be set—"

Hughes nodded. "I'll do my own report. Thanks for the help—and good night, Doctor."

The Navy man glanced at the brilliant flood around them. "I've forgotten what night's like since I've been here. But there'll have to come an end sometime. Be seeing you—"

Hughes had the solution for their return to Carterstown—the lab launch. As they swung out and away from the light and din of the base, Griff noted that the supply ship was still unloading.

"Looks as if they're getting ready for an army."

Hughes studied the laden craft discharging cargo on the beach.

"Might be preparing for a siege. I wonder—"

"Sub base?"

"Could be that. Well, here comes our escort."

The Navy cutter drew alongside, flashed the searchlight beam across them, and then cut throttle, dogging behind the small boat in a warning to get out.

But the radiance that wreathed the base was not the only beacon blazing that night from San Isadore. As they rounded the western bulge of the island and chugged into Frigate Bay, they saw the second illumination, a high leaping column of flame on the cliff ahead.

"The lab!" Hughes shouted.

But Griff was not sure it was that building. After all, the thatched roof, the wooden interior fittings would burn speedily, and the coral block walls could not feed such a fire as they now saw. Hughes set the motor at top speed, and the small craft bounced along on the surface of the water. It looked as if they might run ashore, and Griff moved toward the controls.

Though the dark bulk of the *Island Queen* was not anchored there, he counted four of the weedy hulks of fishing boats, more than he had ever seen in port together before. And the town, which had been dead when he left it hours earlier, was now alive—windows lighted.

Hughes was out of the launch, stumbling ahead on the wharf as his will moved faster than his feet. Griff made the craft fast before he followed. But when he caught up with Hughes, he found the ichthyologist struggling with someone in the dark.

"Mon—don't you go up there. Not now, mon—"

Only extreme emergency would have set Le Marr to that struggle. Before Griff came up, Hughes was down and the voodoo man crouched over him, trying to hold his flailing body immovable while he talked.

"They's gone wild—those mons up there! The debble out o' the night sits in their minds, an' they thinks wild things. You up there—maybeso more trouble—bad trouble—an' that's not good. They 'fraid—an' 'fraid mons hit out at the first thing they see. They don't think, they do! You come wi' me. The commissioner, he talk. When the wild go—these mons be shamed. Then they listen, they walk small for long time."

"Are they burning the lab?" Griff asked. That something he had sensed in the town earlier in the day had now returned a hundredfold. It was thick in the air. He could almost clutch it in his hand, taste it—the fear, the panic of a mob.

"They can't burn the walls—they burn what they find—"

Hughes writhed, and a torrent of raging words poured out of him. But the outburst was short. In a moment he was able to ask in an almost normal voice, "They took everything?"

Le Marr released his hold on the older man and squatted back on his heels. "They missed some things. I tell Heber, Ross, Lechee—take an' hide your papers. They be in my house waitin'."

"But why?" Hughes sat up. He sounded honestly puzzled.

"They 'fraid. The *Island Queen* be missin'. There be debbles in the sea. Before the doctor came, before you came, these things were not. They believe you dive in the sea, stir up bad trouble for island mons. If they burn what is your magic things, then you go 'way and the debble go with you. Now you come commissioner's house, make better plans there. Soon these foolish mons begin to think again—better let them do that then they have more trouble now."

Griff aided Hughes to his feet. "You win, Le Marr," the assistant said bleakly. "But all the chief's work—it's criminal!"

"These mons—" Le Marr arose too. His hand twitched in vague shooing movements as if he would hurry the two Americans on before him to the Government House. "They ain't thinkin' now—they is 'fraid. Mon 'fraid, he do things what he don't do when they think. But when you 'fraid, you do same. Navy mons 'fraid now—they build, build, hurry-hurry, 'cause they is 'fraid."

Griff could feel it—that net of tension. It had been slowly tightening about the island for days; he had begun to realize that—a feeling that they were all perched on the rim of a steep cliff with a wave rising to lick them into the raging water below.

They found the commissioner still in the radio room. He might not have moved since Griff had left. Braxton Wells, the storekeeper, his grizzled, closely cropped hair a silvery cap, sat by the far wall. Without remembering, Griff glanced around in search of the other two who made up the inner circle of San Isadore. But Captain Angus Murdock and Chris Waite were missing. Instead George Hanson balanced timidly on the edge of a chair, jumping to his feet and jerking his tunic into order as the Americans and Le Marr entered. His topee with its patiently shined constable's crest hung on a wall peg.

The commissioner might be in the same position as Griff had left him, but he looked years instead of hours older. His face had a drawn expression. He no longer wore the headphones but nursed them in his hand, glancing down at them now and again as if they were totally strange objects.

"What's going on here!" Hughes burst out. "Those hoodlums smashing up the lab! We're here under the protection of your government as well as our own, Commissioner. You'll hear from headquarters about this outrage—"

The commissioner raised his head. "You are perfectly at liberty to file any type of protest you wish, Mr. Hughes, with your government or mine—if either is left by tomorrow morning." The colorless timbre of his voice, the tone of a dead man, stopped Hughes's protests as effectively as if he had been slapped across the mouth.

"What's happened?" Hughes rephrased his question of the moment before, watching the commissioner narrowly. This was more than any outburst of violence on the island, more than the disappearance of the *Queen*.

"We received a message relayed from Santa Maria. Two hours ago Cape Town ceased to be."

"Cape Town?" Hughes echoed stupidly. What did Cape Town have to do with—

"Cape Town, South Africa, Wellington, New Zealand, Sydney, Australia, Singapore, and"—his tired eyes flickered from one American face to the other—"Seattle—"

"Seattle!" That struck home. "But what—?"

Burrows continued, stating wild facts as if he were repeating the current market prices on conch meat. "There's censorship clamped down tight now, and during the past hour they've been jamming so that nothing at all gets through.

But something happened off the coast of China. They blamed it on the Western Confederation, so they have started wiping out the great seaports one by one until they get what they demand—unconditional surrender—"

"Why not London—New York—Paris?" demanded Hughes.

The commissioner put down the earphones. "Perhaps they don't want to ruin too much before they take over. We've been told enough tales about what will follow out-and-out atomic warfare. The reports which have come in suggest bombardment from hidden subs, not air-borne missiles. And we've heard nothing for the past hour—other cities may be gone by now."

Griff's hold on the back of the nearest chair tightened. He tried not to imagine what might be happening beyond the rim of the sea. Back home they had always sworn they would not fire the first shot. But when they were attacked, there would be a reply the world would remember. Had that attack and reply been already launched?

Hughes was almost shouting. "They said nothing to us about this at the base—but they must have known!"

"Commander Murray said nothing?"

Griff shook his head. "He was speeding up the job there, would hardly listen to me. There couldn't be some mistake?"

"No, the broadcast was official, though we don't know—or they won't tell us—more than a few bare facts. Those cities ceased to communicate—then the ultimatum from the East—"

Hughes shook his head. "They must have gone mad. They know what we'll do in return—"

"They might have gambled on something else," Braxton Wells pointed out in his off-island accent. "What if the Western Confederation does not reply in kind? What if they won't take the risk of using the big ones—?"

"You mean—surrender on demand? That's pacifist reasoning—"

"Some men think it is better to endure a bad government for a space than to turn the earth into a cinder by retaliation."

"And I say"—Hughes rounded on the little man—"that

the men who argue that way should be forced to live in the Eastern Bloc and learn what it means."

"Do you know how many million people signed the last pacifist petition?" countered Wells.

"I know how many million are going to face the firing squads when the Reds take over if we fold up under this! Maybe that's why they've dared to make this move—those mouthy pacifist petitions have the Reds thinking we won't stand up to them."

The commissioner put on the headset and then turned up the volume of the broadcast receiver. From the loudspeaker on the table came a nerve-wracking clamor.

"Jamming—still jamming. Gentlemen"—the commissioner spoke now with a quiet authority—"I believe that we must now assume that a condition of world-wide war may exist."

"And that base may bring it here to us!" Wells snapped.

"Quite true. But it is too late to do anything about that," Burrows pointed out. "And I believe that you will all agree that we have no defense against subs whose weapons can destroy cities such as have already been wiped from the map. Heretofore, wars have been waged and their action has not touched this island. Le Marr, has the real meaning of modern war penetrated to the people here?"

"No, sir. Tonight they fear the sea debbles—they don't fear war. War don't mean nothing."

"Then I must ask all of you here"—Burrows' gaze caught and held the party in the room—"to let it continue that way. We can welcome the disturbance at your laboratory, Mr. Hughes, wanton as that destruction may seem to you. It will occupy their minds. Tomorrow all who took part in it will lie low. But there shall be arrests, fines; we shall be very busy with it. But can we afford a panic—the whole island going mad with fear? You understand that we cannot!"

Braxton Wells opened his lips as if to speak and then closed them. Hughes wore a defiant expression, but reluctantly he nodded.

"All right. I promise to go along. But we must get some sort of news!"

"Most certainly. So I suggest, gentlemen, that the five of us now here will do sentry duty at the radio—but that we alone shall have access to it. Unless the Naval party takes us into their confidence, we have this as our only link with what is happening out there. And since you are homeless, Mr. Hughes, Mr. Gunston, please take quarters here. We shall arrange time for each to be on call here. Do you agree?"

"Do we have any choice now?" Hughes wanted to know.

IX

WAR TWO WAYS

GRIFF SWALLOWED and then ran his tongue over dry lips. He had a stale taste in his mouth; his body ached as he moved stiffly on the hard chair. He must have slept; there was a bar of sunlight advancing from the window. Getting clumsily to his numb feet, he stamped to hurry the return prickle of circulation and went to that window to look out upon Carterstown.

The sour smell of the town hung heavy with no wind to lighten it. He became conscious of that—no wind. A bird chittered in the foliage and was answered by the squalling bray of a distant donkey. But there was no sighing wind, and a dank cloak of heat had fallen heavily on the houses.

His shirt clung to him stickily. Griff wanted a shower, a change. Then he remembered the fate of the lab and all their possessions there. At least it would do no harm to go up and look around.

Not wanting to meet anyone, to have to talk, Griff hurried down the hall and out of the door. A woman in the road outside glanced up at him and then away, staring straight ahead of her as she scuttled by.

But the American strode on unheeding. In the darkness of the previous night he had been able to agree with Le Marr that it was best they stay away from the scene of disaster. But in the brassy sunlight he could not be so moved.

And the sunlight *was* brassy. It glared down with an intensity that kept him in all possible bits of shade. Perhaps it was only his reaction to the past hours, or perhaps there *was* some actual change in the quality of the air. Then, with the memory of what might have happened elsewhere striking home, Griff stopped, one hand against the reasonable, sane roughness of a coral block wall, keeping that touch with reality as he fought a surge of panic. No man could honestly foretell the result of an atomic conflict. There had been so many imaginative constructions, so many learned opinions talked about during the past twenty years. Men had solemnly built ghost towns, peopled the houses with dummies, and then rained this new destruction upon that handiwork to study the consequences. But none of those experiments could equal the real thing!

The burrow of a land crab showed at the roots of a palm a few feet beyond him. If the occupant of that hole were caught in the sun, prevented from seeking the cool dark of its daytime hiding place, it would die—speedily—from the heat baking its shell. Were all of his own kind now caught in the open—without any burrows of safety?

A lizard flashed, a streak of brilliant coloring, jet black, yellow, ultramarine, along the rut of the road. Mechanically Griff began to walk after it. The heat was a flame funneled down upon the island. Without the usual alleviation of the wind, it became torment. Griff's body steamed. He was forced to halt now and then, panting, as he made the climb to the lab.

Now he could smell the stench of the fire, and within moments he came through bushes withered by its heat. Someone else was there before him, digging with an energy that made Griff marvel. To one side lay a pile of wreckage the other had apparently drawn out of the charred mess, and he was pulling out a tangle of blackened metal Griff identified with a flash of anger as one of the diving air tanks. So they had destroyed those too!

Hughes wiped his arm across his face, branding himself

with a smear of black. Beneath that he was drawn, haggard. His eyes met Griff's dully.

"They made a clean sweep." He poked the air tank, pushing it to his salvage station. "We're finished here—unless we can get new supplies."

Finished here—that meant return to the States. For a second or two Griff was wildly excited. That was what he wanted. But how could they go to the States now? Was there—was there anything at all left there? If the worst had happened—Resolutely he tried not to think of his father, or others he knew back home. Back home—was there a "home" now?

"Any more news?" The ruin about them had no meaning if what they feared had occurred.

"All wave lengths still jammed, or were when I came up here." Hughes was indifferent. Then he paused, looked straight at Griff with a measuring that held some of his old conscious superiority.

"Maybe everything *has* blown up. But we're still alive."

"No—not dead yet." Griff was wryly amused at the change in Hughes's expression. Did the other believe he was going to have an hysteric case on his hands in the younger Gunston?

Griff stooped, hooked his fingers under the flame-grimed tank, and heaved it over with the rest of Hughes's rescued odds and ends. Who knew—they might just find a use for it sometime.

"Did you get the papers from Le Marr?"

"They're the only thing that was saved. They stole the skull of the sea serpent." Hughes had fallen into the habit of giving that beached monster the traditional name. "I suppose it's on display in their devil-devil sanctum sanctorum! Every other specimen went into this." He toed the malodorous, half-burned rubble.

Griff wandered over to the spray pool. A black and ugly wad lay on the once clean sand of the bottom, and fish floated belly up, washing in a scummy deposit on the surface. He searched for the small octopus. But it was a moment before he saw the limp tentacle trailing from beneath a stone.

Chance had crushed the cephalopod. Two of the crabs, whose clan had furnished its favorite prey the day before, were now tearing at its flaccid arms.

A shout brought his attention back to the plundered lab. But Hughes was pointing up—into the molten blue bowl of the sky. Griff saw those white bands of exhaust—four—no—five of them! Jets! He was on his feet, watching those traces of the planes they could not see fade from sight.

"Headed south—"

Sure, they were headed south—South! But why south? Why not north toward the States? Were they in pursuit of some enemy, or fleeing—ships that no longer had home fields—seeking a place to land?

The air trails were lost. Griff's eyes fell to the sea. Down in the bay the full fishing fleet of San Isadore was still moored. No one was to be seen on the wharf or along the beach. But Frigate Bay did not look natural. Though the surf was no higher than it had been, the waters inside the circling reef showed movement. A school of flying fish—and there must have been more than a hundred of them—broke the water so close to the shore that most of them skidded onto the sands.

"What in the world—!" Griff could spot the swirls beneath the surface, but he could see no logical explanation. "Frank—look here!"

Hughes moved up beside him as triangular fins cut the water. Griff began to count aloud. "Ten—twelve—fifteen—Fifteen sharks down there!"

"Fish!" Hughes's wonderment was open. "The whole bay's filling up with them!"

The turmoil under the water was increasing. More flying fish soared aloft, flopping miserably ashore. Someone shouted in the streets of Carterstown, and people ran for the water's edge. A squid launched into the air, struck upon the deck of one of the fishing boats, and lay there writhing. Venturesome children waded into the shallows scooping out fish with their hands. But very shortly they were being snatched back by their elders. There was too uncanny an air about this;

the islanders wanted no part of the abundance being driven into their own dooryards.

"What's bringing them in?" Griff asked Hughes, the authority. But the other man only shook his head.

The confused shouting of the islanders was fading to a murmur as they drew back from the shore, retreating slowly, always facing the bay as if ready to defend themselves against sudden onslaught. There was a hail from the sea. The Navy cutter was coming in to the wharf, but the men on board it were striking down into the water, levering off the masses of sea dwellers crowding in. The fins of the sharks drew in about the cutter quickly.

"They're eating those cut to pieces by the propeller," Hughes said wonderingly. "If those Navy chaps don't watch out, they'll be swamped! Swamped by fish!"

Somehow the cutter reached the wharf. And Griff watched the foreshortened figure of the commissioner, his white ducks as rumpled as if he had slept in them, go down to meet the men who came ashore. Then the whole party started toward the center of town.

As they went, the islanders stood aside. It was plain that they wanted no contact with the Americans.

Hughes and Griff came down to the shore line. To Griff's startled eyes, it appeared as if all the fish for miles around had been herded into the circumscribed area of the bay. Yet they had not been drawn naturally as by some oversupply of food—as he had seen them gather so quickly when a diver had broken loose sponge creatures and flat worm cases. But these, now so thick in the water that it was being whipped to froth, had fled in panic from some danger greater than had existed in their world before.

Scaled bodies rose in the air, plumped aboard the anchored boats, to flop over already comatose brethren. And above their heads, the sea birds were screaming themselves hoarse as they dived for such a rich feasting as they had never known before. A flea-bitten mongrel trotted by Griff, nosed at a dying fish, and snapped it up, to go on to the next.

"What brought them here?"

Hughes shrugged helplessly. "I don't know. Never saw anything like this in my life!"

"Mistuh Hughes—Mistuh Gunston—" The constable, his topee pushed to the back of his head, but with his tunic correctly buttoned, bore down upon them. "Commissioner say—please to come along Government House now."

The islanders were in retreat, vanishing into their homes. And shutters were being banged shut in spite of the heat.

"The fish go mad. Now maybeso mons go mad, too," the constable muttered. "This be bad time—"

Like the roll of the sea, the murmur of voices rose and fell in the hall of the commissioner's office. Braxton Wells, Le Marr, and Burrows represented San Isadore on one side of the mahogany table—while facing them were Commander Murray, Lieutenant Holmes, Casey, and a young officer who wore pilot's wings clipped to his shirt front.

"I'm laying it right on the line, sir," Murray was saying as the two Americans entered. "War has been declared. What is going on in the north now is your guess as well as mine. The radio is jammed, and there's interference on all bands. Our supply ship chose to take a chance and head back to the States this morning. She was following her orders. Our orders are—"

Holmes put out his hand as if in protest. Murray did not even glance at him.

"Our orders—the last ones—were to stick on the job here. But it's a hundred-to-one chance whether what we are building will ever be put to use. In fact—I'm being frank with you, gentlemen—I don't honestly know the reason for the base. We have a mountain of supplies and certain installations that cannot be completed—or won't be—unless we get another shipment from the north. Until we get reliable news of some sort—" His voice trailed off.

"That is your problem, Commander," the commissioner replied. "Frankly I feel that it does not concern us. But what is of importance here is the morale of my people. Already they have destroyed the Gunston laboratory. Had there been no further unusual happenings this morning, we could have brought them to order. But now—with this disturbance in the bay—I have one constable, I have the support of Mr. Le Marr, Mr. Wells here. Captain Murdock, upon whose influence we could have depended to a very great extent, is missing, and his disappearance has only added to our burden. In Carterstown we are now sitting on a keg of gunpowder while a lighted match is being applied to the powder train. And, while gunpowder may sound ridiculously old-fashioned in this atomic era, it does explode with unpleasant force. I am going to ask you, Commander, to stay at your own end of the island and keep your men there. You have the right to defend yourselves—but the last thing I want is riot here!"

"Amen to that!" Murray agreed. "All right, we'll stay at home. You won't see us—unless there is need. But I'm going to leave a walkie-talkie unit with you, linking us. It may be necessary to get in touch in a hurry."

"For that I will thank you, Commander. Given a short spell of normality, we of San Isadore will settle down. In the meantime, the unit will suffice to exchange news. I have a steady watch on the wireless here—should I pick up anything—"

"It is the same with us. We'll let you know." Murray arose.

"Commissioner!" The constable hovered in the doorway. "The boat of the Navy mons—it sink! The fish fill it all up!"

"What—!" Murray pounded into the hall, but his running strides were matched by Casey. And the rest raced behind them. As they burst out into the day, Griff gasped. Where the brassy sun had beat down, there was an odd greenish light under massing clouds. It was unnatural—somehow horrible. Yet it reminded him of the water world into which he had dived—what arched over them now might not be the sky but the bowl of the sea!

A family party, their belongings lashed to the backs of three donkeys, came out of a side lane and then dodged back swiftly as the men from the Government House ran by. Where there had been an absence of wind, they now plowed through rapidly thickening gloom into the salt spray driven inland by gusts, which almost knocked the runners from their feet.

Clearly a storm was coming—such a storm as Griff had never experienced before. Yet it had none of the characteristics of a hurricane. The greenish gloom was now a dusk as dark as nightfall, yet it couldn't be noon. Griff blundered into a figure, heard Casey swear—an oath that was bitten off to become the muttered words of a formal prayer.

They did not reach the wharf. There was no longer a wharf—no longer fishing boats, Navy cutters. There was a writhing sea, which bore struggling bodies ashore to slam them on the rocks, bash them against the walls of two crumbling houses. The men stopped, and then retreated slowly. An eight-foot shark struck the ground beyond Murray and twisted, its murderous teeth slashing. Someone screamed, the wild cry of panic, and a figure ran back up the street. Griff was engulfed knee-high in a curling wave; a sharp pain scored his leg. He leaped back, dragging the nearest man with him.

A sharp explosion sounded even above the howl of the wind. One of the party was firing into that murk of water— though why, Griff, in a moment of rational thinking, could not understand.

They were back again, almost to the open space before the Government House, a knot of men who could not believe the evidence presented by their eyes. Palm fronds torn from buffeted trees were hurled lancewise through the air. Yet it wasn't a hurricane—it wasn't anything San Isadore had ever known!

"Oh, Lord—look!" A voice hardly human in its abandonment to raw fear shrilled weirdly.

This wasn't true, Griff assured himself. Nightmare! It had to be a nightmare! That—that *thing* wallowing down the streaming road, the water curling before it as it came—was nothing for any sane world to spawn. Lightning ripped across the sky, a jagged purple sword. And a monstrous head swung; fanged jaws opened and—closed! A ragged scarecrow thing mewled and squirmed and then hung limp between those jaws, as the dark came down once more.

Griff was running now, but when he felt the lift of the Government House steps, he stumbled and went down painfully. Some inner urge made him twist about. At the foot of the slight rise, which formed the core of the town, four—no—five white-clad figures wavered ghostlike in the dusk. Then Griff heard the crack of side arms. Whatever horror was following them was being met by fire.

But they had not yet faced the worst to be hurled at them that day, for under them the very stuff of San Isadore heaved. Griff, recalling the caves that underlay the island, thought that this was the end—that they were fated to go down with a sinking land. And it was in that moment that light came in a burst—not the lightning of the sky, but a pillar of flame out at sea, hurtling skyward, bathing them all in a bloody glare.

Griff crouched without knowing that he was sobbing. He watched while weatherworn houses collapsed—some in a sudden flattening, some slowly, stone by stone. There were screams lacing the fiery murk. But he remained where he was, seeing the men at the other end of the plaza break and run at what came through.

Death, monstrous because it lived and wallowed forward on flipper feet, death such as no man had faced before. And on its back—! Griff whimpered and buried his face in his shaking hands.

Again the ground rolled and wrenched. There was a trumpeting of anguish, a roar of titanic pain. Griff dropped his hands. From a mound of rubble that horrible neck trailed and wriggled convulsively. The thing was half-buried, struck down. But Griff was only thankful that he could no longer see what had ridden it in.

The blazing torch at sea had not been quenched. And the land was still moving. Then hands fell on his shoulders, jerking him upright. A voice shrieked in his ears words without meaning. But he turned, obedient to those tugging hands. This was the end of the world; why try to escape? Only some instinct far inside him kept him going over the reeling ground, even led him to stop and help claw another staggering figure to its feet. They were out of the town now. Scrub thorn and cacti tore at them as they pushed unheedingly through it. The red fires of hell blazed to light them on—on where? There was nothing left for man—no hole to hide in.

PART TWO

Operation Survival

I

THE GREAT SILENCE

GRIFF GUNSTON stood once more on an island cliff. But this was not the San Isadore of the past, and his memories of that peaceful stretch of salted land and reef-bound water were now so dimmed by what lay between that it was difficult to believe that other island had ever existed, or that he, Griff Gunston, had led such a carefree—or reasonably carefree—existence there.

A thick grayish dust covered the ground, clung to tattered bushes, and made a murk in the air through which the sun had not been able to penetrate until yesterday. It packed as mud on the mask he had improvised from salvaged diving materials, and he had to keep scraping it away in order to see. Somewhere not too far to the east a volcano born out of the ocean was still spouting throat-searing fumes, dust, and molten rock into the air. And the same action that had given it birth had rocked and broken San Isadore, bringing a mass of new land from beneath the waves and plunging other sections into the depths. They did not know even yet how many of the islanders had survived the night and day of agony when that change was in progress. Yesterday at the first hint of clearing the Navy party had started overland to discover what had happened to the base, but as yet they had heard nothing from them.

Overland—Griff had crept to the edge of the racked rocks

of the cliff to catch a glimpse of the sea. That was the worst—the sea was no longer under the rule of his kind. He knew now that he had not lost his mind in that instant when he had seen the sea monster advance into sinking Carterstown under direction. Under direction! There was a menace lurking out in the bay—about the shallows. A creature with a mind, with intelligence, directing thought-out attacks upon any human being who ventured within range of its weapons. Only yesterday he had seen what happened to an unwary islander who had paused beside one of the inland sea wells. A loop, or it might have been a suckered arm, cast about the man's legs, snapping him into the water from which there was no escape, leaving his two companions to flee in mad panic.

Hughes, the only expert they knew, had no answer for them. He had made a daredevil venture down into the water-logged town to inspect the remains of the thing that had been caught by the falling house. It was of the same species as that found on the beach, but that was all he could tell. Of that which had ridden it he found nothing, for he did not try to dig into the half-awash rubble. Though octopi had been known in the past to exist out of water for short periods, that creature which had directed the sea serpent was a breed with even greater powers of endurance.

There had been no more earth shocks for three days now, and they had begun to hope that the worst of that particular phase was past. The survivors were camping out on the highest point of the interior, the salt plain where the lake of the flamingos had existed a week or so ago.

Luckily, on the second night, there had been a heavy rain. And they had caught the water—which was partly mud and stank of sulphur—but it kept life in them. It was Casey and Murray, with less skilled help from the islanders, who had rigged a crude apparatus for distilling fresh water from salt, and though the yield was small, there were those precious drops garnered to be used for the sick, the women, and the children.

They had organized parties to gather supplies from the

town. And the three shotguns found had proved useful in halting the stampede of wild cattle, which had threatened to beat out their camp on the third day. Perhaps fifty people huddled there, fifty out of—how many had Carterstown sheltered—at least several hundred. There might be other survivors in the bush who would eventually drift into the settlement.

Some trick of the wind blew aside the drifting dust, and Griff saw what had once been Frigate Bay. The line of the reef tilted up in one place to form another island, its upthrust rocks slimed with dying sea things. And smashed squarely down upon it was a small boat—an island yawl or a fishing smack. But the dust curtain dropped again before he could be sure.

With a sigh Griff turned to plod along, using a fishing spear to test each suspicious patch of ground as he limped forward. His task was to explore the southern portion of the island, bearing westward, to locate any survivors and start them into the central camp, and, incidentally, to mark down any garden patch, any coconut palm, or other food that could be harvested.

He came out onto a strange strip of land, where the former beach had been raised elevator-fashion several hundred feet into the air. He walked over sand that the week before had been washed by waves now dashing on a new strand far below. His mask kept out some of the stench of the decaying sea life already half-buried under the soft cloak of the dust. But crabs scuttled and tore with clicking claws at the rare feast.

Wind! His head went up as he felt that familiar ripple in his matted hair. Wind! He turned his back to the force of it, very glad for the mask that protected his eyes against the blowing grit. Maybe it would clear the air.

But instead it whipped up the light stuff and thickened the murk until Griff, battling through the soupy substance, fetched up against a rock with a force that brought a grunt out of him. He decided to shelter there. No use fighting through this when a misstep might plunge him to the bottom of a crevice.

He crouched on the lee side, wedging his shoulders against the comforting solidity of the stone, his head down on his knees, waiting with all the patience he could muster for the storm to clear. Rain came—a visible curtain of water, washing the grit from his body in a warm flood, channeling the muddy silt away except where it was caught in brown pools.

Griff ripped off the mask and held his face up to that downpour. He drank his fill from a rock hollow, filled the gourd that was his canteen from another. The bushes, the clog of dust washed from them, showed their natural silvery gray. Griff got up, eager to take advantage of this break in the dust fall.

He came to the end of the lifted strip of beach and, faced by a jagged stretch of rock, doubled back to an easier climb. A streamlet born of the rain was already dripping from the upper levels, and twice he stopped to drink for the sheer pleasure of rolling the water in his feverish mouth. It was the stream that guided him into the valley.

Through some freak of the earth's settling, this cup had been born. A ragged row of palms was rooted strongly enough to be still standing. Here the bushes and ground shrubs, washed clean of the dust, were new and green. A trough of rock was turning into a pool of rain water. But beyond that was one of the single-room coral block houses. It's thatched roof had been ripped away, the walls were cracked—but it stood. And against it huddled three donkeys. Wtih them were two of the wild horses, hardly larger than ponies. They stamped uneasily as he came, but they did not bolt.

"Who come?"

Out of the twisted hut crawled a woman. Her ragged dress was plastered to her body; a battered straw hat kept the worst of the flooding streams from her shrewd brown face.

"Oh," she identified him, "Mistuh Gunston, from the fish place. Well, there's a plenty fish now, ain't there?"

"Liz!" He recognized her as the sturdy and independent widow who had done the lab laundry, cooked for them on occasion, and had been their mainstay for general help until the month before when she had been sent for to nurse an ailing daughter-in-law.

"That's me." She smiled. "We done have ourselves a time, ain't we?"

"You here alone?" Griff leaned on his spear to rest his leg. The tear he had received the night of the disaster was healing, but he still had to favor it.

"No, sir. We all done got 'way. Lily—she's ailin'—" Liz jerked her head back at the cabin. "She's got Jamie an' Jess wi' her. Luce—he took the boys 'long him. They go off see they find water." She laughed richly. "They come back an' find water done come to us!" Thiumphantly she pointed to the growing pool before her.

"We've a big camp up on the salt flats," Grit told her. "Commissioner wants people to come in there if they need anything." Glancing about the valley, Griff privately thought that Liz and her clan were better off here, and she said so herself.

"This here's a goodly place, Mistuh Griff. Thank you kindly for tellin' us. Now we got us some water we don't need nothin', nothin' at all. Come in, sir, an' have yourself a rest time an' tell the news—"

He allowed himself to be shepherded into the hut. On a pile of palm fronds and dubious bed coverings the ailing Lily lay, her attention all for the answers he gave to Liz's flood of questions, while the two youngest of Liz's grandchildren crawled out of the same nest and crept across the floor to sit staring solemnly up at him. He nursed the thick mug of some herb brew Liz had pushed into his hands and sipped it gingerly as he tried to satisfy her curiosity.

"Carterstown be drownded daid?" She pursed her lips. "An' the fish done gone crazy—"

Griff hastened to pass on the needed warning. The children—he looked down at them—the children of San Isadore had always played along the shore. Most of them could swim almost from the time they could walk. But now—!

"There're worse than crazy fish out there now, mistress." He used the old formal island address to underline the seriousness of what he had to say. "Something's come out of the sea that is dangerous. Keep away from the shore—and above all, keep the children off the beach!"

"Debbles," Liz remarked calmly. "Done raised us a mischief. You needn't fret, Mistuh Griff; nobody in this here family is goin' down near that water! Not 'til those debbles done gone back to where they camed from."

"It be the last days o' the earth!" A thin wail burst from Lily. "This be the end o' all mons!"

Liz swung around, and her voice was sharp. "That's enough o' that foolishness, gal! As long as we has legs to walk on an' hands to work wi'—an' wits in our heads—we ain't daid. We is shook up some an' scared right plenty, an' there's a new world out there. But we ain't daid—an' the good Lord above be bigger than any debble-debble or dupee ever raised! Me—I say we ain't daid, an' we'll git the better o' these bads—"

Griff had the sudden conviction that Liz and her kind would. When he went on, cutting across the countryside where the rain had deadened the dust and brightened the vegetation, he paced almost jauntily. They weren't dead, as Liz had pointed out. And those who had not broken under the extremes of the past few days were all right—as the growing things were straightening up from the buffeting they had taken. There was no use speculating about what was happening—had happened—outside the boundaries of San Isadore. For the time being the world had shrunk to the island and its immediate surroundings, and it was better for them to keep it that way.

The rain continued for the rest of the day, turning some sections into sticky morass, filling pools. Griff came back to the settlement, where the huts, constructed of brush, had to be abandoned to the rising water of a new lake. Bedraggled and dripping, the survivors loaded their supplies on the few donkeys and straggled on across the plain, heading for the base to the north. If any of the construction there had survived the twisting of the island, it would provide the shelter Carterstown could no longer give.

They camped in a weary huddle that night, sheltered by a stand of twisted trees, from which dripped the steady stream of rain. Tins were pried open with knives and their cold contents shared out apathetically.

There was a low keening from where the women and children crouched together. Very few of them showed Liz's spirit, and the constant rain and the lack of fire or protection was beginning to tell on a people already in a state of shock. Griff chewed a mouthful of beef as with stiffening fingers he tried to weave some palm fronds into a lean-to. The rain, which in their ignorance they had welcomed as a relief from the scourge of the dust, was becoming as great a curse. During the latter part of their march today he had helped as a rear guard, working with Le Marr and Wells to keep the pitiful train of refugees moving. Several had lain down, refused to keep trying until they were actually booted or beaten to their feet, and Griff knew that anyone who gave up now was lost. Without the will to live, they would, as travelers lost in a snowstorm, drift into unconsciousness and death, some inner spring broken past repair.

Two women, one child, and an old man were lost from the count the next morning—four graves scooped out. The commissioner, showing a skull face with shrunken eyes, walked like a man in a nightmare, but he never ceased to exhort, to urge, to keep that straggling column moving. Griff wondered what Burrows would do, what they would all do, if they had their hope extinguished by finding in the north no remains of the base, only a new desolation as great as the one from which they fled.

But the answer was not to be that brutal. Through the ever-present drone of the rain broke another sound, the crunch of metal over rock. And one of the powerful caterpillar tread haulers he had last seen at work with the supplies on the shore crawled steadily into view, pulling behind it three of the carriers. Men dropped from the tows as the soaked line of islanders was sighted. Donkeys brayed, dug in their small hooves, and refused to approach the monster, while their owners were half-led, half-carried, to be tumbled aboard the platforms as if they also were supplies.

"Hello, Gunston! Hop a ride!" Casey, red stubble still visible on his jaw and cheek, matched step with Griff. He caught the younger man's shoulder and propelled him toward the carrier.

"I take it the base made out all right?"

"After a fashion." Casey lost some of his cheer. "We've a few bad holes here and there, but we're still in running order. Atomic power has its points."

The crawler, with its escort trotting easily beside it, made a wide circle to retrace its trail, the babble of the islanders rising at the novelty of the ride. This had shaken them out of their apathy. Even the men who had elected to walk and lead the donkeys were moving at a smarter pace. And after a short rest Griff slipped off the slow-moving tow to join them.

"Big changes," Casey was saying to Braxton Wells. "I'd say there are some new islands off that way. We've started work on the plane. When she's repaired, Whit'll take her up for a look-see."

"—trouble from the sea, mon?" Griff caught only half of the question.

Casey was sober. "Pretty bad the first night—until the boys got defense wires up. Now we can burn them off when they try it. And they haven't for two days. We've got a landing section cleaned out in the bay, run shocks through the water. But we can't do the whole ocean!"

"This condition may be local." Burrows trudged up to join them.

"Might be, sir," the American agreed, but plainly only because he thought that that was what the other needed to hear. "The radio is okay now—no more jamming. Except what's natural after—after—" He hesitated.

The commissioner stooped more, as if his shoulders were sinking under invisible blows. "After an atomic war—" he supplied in a low voice.

"Well, yes, sir. I guess we have to face that. They've shot the works. So far we can't get any messages through, and we haven't been able to pick up anything except one South American station. The fellow down there sounded hysterical—kept wanting to know what had happened and why someone didn't answer him."

Griff swallowed before he was able to ask his own question. "Nothing from the States?"

"No. Sorry, kid. The skipper's been asking for news ever since the jamming cleared. He gets a gabble now and then—crazy stuff—but even that stopped early this morning. Today nothing but quiet. Looks as if everything has gone off the air. That's why we're working so hard to get the plane up for an exploring party. They're converting her with one of the new experimental motors—means she can only carry a pilot. But she'll be able to go farther. We certainly can't make a try by sea—not 'til we find some way to brush off those things hiding down there. I'd like to know what they are and why they've got it in for us anyway—"

"The sea have big secrets. Mons, they float about on top the sea, they dive down little way, but how they know what be down there? Mons think they know everything. But they don't. Maybeso other things, they tired of mons an' his big mouth—thinkin' he be the king o' the world." Le Marr dragging at the lead rope of a reluctant donkey had joined their small group.

"Fish with brains yet!" Casey shook his head. "Well, they're mean enough, and they sure go for anything within their reach. Crawl out on the beach—that is, they did, 'til we tickled them up with a rapid fire—then they stopped that. Octopi—only not like those we saw hanging around the reef before all this started. I'll believe they can run us off the earth when I see it done! We'll get their number—drop a bomb and where'll they be—"

"Too many bombs have already been dropped, sir," the commissioner said dryly, and Casey was left without an answer.

The crawler and its laden carriers creaked and crackled down a slope that led into a wide valley. Griff was not very sure of this end of San Isadore, and the recent quakes had destroyed many of the usual landmarks. He thought that they were several miles inland from the original base, but he could not swear to that. A river of rain washed about the treads of the machine and was ankle-keep about their feet. Then they came out where the labor of man was again changing the shape of nature.

White beams from working lamps cut the gloom of the rain, and machines were busy. Shelters of rock blocks were growing visibly as they watched. It was apparent that the builders had cut their losses in the vanished erection by the sea and were in full progress to copy it here. A settlement was coming into being.

They were all shaken out of their own private miseries. The activity before them was in such contrast to their own toilsome harvesting of the shreds disaster had left them. This was a refusal to admit that there was any reason to give in to anything that had been hurled against San Isadore in the past five days.

Griff limped forward, drawn by that burst of light, that aura of confidence that overhung the whole scene. There was that about it which argued that, as bad as the news was, *they* were not licked! Here were Liz's boasts of the day before acted out. No, they were not dead yet.

He was still clinging to that when an hour or so later, under a roof where the rain drummed but could not enter, in a building that was half-erected, half-hollowed cave, he ate and drank, resting in comfort.

Murray was there, Hughes, the doctor, Burrows, Wells, Casey—only Holmes was missing. But the rest were seated on packing cases, poring over the map Murray had pegged out on one wall. The outlines were those of San Isadore as the island had been a week before. And some alterations had been added with a bold black crayon.

"Volcanic action without a doubt—" That was Murray's comment. "Don't know what set it off—might be the result of bombing. At least one new island here." He stabbed with the fish spear he was using as a pointer. "We'll get a plane up."

"No radio yet?" That was Hughes.

"We have men on there—twenty-four hour duty. So far we've heard nothing—"

His words fell into a pool of silence, as for the moment even the outside din was hushed.

"Nothing—" Griff repeated that to himself. His thoughts shied away from all that implied. Did that describe what now lay to the north—nothing?

II

NEWBORN WORLD

GRIFF AWOKE to lie uneasy in the dimly lighted space. Under the slight movements of his body the hammock swung. But it wasn't the unfamiliar bed that troubled him. Something was missing—and its absence had brought him out of the depths of exhausted sleep. The drum of the rain! That incessant downpour, which they had almost come to accept as the natural order of life, was stilled at last.

He heard a faint snore, a sleepy mutter, and raised his head. Pallets on the floor, hammocks aloft—as many sleepers had been crowded into that room as could find space. Cautiously he slid out of his swaying support and crossed the room with care.

His watch had stopped. He had no idea whether it was now night or day. And as he came into the open, he was even more befuddled. There was still work in progress some distance away. But, though he saw machines building, dragging supplies, he could see no men. Overhead the sky was a frightening, sullen yellow-gray. Not night—but not like any day he had seen either. Except for the clamor of the machines there was an ominous silence. No wind, no rain—even the ever-present boom of the surf was muted.

An eerie call of a sea bird startled him. He could see a single pair of wings wheel and dip overhead. Trouble was on the way, trouble San Isadore could not escape. It was hot, stifling hot, yet there was no sun. Griff was panting; a trickle of moisture crept down his chest.

Somewhere up there, out there—he had turned to face north—danger was building up. The clouds massed like a giant sledge hammer over the wracked bit of land that was the island.

"Nasty-looking, isn't it?"

Griff started. Crepe-rubber soles had made no sound as Breck Murray had come out. The commander wore his uniform cap and a pair of work slacks—with a long tear down one leg. He also had a wide bandage across his upper arm, and about his waist hung a belt supporting a service side arm.

"What do you think is coming now?" Griff asked. The past days had taught him one thing—that one could live through panic—live through the blackness of such fear as he had not known could exist—and come out on the other side. It could only be done by living one moment at a time, by not looking ahead. Yet here he was breaking his own rule for safety.

"Storm of some kind," Murray said. "It'll be the worst yet."

He strode unhurriedly to the side of one of the tanklike machines and opened a door. Griff trailed along in time to see the commander seat himself inside before a microphone.

"All hands!" Murray's voice, magnified into the roar of a giant, split the air. "All hands to work area—on the double! Hit the deck! Assemble at work area—"

Men came, fast enough. And after them followed the islanders until the whole populace of the new settlement was assembled.

"By the looks of this"—Murray went directly to the heart of the matter—"we're in for trouble. The meteorological equipment we've been able to salvage has gone wild. We've got to dig in. As long as the island itself doesn't go, we'll have a chance. Now—on the double—get those diggers going. I want everything undercover—if we can do it. This is Red Alert Two—follow plan Red Alert Two—"

If the activity they had witnessed earlier had seemed frenzied to the islanders, what happened now made them gasp. And they, themselves, found refuge in the new caves into which Burrows and his unofficial committee urged and drove them.

The wind was back, rising steadily. Griff, helping to manhandle boxes, bales, and crates into hollowed storage places, heard the howl of its coming. Though the rain had not returned, spray, whipped out of the sea and borne across the rises between, was a mist in the air.

"That does it here, kid!" A man clapped him on the back, pulled him away from the last stowage job.

The blare of a siren howled across the area as the lamps went out. Griff helped his unknown co-worker to unhook one and roll it under cover.

"Second warning," the man mouthed in his ear. "We got about five minutes more, kid, then it's hit dirt. Lord, this is going to be a dirty blow!"

Machines clanked by, on their way to such anchorage as had been devised for them. A steady stream of orders, mangled by the scream of the wind, poured out over the loudspeaker in the com truck. Most of them were incomprehensible to Griff, but he ran along with the men he had joined, helping wherever strength to push or pull was needed.

Two blasts from the siren this time. And now the com truck itself crawled through the murk. A Seabee caught at Griff, pushed him ahead with a force that made him stumble.

"Time to go—"

But there were still two lamps—a pile of boxes. However,

that grip compelled him to enter the nearest half-built house. He clattered through it, one of a group of four, across the roofless large room, with the wind sucking at them, to a doorway, which was close to a hole, popping through that into light once more—a cube chamber cut in the rock, half-filled with a jumble of hoarded apparatus and supplies.

"—the skipper—?"

"He took the truck out—he'll make it. Listen to that, boys!"

The wail of the wind transcended anything Griff had ever heard before. He half-crouched against a crate, his hands over his tortured ears. Dimly he was conscious of activity by the door, of a chain of men hastily linked hand to hand who edged through to drag a streaming, wind-buffeted figure into their own hiding place. Then came the building of a barrier, heaping up of boxes before the one opening on a world gone mad.

Under him Griff could feel the trembling of the rock, as if the island pulsed with life. Then he remembered—Liz and her small clan! There was no use telling himself that no one could have crossed the island in time to rescue the family in the southern valley. If he had remembered in time, they might have had a thin chance. Now—

"Well, here's where we prove whether the idea boys were right or not." Murray's voice was almost a drawl. He leaned against the barrier they had built to cover the door. Under the light his bare chest and shoulders were glistening wet. His cap was gone, his hair a bushy tangle as if the wind had tried vainly to jerk it out by its too tough roots. "We can see if shelters designed to withstand air attack are going to best old Nature herself."

"Just a buncha guinea pigs," murmured one of the Seabees.

"Live guinea pigs," a fellow hastened to point out.

"Yah—so far!" was the pessimistic answer.

But they were on the move about their constrained quarters, pushing supplies into a line about the wall, dragging other boxes into the open.

"Gunston!" Murray seemed surprised. "Thought you were with the island crowd— What's the matter, son?"

"There was an island family down in a valley to the south. I found them when Burrows sent us out to round up stragglers. They were safe enough then and didn't want to move in. One of the women was ill—so—" That jar vibrating through the rock reminded him of that other valley he had explored with Le Marr, where the contents of the sea's floor had long ago been dumped through a storm's wild fury.

"Nothing we could do for them, Gunston." Murray repeated the same argument his own mind had presented. "We couldn't have brought them here in time. And there's no assurance that we're going to weather this ourselves. Also— this storm is driving from the north!"

Griff's incomprehension must have been plain, for the commander added a terse and frightening explanation.

"If there has been an all-out atomic attack up there— we've got to face the possibility of fall-out. And it may be headed here."

Fall-out! The radioactive debris blasted into the highest heavens to drift or be driven by storms, to settle at last maybe thousands of miles from the site of the actual explosion—but equally deadly to its victims.

"The dust!" Griff blurted out, that gray cloud which had been with them for days—was it—? But Murray was shaking his head.

"Not the stuff that's been dropping here. That was mostly volcanic ash. The counter did a little jittering, but not enough to hurt. Doc's played it safe and taken hourly readings for a while. And we'll play it even safer if we get through this blow."

The hours spun wearily by. All of them wore watches, but, except for that measurement of time, they had no idea whether it was night or day. There were instruments chattering at one end of the rock room. They must have had some meaning for Murray, for the two men who watched them constantly.

Once an ugly serpent of water curled from beneath the

door barrier, setting them busy damming its advance. It gathered, crept, and then stopped. Moved by impulse, Griff dipped his finger and touched it to his tongue—salt! Had the sea reached them?

But there was no more water. They slept, ate sparingly of concentrates. A card game ran for hours. Books passed from hand to hand. But Griff was sure that few of his companions were able to concentrate any better than he was. He nodded into a nightmare-tormented sleep, aroused to find himself being shaken none too gently as one of his exasperated neighbors demanded to know why he was groaning.

There was a period when Murray hunkered down beside him to ask a series of questions about the sea life in the lagoon. Griff answered as best he could, with a dull wonder as to why this should matter now.

"Squid—octopus—what are those things after us?"

"Octopi, I think. They could always exist for a short time out of water, and this new breed apparently can do even better. Also those we saw along the reef before the blowup were acting oddly—"

"How oddly?"

"When I was diving with Casey—on that last morning —they ringed us in, watching to see what we were doing. Octopi are normally afraid of divers—they'll slip into crevices and hide—"

"So those were the new super-octopi? Did your father have any explanation—"

"I never had a chance to tell him about them. But those along the reef were much smaller than the type attacking now. The red plague, the dead sea serpent we found were both 'hot.' You've heard the old arguments about mutation forced by atomic radiation. Maybe this new type are mutants. You'll have to ask Hughes—he knows more about it than I do."

"Hughes is with Doc. And I know that they were working on it," mused Murray. "Maybe they *can* give us the dope— if and when we get out of here."

How much later it was that the end came Griff could never afterwards determine. Maybe hours—days were lost in that period of vicious upheaval. But the rocks were stable once more, and men arose to pull aside the barrier, allowing a queerly dressed figure out to explore. The stiff white coveralls, with the windowed cowl covering head and face, made a robot out of a man—a robot who walked with the clang of heavy boots, the rigidity of the thick material weighing down his limbs.

The explorer clanked out as the atomic-powered lamp was switched off. Sun—yellow sunlight—lay in a shaft through the door. Thin and disembodied words came from the walkie-talkie.

"So far—so good, skipper. But—boy, oh, boy, there've sure been alterations! Hey—here's a pal! Out of Doc's burrow—"

"Stanley reporting, Commander," another voice broke in. "All okay in burrow four. But there're 'hot' signals from a drift here."

Murray picked up the small mike. "Bad?"

"Not to danger point. Looks, sir, as if this whole area had been scrubbed right out. Well, I'll be—" The report broke off in a bewildered exclamation.

"What is it?" Murray prompted impatiently.

"Crawler planted right on top of the cliff—upside down! How in the world—!" That was the first explorer answering. "Wait—getting something new, skipper—"

Magnified through the walkie-talkie, they were all hearing that click, click, faint and regular at first and then rising to a furious chatter of warning sound.

"Where's that coming from?" Murray demanded.

"Wreckage, sir. So banged up we can't tell what it was— some sand and dust caught in drifts around it."

Again the counter gave the radiation chant.

"It's the wreckage all right, sir. None of our stuff—"

"That's the tail of a jet!" His partner in exploration cut in excitedly. "What is it doing here?"

"What's anything doing here? Including that half of a

horse hung up in what's left of those palms? But this jet can be cleared, skipper—and it's the source of the infection."

"Good enough. But quarter the area and let us know if there is anything else. How about the sand—are there any dust deposits?"

His first answer was a sound that might have been laughter.

"Skipper, except around a few rocks there isn't any sand. This place has been scoured right down to the bottom. If there was a fall-out, it was washed and blown right off our map again. Shall we try to break out one of the crawlers and lug this wreck off?"

"Not yet. Go over the area first. We want to make sure—"

But the report continued to be negative. And the others were free to crawl out and stand blinking at the pallid sun, seeing the scraped world that bore a sharp resemblance to the lunar landscapes drawn by painters of the fantastic.

A working party headed for the place where they had parked the machines that had built this refuge, only to discover that the storm had been there first. There was a jumble of metal, tangled and jammed, thrust into a split in the wall. And there was the single crawler perched upside down on the cliff. Perhaps others would be found later, but for now that was the total machine survival.

In the end the dangerous, radiation-'hot' wreckage was dragged away by hand, the lead-suited explorers fixing the ropes, the others lending their weight at a good distance. It was snaked up and over a ridge and wedged into a crevice, which could be walled up against future accident.

"Jet tail, right enough," was Murray's verdict. "Wonder where it was blown from?"

Decom chemicals were sprayed on the section where it had lain, on the sand pocket that had gathered about it. And then both men in their grotesque suits stood in the heavy stream of cleansing liquid.

Now that the all-clear signal had been given, the other burrows spilled out their inhabitants. But while the Naval personnel poured out eagerly, the islanders came slowly, moving like people caught in a bad dream. The sight of the stranded crawler on the cliff, the changes in the valley, added to their stupefaction.

A child whimpered; a man swore softly in the island idiom. The commissioner came up to Murray.

"Thanks to you, sir, we've been saved. I gather that radiation is not to be feared?"

"There was a piece of 'hot' wreckage, but we've cleared it. Tell your people to take it slow leaving here. We are sure of nothing beyond this valley."

Burrows smiled. "Look at them, sir. They are not yet ready to take up life again. In fact, they must be shaken into it. They are a simple people, Commander, and much which has happened to them in these past terrible days has been beyond their comprehension. Now many of them are in a state of shock. We—" he hesitated and then continued— "already we have two who are totally insane. But the rest— I think that they will be all right. If this last storm is only the end to our misfortunes—"

Murray turned his face to the sky, bright and clear, untroubled. The trade wind was blowing again, although its touch did not dip into the valley where the survivors were gathered.

"We can hope that the worst is over. Luckily we do have supplies—concentrates mainly—which will do for some time. I don't believe that we may expect any help from outside soon—"

"If ever," the commissioner agreed. "But there is no use thinking about that now, sir. I gather we are fronted with the business of taking stock and seeing how we can put to the best use all that can be salvaged."

"Just about that. I'm sending out exploration teams as soon as it is practical. They have to go slow and carefully. We've escaped fall-out here, but elsewhere—"

"It may be a different matter? Just so, Commander. Whatever we can do to aid in your plans, please let me know at once. Le Marr has a very intimate knowledge of the island—as it was, of course. There were certain native plants which might be added to the food supply—if they are still in existence." The commissioner smiled ruefully. "One's speech nowadays becomes overburdened with 'ifs.' Men have been accustomed to taking so much for granted, as a part of their personal security. We shall have to learn that nothing can be lightly accepted now. But consider what little we do have to offer at your service, Commander." His hand sketched a gesture close to a salute as he turned away.

Murray gave orders; the Seabees carried them out as precisely as if they were the robots now. But Griff, with no assigned duties, climbed the cliff wall. When he reached the top of the knife ridge, he swung to the north, dreading what he might see, yet forced to that inspection.

He shaded his eyes from the sun. Less than half a mile away he caught the rainbow lights of spray beating into the air against a new coast line. The site of the first base must now be under water. But to the east there was an even stranger sight. He had expected land to disappear—he had not expected it to rise above water. Yet a long strip steamed there under the sun's heat, dotted with clumps of decaying ocean vegetation. It stretched out far beyond where the reef had once encircled this end of San Isadore. Newborn land indeed!

III

PORT OF REFUGE

"WELL—THAT'S THAT!" Casey leaned back against a convenient rock and absent-mindedly smeared dark streaks of grease across the shorts that were his only garment. "We can take her all apart, but she'll still be scrap as far as doing her regular job is concerned."

However, he did not appear in the least downcast by his own verdict as he surveyed with narrowed eyes the smashed and twisted wreckage just disinterred from a wind-sculptured sandbank. Undoubtedly he was already mentally tearing the defunct machine to pieces and assembling from its parts a new and efficient tool, which would aid in the reconstruction project. Griff could see no such possibilities. But then, Griff thought bleakly, he had taken on his present role of survivor with very little practical preparation. And the one thing he could have contributed to their general store of knowledge—the lore of a diver—was of no use at present.

"We'll have to dismantle her right here—" Casey was continuing buoyantly. "You know, kid, we have one thing on our side. Maybe it was atomic bombs that got us into this mess, but it's atomic engines that are going to pull us out. In the old days we had to have gallons of fuel to run things. And a slam-down like we had would have finished off all machines—no gas—no oil—we couldn't have run them. But now—we still have plenty of power, and that'll bring us through. Unless—"

He glanced downslope to the distant line of blue. That earlier experimental installation, which had given man a short domination of a strip of that blue water, had gone out in the big storm. Another might be improvised in time. But for the present they were leaving the sea alone, for the menace still lurked there. Two islanders, attracted beyond caution by the jetsam strewn along the strand after the storm, had ventured into the water to haul at a waterlogged boat, to be dragged under shrieking before their companions could move to their aid. And when the others did come to the waves' edge, there was nothing at all to be seen. Hunters and prey were gone.

For a people who had lived on and by the sea for generations, this peril, this divorcement from their usual way of life, was doubly terrifying and at last induced such a shrinking from the boundaries of the ocean that they even avoided the beaches, though the wealth that came drifting in with every thrust of the changing tides was bewildering in its range and value. The inhabitants of San Isadore had benefited from storm salvage ever since the island had been first settled. But now they had to be herded down to the work under supervision and then would go only in full daylight.

The Naval party kept aloof from that task. They had their own repair and rebuilding problems left by the fury of such a storm as this section of the world had never seen before.

And the diversity of the shore gleanings underlined vividly the crash of the civilization that had nourished them. None of the finds were ever approached until after they were checked for radiation. But the pile of loot grew high and pleased both islanders and Americans alike because of future possible uses.

Hughes prowled the dunes on his own project, sharing only with the doctor the secret of his finds, spending long hours afterwards in the improvised laboratory.

Casey dropped down cross-legged, still contemplating the machine they had uncovered. He fumbled in a pocket, pulled out a badly battered pack of cigarettes, regarded it wistfully for a moment, and then stowed it away again.

"It's the little things you miss first," he mused. "Did you hear Lawrence telling off the supply officer this morning when he couldn't promote a tube of toothpaste? We can rebuild old Arabella here—or at least make her earn her keep in some way—but we can't produce a pack of smokes or some toothpaste. Funny to think that there'll be no more zippers, Coke, or disk jockeys—not in this lifetime. The very props of civilization come to dust! What were you in training for, kid—to be a fish hunter like your old man?"

Griff rubbed his hands together. Blisters were shaping nicely along the palms. He hoped some day that they would be as resistant as Casey's hard paws.

"I was hoping for an appointment to the Air Academy." He was able to mention that dead and gone ambition with a sardonic kind of humor. How long had it been since he had walked along the cliffs above Carterstown pouting at his inability to manage his future? Well, his future had been managed—but good!

Casey chuckled. "Off into the wide blue yonder." He made flapping wings with his hands. "I don't think! Nothing less than a jet, I suppose."

Some tight string within Griff loosened. The apathy with

which he had worked, obeyed orders, faced the strange new life, was fading. Casey hadn't changed—there was something easing in his attitude. To be with the islanders was to return to the tenseness, the watchful waiting. With Casey it was like being at home, the home he could not yet force himself to believe had ceased to exist.

"Nothing less than a jet," he echoed. "Maybe some day a space ship—" He laughed self-consciously. "Kid stuff!"

But Casey shook his head. "Maybe yes, maybe no. We had what it took to get us out there—everything but the sense to try that instead of building for the grand smash. Now—no stars—and we start over."

"Casey." Griff dared to put into words the question he had not voiced before. "Do you think it's all gone—everything?"

Casey rested his bristly chin on his fist. " S' funny, kid, you tell yourself that everything went up—smash!—just as all the croakers always said it would. But sitting here you can't really believe it. You're sure inside that off there"—he waved his other hand to the north—"New York still stands—and St. Louie, Frisco—all the rest of them—just as they always have. As long as we don't see the holes, we'll go on with the sneaking feeling that they're there. Maybe it's a good thing we'll never be able to take it in—to see what's up there now."

"As long as we believe in it, maybe it *is* there—in a way—" Griff thought he had not put that into words very clearly, but Casey understood.

"Maybe you got something there, kid." His mouth pulled tight. "Anyway we can keep on an even keel if we keep busy. Our supplies aren't going to last forever, and we have mouths to feed—to say nothing of those jokers hiding in the drink to grab off anyone dumb enough to go fishing. I wouldn't be a bit surprised if they start throwing bait up on land to hook us down to where they can get us. They may be some sort of octopi with brains. But we've had brains longer, and they can't come out here after us, any more than we can go in after them—now. Too bad that last blow got the plane. It'd be good now to have a bird's-eye view of the surrounding territory. I'm betting that this island is half again as big. Whatever spouted fire out there humped us up a lot. Did pretty well for itself too—regular mountain."

With the aid of binoculars the curious had been able to identify a distant smudge as a towering mountain-island, born from the sea in a burst of flame and lava. Steam still arose from its flanks, and there was a curl of smoke at its cap. The internal fires were alive. Whether it was a transient phenomenon that would sink again or whether it was there to stay, they did not know. And so far a closer examination was out of the question.

"Now to work." Casey unstrapped the canvas roll of tools. "We'll pull off her all we can—"

He never finished that sentence, for out of the sky above them came a sound neither had ever expected to hear again—the drone of a plane. Griff was on his feet shading his eyes as he tried to trace that sound to its source.

"Transport! And she's landing here!"

"Where?" Griff glanced around. There was no possible landing strip on San Isadore—unless the pilot in that lumbering ship was headed for what was left of the salt plain, which had been in the interior. Yes—he was trying for that!

Griff began to run, Casey thumping beside him. There was shouting from other points. Griff saw others head inland. He skinned his hand on coral, felt the grit of salt-encrusted sand under his sandals. The plane was overhead now, moving in a wide circle. Something awkward in that suggested that it was either overloaded or in trouble. Then it came in to land.

"Crack-up!" panted Casey. "They're going to crack up!"

There was noise but not the splintering crash Griff had expected. He continued to climb over the sun-heated rock toward the salt-floored basin, where the lake of the flamingos had once rippled. And, thrusting his way recklessly through the thornbrush, which left oozing gashes on his arms and ribs, he came into the open. The plane, undercarriage gone, rested flat on the soil.

"He made it!" whooped Casey. "That bird's something special as a pilot!"

As they ran toward the plane, Griff identified it as one of the passenger ships belonging to the inter-island tourist trade. One of the Seabees was tugging at the hatch as they came up. It gave, and he retreated a step or two as a tall man, his eyes bloodshot and infinitely weary, his once-white shirt filthy and spattered with an ominous red, edged through.

"This—is—?" He framed the question slowly.

Before they could answer, they heard the pitiful chorus from the interior of the plane—the crying and whimpering. Casey reached out to support the pilot. The man winced under his touch.

"This is San Isadore, fella." Casey's voice was gentle.

The tall man crumpled, his legs folding under him and letting him down to the sand, his hands covering his twitching face. He was breathing in long, shuddering sobs, which shook his body.

"Never thought we'd make it! Never thought we'd make it!" His words trailed off into sounds that hurt. But one of the others had pushed past to look inside the plane. He came out faster than he had gone in.

"Kids!" he burst out. "There's a whole load of kids in here. Help me get them out, you guys!"

Not all of those handed out of the plane were children. Four women, each holding a baby, staggered out into the sunlight. But some twenty children, ranging in age from toddlers hardly able to stand to three almost in their teens, were led from the confines of the cabin, where they had been lashed for safety in bundles of blankets and foam-rubber pads.

It was from the older children, rather than from the adults, that they got the story. A boy, his grimy hand bandaged in a strip of dirty gauze, held onto Griff.

"Did—did my dad come?"

"In the plane?"

"No. He had to try the boat. The rest all had to take the

116

boats. There was only one plane left, and they made us kids go in that."

Griff knelt so that his eyes were on a level with the boy's. "Where did you come from, son?"

"Santa Maria." He was shivering now. Griff drew him into his arms.

"It's all right, sonny. You got here safe. And Santa Maria isn't far. So your dad'll be along."

"They're things in the sea—" The boy's shudders were a dry sobbing. "They get the boats—"

Griff was silenced. As far as he knew, there was no soothing answer to that one. He could only gather the lad closer, carry him as the cavalcade of children and Seabees moved away toward the settlement in the valley.

"Has the water stopped coming here?" the boy asked suddenly.

"Water? What do you mean, son?"

"It came and covered a lot of Santa Maria. Then it came again, more every day. And Dad said we'd have to get away and get away quick or there wouldn't be any island left! The water just came and came—"

"Well, it isn't coming here! In fact, the water went away and left us a big piece of new land. You can see it from the top of that next little hill. You don't have to worry about the water—"

"And there're no bad things in the water here to get people?"

"You don't have to worry about them now," Griff said firmly. "These men here are from the Navy, and they're preparing some surprises for those things in the water. You're safe. And your dad'll be here soon. You wait and see—"

"What's your name?" his charge asked.

"Griff Gunston. And what's yours?"

"Jimmie Marden. You're an American, too—like Dad—aren't you?"

"Yes." But Griff wondered if it wouldn't be more correct to say now, "I was an American."

"Dad works for the Fruit Company. Are you a sailor—in the Navy?"

"No. I was doing other work here—diving—"

The youngster swung about in his arms to regard him with big eyes. "You go down in the water? But didn't the bad things try to get you?"

"There weren't any bad things here then."

Jimmie nodded. "I remember. It was before the storm. I went out sailing with Hippy. He had a boat—he fished. But I never saw Hippy any more after the storm. Dad knows how to sail a boat, too. He's about the best sailor on Santa Maria—"

"Then he'll be turning up before you know it," Griff suggested.

But Jimmie's head went down on Griff's shoulder once more, and he felt the boy shiver. "—bad things—" His muted whisper could hardly be heard.

Griff studied the tangled hair and the thin little body with a helpless feeling. There was nothing he could say that might not be a lie. If some desperate party had left Santa Maria by ship—was it possible for them to reach San Isadore? The whole seascape had changed. There were new islands, uncharted reefs—besides the sea enemy. Did such a party have the least chance of winning through?

When they reached the settlement and turned the refugees over to the island women under the supervision of the doctor, Griff and the rest patched together bits and pieces of a horror tale that exceeded anything they had been through. Jimmie's story was only the bare bones.

Volcanic action had wracked Santa Maria to a far greater extent than it had San Isadore. A part of the other island had vanished within an hour as a spouting cone of flame and dust had broken through the outer reaches of the harbor. After that disaster the survivors who had fought to a perilous safety discovered that the doom of the island was sealed. In a series of landslips what was left of Santa Maria vanished hour by hour.

Their escape had been forced upon them. Luckily a

section of the airport remained above the water line. There men had labored almost in a panic to cobble together out of the wreckage at least one plane that could take to the air, while others, with little hope of success, fitted up two fishing boats for a try by sea. Most of the island's population had died in the first upheaval, or been lost in the fury of the storm, which had struck when the island was in its death throes. Out of thousands a handful by lucky chance made their way to the last stable land.

The children and three women with newly born babies were given the best odds in the patched-up plane, which a veteran pilot, Henry Forbes, volunteered to fly. Those left behind would take to the boats as the rising water forced their withdrawal. They would try to make San Isadore, though they had not been sure that that island was still above water.

"We're just plain lucky." Casey summed up their own reaction to the news. "Lord, we had it easy compared to them. What're we going to do about those boats, skipper?"

Murray looked in turn to the Navy pilot. "Any chance of getting that plane up again, Whit?"

Hooker shook his head. "Not without a machine shop. Oh, we might do a lot of patching and hope. But it'd take days. You've that one LC 3—"

The LC 3—an amphibian, tanklike vehicle made to plow through water and crawl over coral reefs—which by some freak of luck had survived the storm, was parked on the beach. Just that morning her internals had been checked by mechanics, and she had been proclaimed seaworthy.

"That's a thought," Murray conceded. "If we can rig up some sort of protection—"

"Skipper." Casey leaned forward eagerly. "How about shock waves out from her bow. No," he corrected himself, "we couldn't try that—too risky. But we could mount a couple of spray guns on her fore and aft. And maybe those things wouldn't attack in force if we tried a run by day. They like evening—or when it's gloomy—better."

"How about it, Hughes?" Murray asked the ichthyologist's opinion.

"How can I tell?" Hughes's mouth was set, a permanent nervous tic twitched with clocklike regularity in his thin cheek. "I don't know what makes those things do what they do! Until we can capture one, we won't know anything. And so far none of our traps and bait have worked. They think, I tell you; they can reason out just how to beat us!" His voice rose, and he was on his feet kicking at the packing case that served him for a seat. "Maybe you can shoot them out of the water. If you do, grab a body and bring it back; then maybe we'll be able to get somewhere."

"Commander, you have no idea what course to set." Holmes entered. There was a bandage turban about his head, and he sat down quickly. "To go out on the mere chance of contacting one of those boats would be acting directly against our orders. We were told to establish this base and wait—" He stopped suddenly as if he realized that he himself had almost committed the cardinal sin of supplying top-secret information.

Casey laughed outright and Murray smiled.

"Wait here for what, Lieutenant?" jibed Casey. "More orders? From where? We're on our own now, and we have to do our thinking for ourselves. That feels kinda good." He stretched.

"You have no real proof of that," snapped Holmes. "Commander, I would suggest that you'd be wiser not to take decisions on yourself so quickly. We have had no official news—nothing releasing us from our original duties—"

Breck Murray levered himself off his crate. "There's such a thing as common sense, Lieutenant. And there're also some people out there, men and women, who have had it worse than we have. If we can make this their port of refuge, then that's for us. All right, Casey, you get Evans, Marshall, Hall, and Koblinski and see what you can do about arming the LC. The sooner you can have her ready the better!"

IV

SOS AMERIKANTSKY!

"THERE'S A VOLCANIC island here." The pilot from Santa Maria, propped up on the cot, moved his bandaged hand to mark a cross on the chart Murray had given him. "And shoal water showing here—"

"They'd have to swing to the south then—" mused the commander.

But Griff spoke up. "Who were the captains in charge of the boats?"

Henry Forbes frowned. "There was an islander—Pedro —Pedro Farenez. And Goodrich was slated to take out the other. Farenez knows these waters—he was to lead."

"Pedro Farenez was a runner—at least Murdock always claimed that. He'd head north instead of south; he knows that route better."

"A runner?" Murray was puzzled.

"Smuggler, running contraband to the States, even men who wanted to enter illegally. And he's been busy lately. Murdock said it was common talk among the islanders."

Murray showed Griff the map. "What's the northern route? Did Murdock ever outline it for you?"

"I sailed part of it once in the *Island Queen*. But with these charts no longer accurate—" Griff surveyed the creased canvas and paper square before him with studious attention. He checked place names, the lines of solitary cays and half-hidden reefs. Slowly with his forefinger he traced the course while the commander watched, narrow-eyed.

The route did avoid the recent blocks to navigation that Forbes had sketched in. On the other hand, the pilot had not crossed that section of sea, and more surprises might lie to the north. Murray rubbed his chin thoughtfully.

"And that's Farenez's route?"

"Pedro Farenez put in at Carterstown two months ago."

The commissioner spoke for the first time. "He was always secretive about his business. Yes, he was known to be operating outside the customs laws, and perhaps against the American immigration laws, but nothing has ever been proven against him in court. However, his knowledge of the northern cays is that of an expert. He might instinctively seek a passage through sea he knew well."

"Like hunting a needle in a haystack! If we head off into the blue northward and they do come in from the south—! No chance of contacting them by radio, I suppose?"

Forbes shook his head. "The boats are old—fishing luggers. One was not equipped with a radio at all, the other had one with parts missing. When we took off, it had not been repaired." His ghostly smile held no humor. "Why should they spend the time on it then? As far as we knew, there was no one left to pick up any calls. After the last day we had begun to believe that we were the only survivors—"

"That makes it tougher. No radio— We could have beamed them in—though there's still a lot of static."

"If we had two LC's—"

Murray snorted. "If we had the fleet and a carrier on tap, we wouldn't have to worry at all." He swung to the commissioner. "What're the chances of picking up a pilot for this northern route from your people?"

"Very poor, I am afraid. The only men who might have assisted you were Murdock and his crew. They're missing. I don't think you could force any of the others to sea now. They have too great a dread of what lies in the water. And superstition adds to that fear."

"I plan on a five-man crew." Murray went to the window to watch Casey and his crew laboring on the LC. "Two on each gun if trouble comes, the other to operate her. But a pilot would be a help—someone who knows these waters—"

"I'll go—" Griff was startled at his own words. But the compulsion to say that had been as strong as the compulsion that had sent him into the inland pool in that reckless dive.

Murray turned around. Griff could read dissent on the

commander's face before he spoke, and he had his own argument ready.

"I've been out there with the *Island Queen*. Made the run in her to Santa Maria four or five times, and once we went north along this same course. Captain Murdock briefed me on it, and I know the charts." He thrust the one they had been studying at Murray. "Listen!"

Closing his eyes to picture mentally the lines on the map, he began—first slowly, and then with rapidly growing confidence—to recite sailing directions. Why, he remembered far more than he thought he had! The long sunny days when he had lounged on the deck of the *Queen,* listened to Angus Murdock's unhurried speech, to Chris Waite's stories, were now paying off. When he finished, he found himself the center of a surprised circle.

"All right." Murray re-rolled the chart. "You've proved something or other. I may be five kinds of a fool for letting you go. But maybe you'll provide what we need. I have a hunch about that."

Burrows was nodding, too. "We can—we must depend now on such things—your hunch, I mean. I, also, think that it is meant for this young man to do us this service. But you do not leave tonight?"

Forbes stirred on his cot. "They must have sailed this morning—"

"It would be too easy to miss them in the dark," Murray pointed out. "There's no help for it. We'll have to wait for dawn."

Griff tried to sleep but found it hard. The glow of light from where the LC was being prepared was one irritant. But more important was his distrust of his own proposal. Had he been too sure of Farenez's route? Would the island smuggler try this time for the southern course? Suppose, following Griff's suggestion, they headed in the opposite direction from the party they were trying to help! His fault—it would be his fault.

"Griff—?"

Griff felt a hand touch his arm, slide up to his shoulder, pressing there.

"You have fear—" The words had only a faint touch of the island slur, but he recognized the voice.

"Le Marr?"

"Yes, Griff, you have done what is right to do. There is that which must be done waiting for you. But the end is not failure."

There was conviction in those words out of the dark. Griff had always believed that Le Marr had his own sources of information. There were odd quirks in many human minds that led to a measure of foresight—cases were known, but as yet no one could explain how or why. And the very inability to control such a talent made it more a curse than a gift.

Now he asked without disbelief, "What waits for us—?"

There was a sigh. "That I cannot tell you, my son. But you will return, bringing with you what you seek, also much else."

"Le Marr—who are you?" Griff demanded impulsively.

This time the answer was akin to a chuckle. "Have I not asked myself that these many times, mon? I am a son of San Isadore, also I am a Papa-loi, the ignorant witch doctor of the mixed bloods."

"You're a lot more than that! Dad thinks so anyway."

"Dr. Gunston is a seeker of the unknown. In my small way I walk the same path. Thus are we fellow travelers, owing each other the courtesy of the road. Now do you sleep, for the morning will bring much to be done."

The hand exerted pressure, and Griff yielded to it, sinking back. Then the warm palm went from his shoulder to his forehead unerringly, as if the other could see in the dark, and rested there in a light touch. For the first time Griff was able to relax.

"—can't use the regular stuff. It's not for a job like this." The protest came unmistakably from Casey.

And Griff, as he came downslope through the gray light

of predawn, was not surprised to see the chunky Lieutenant, J.G., facing up to the leaner figure of Lieutenant Holmes.

"Sure I told Henley to break open those crates. We gotta know what we have. Maybe some of it can be adapted to this job. All right, all right, so I broke about nineteen dozen regulations when I said rip off the packing! Who in Hades cares now? Go tell Washington, if you can still find it—" His round face was almost as red as the thatch of hair above it as he stood, hands on his hips, a ring of Seabees for an audience and a row of small, sleek, torpedo-shaped canisters laid out on the sand.

"I shall make a full report—" Holmes returned coldly. He must have heard that snicker from one of the group, but he gave no sign.

"Report your head off!" was Casey's hot retort. "I was given a job to do, and I'm doing it—to the best of my ability. I don't care how many reports you make, or to whom. You'd better get it through your head, Lieutenant, that the Navy's washed up. We're on our own—"

"You forget yourself, Mr. Casey." Holmes swung around, his face set in stiff lines. He marched back toward the settlement, passing Griff without any greeting.

"Now." Casey shifted his attention to his working crew. "We'll let this stuff go." He indicated the row of cylinders. "For all we can tell it'd send us to hell and gone if we tried to make it into depth charges. Put in that box of grenades along with the extra ammo. We want to get rolling as soon as the skipper gives us the high sign."

The LC was not trim in line. On shore she had the ponderous shape of one of the crawlers, suggesting brutal power rather than speed or great mobility. During the night the workmen had rigged wire nets along her sides, nets which would offer no deterrent to the firing of the guns now mounted at her bow and stern, but which might give pause to anything trying to clamber on board from the water line. Since the LC was made to carry cargo or a sizable landing party to shore, the six-man crew Murray had designated occupied very little of the cockpit-like interior. But some of the empty space was being filled with boxes of supplies.

"Hello, kid. Come aboard!" Casey had sighted Griff from his commanding position by the wire barrier, where he was now overseeing the last-minute stowage.

As Griff dropped down into the cockpit, the other pointed to the guns.

"Good stuff. They were hush-hush—rapid-fire atomics—something new. Probably planned to use against subs."

"Yeah." One of the Seabees at the nearest gun spoke over his shoulder. "*If* they work. Me, I'm glad we've got a full case of *them* aboard in addition—" He jerked his chin left to indicate a line of automatic rifles of new design leaning barrel-up along the edge of the cockpit.

"Can you handle one of these?" Casey asked.

"I've used a shotgun," Griff returned, willing to admit his own greenness, if it were necessary.

"They've got a kick, but their fire power is great. Here comes the skipper—maybe now we shove off."

Murray's last-minute orders were few enough. Apparently having selected Casey to captain the expedition, he was willing to allow the proceedings to be at his subordinate's discretion. Years of working together in and out of the service had made them a team; each knew and depended upon the abilities and character of the other. The commander's one instruction dealt with time.

"Three days only. Then whether you have made contact or not—come in. We'll try to keep in touch by radio. Any sign of a storm, and you head back at once!"

"That's for true, skipper. We won't try to ride out any blow in this old mud turtle. Okay, Barnes, give her the gun and let's push off!"

There was a snort as the LC motor came to life. She started a slow progress over coral rock and sand, a progress that was close to a waddle but that brought them into the washing waves.

"Come up here to the lookout, kid," Casey called. "You

know these blasted fish and how they move. If you see anything coming—sing out!"

"Lookout" proved to be a wide water glass set into the LC itself so that they could watch below the wave line as the amphibian craft took to sea. When the treads no longer caught, she began to chug, a floating tank.

To Griff's surprise the sea world he viewed through the glass was much as it had always been. The rainbow fish, the animal-vegetable foliage of the underworld was, as far as he could tell, normal, apparently untouched by the blasts of storm that had so beaten the island. But he watched alertly for the first hint of trouble.

Sun banners flooded the eastern sky. Was that coming light a threat to the enemy? And who or what was the enemy? Mutants caused by atomic radiation from earlier testing? Such a neat answer, but probably they might never know for certain.

Griff froze. That dark trail—it could be a twist of weed, an extra-long sea plume half torn from its moorings—But it was not!

"Casey!" He gave the alert, still tracing that rippling, ropelike thing back to the crevice from which it protruded. It was a tentacle right enough, but the largest he had ever seen. The squid or octopus it belonged to was far more formidable than any of the creatures he had watched along the reef in the old days.

"What is it?"

"Octopus—very big one. See—it must be holed up there—right behind that big stand of red sponge!"

"I don't— Oh, that's one of its arms waving about. But— Good Lord, kid, that arm must be about twelve-fifteen feet long! I didn't know they grew so big around here."

"As far as I know, they didn't—before. Ink!"

The murky cloud shot out of the crevice, forming a screen through which even the water glass could not aid their vision. Casey went into action.

"Barnes, let's have the best she can do! Hall, you and Briggs stand by—"

The LC's crawl stepped up a notch, but her speed was no better than a snail's compared with the agility that any of the great cephalopods could show, as Griff well knew. He reached for one of the rifles and saw that Casey had already picked one up.

"They shoot that ink when they're afraid, don't they?"

"It can also be a signal. With no speech, no hearing, it's their means of communication."

"Maybe we've alerted a lookout." Casey peered fruitlessly into the glass. "It sure muddles things for us."

Griff watched that murk, hoping that soon the LC would be beyond its fogginess. Minutes passed with dragging slowness. Nothing broke the waves, showed any desire to challenge the LC. Leaving Griff on duty by the glass, Casey went back to control to check their course. It had the look of a calm day. The sea moved in lazy swells. There was only a fair wind, hardly more than a breeze, and the sun was rising into a cloudless sky.

Behind them San Isadore became a black smudge on the horizon. They approached within a mile of the new volcanic island cone and coughed in the sulphur-tainted air blown toward them. Storm wrack, in the form of dead fish, matted weed, and wreckage, floated by, caught along the LC, and had to be pushed away. There was an unpleasant odor, partly from the flotsam, but alien to the clean scent of salt and sea wind.

Then that cone drew astern, and they were in the open. Gulls beat over them; one of Mother Carey's neat black and white chickens escorted them for a moment or two before tiring of their slow pace and flashing on.

Casey held the headset of the small radio so that one ear could catch any message from shore. At half-hour intervals they tapped back their own monotonous record of no action. As the sun beamed down, they put on dark glasses and covered their heads. But, save for the birds, they might now be traversing a deserted ocean.

"If it's this quiet," Barnes spoke up, "those guys from

Santa Maria won't have it so bad. Maybe there ain't all the trouble that we think there is."

"Or else it hangs about land, around the islands," Casey replied. "Wait!" The rifle slipped from his loose grasp. He had clamped the earphone tighter to his head with one hand, and his sun-reddened face was the picture of blank astonishment.

"Something coming in?"

"The Santa Maria crowd? Maybe they got that radio fixed! They can give us a beam to ride, and we'll be right with them—"

Casey held the earpone away, surveyed it as if he could not believe he had heard what he did, and clamped it back in one fluid movement.

"Not Santa Maria—?" queried Griff.

"Not unless they speak Russian there!"

"Russian!" Hall fairly spat out the word, and his hand fell on the mounted gun he was to operate.

"I learned some. That's Russian right enough." Casey was emphatic.

"Expeditionary force—?" Barnes gazed bleakly ahead at the still empty sea.

"Did any expeditionary force ever signal 'SOS Amerikantsky'?"

"They're asking *us* for help!"

"Seems that way." Casey's grin was back. "Sounds as if they'd like to see us quick, too. Well, boys, what do we do? Ride their signal beam in—it's in the general direction we're steering—"

"It's a trap!" That was Lawrence at the bow gun.

But Casey shook his head. "I don't think so. They may not know there's anyone around. Sounds to me like a general appeal. How about it, boys, do we go or don't we?"

"We don't!" Barnes's retort flashed.

"I don't know." Hall fiddled with the ammo belt of his gun. "We're armed, and they can't take us by surprise. After all—if they did plaster us—they must have got it as good. We're both finished—why keep on fighting? Kinda silly to do that, seems to me. And if it's in the same direction, we may run into them anyway. I'd say—have a look."

"Suppose we vote." Casey spit overboard one of the slivers of wood he had taken to chewing in place of the vanished cigarettes. "We ride in on their beam and look them over— Ayes?"

There were five "ayes" to Barnes's still defiant "no," but the dissenter accepted the decision with good grace when Casey pointed out that they would advance ready to open fire at the least hint of treachery.

With the call signal ringing in his ears, Casey set about the delicate task of guiding the LC along the flickering beam, hoping to contact those transmitting it.

V

WHO IS THE ENEMY?

"WHAT'S BELOW?"

With a guilty start Griff looked from the horizon to the glass, which was their spy-hole on the sea. But, though the murk of ink was missing, there was no clear glimpse of what might lurk there. They were out of the shallows, as the color of the waves about them testified. Any ocean flooring now went down to the big deeps, where even the armored divers dared not penetrate. An occasional fish was all he could see, and so he reported.

"How are we doing, sir?" Barnes asked Casey.

"We're still on signal—"

"Do they say anything else?" That was Hall.

"Not so far. The broadcast may be automatic."

"Bait." Barnes still held to his negative opinion. "New type booby trap—"

"Maybe." Casey cupped the earphones closer. "Two points starboard—yes—" As the LC swung on the slightly altered course, he nodded. "That does it—beginning to fade a little. We must have it dead center now."

"Something dead ahead!"

It was a dark smudge on the water.

"Reduce speed," Casey ordered. He produced binoculars from the case hanging on his chest and tried to adjust them with one hand. Unable to do so, he held the glasses out to Griff with an impatient grunt.

"What is it? A wreck?"

Griff dropped his sunglasses and used the binoculars. Rocks, slime-green velvet in places with sea growths, leaped out at him—undoubtedly a newly born islet. But projecting from its crown, as a finger might point to the unclouded sky, was something too sharply edged, too smoothly sided, to be natural.

"Island. Just heaved up, I'd say. Something on it—might be a wreck."

He was still not satisfied. A wreck would be more irregular as to outline. This showed no breaks. He saw something move, flip up from the water's edge toward that smooth pinnacle.

"Look out! Lord—!" Was he really seeing that—that ropy *thing* lift from the water to hurl an object at the structure above! "They're under attack!"

Casey snatched the glasses. But Griff could see the islet without their aid now. And he could distinguish movement along the shore line.

"They sure are! Quarter speed, Barnes. We don't want to hit a reef in these waters."

The LC crept while Griff leaned over the vision glass alert to any movement beneath. The ocean floor shelved suddenly, and now he could see ooze and fish. But the shallows were too new to harbor the life forms of the San Isadore lagoon.

"Port—look to port!"

The thing broke water, its long neck curling up into the sunlight, the dark skin rough and warted, the fanged jaws open. It gave a whistling scream and snaked forward with a speed out of proportion to its bulk. But the guns were ready, and the chatter of their defiance crackled.

A thin steam of red spurted high, the neck twisted, and

the head flopped back and forth until the rags of skin, torn by the guns' fire, snapped, and it splashed into the sea on the other side of the LC. The convulsions of the dying monster rocked the heavy craft while Barnes fought the controls and tried to back out of the blood-frothed water.

"Lob an egg over." Casey stood braced in the center of the amphibian. "Anything else bound our way, Griff?"

Griff, clutching the rifle, had an answer. "Plenty! Octopi—big ones—Ink!"

Again that cloudy murk cut off his view.

"Maybe this egg will give them other ideas!" Hall hooked a grenade from the box at his side, drew its firing pin, and pitched it over in the general direction of the islet.

Water—water and other things, grisly flotsam—fountained. But a tentacle flushing yellow as it flipped into the air was planted against the side of the LC. Another joined it, and a third!

"They're over here, too!" shouted Lawrence. Sucker-armed muscle and flesh smacked against the wire netting and shook it.

"Stop the engine!" Casey ordered. "We don't want them wrecking the vanes—"

"We're being pulled down!"

"We are, are we? Well, we'll give them something else to think about. Get out that torch, Briggs. You—the rest of you—plant some more eggs. Nothing like discouraging reinforcements."

The LC was rocking heavily. With the same precision as if he were repairing some part of his beloved machinery, Casey aimed a welding torch at the nearest length of tentacle and let go. There was the stench of burnt meat as muscle and flesh crisped and blackened. The length fell away, the charred strings floating for a second or two on the surface of the water, and then disappeared. Methodically Casey turned and applied the heat to the arms showing on the opposite side of the LC, while his crew obeyed orders with zeal, lobbing grenades out in a circle about the bobbing craft.

How many of the octopi attacked them they were never to

know, but, as the sweat channeled in streams from the men in the heat generated by Casey's torch, there came a time when no new arms clutched at the amphibian, no shadows drifted toward them through the ink-tainted water. Casey leaned panting against the combing of the cockpit.

"Did we win the war?" he wondered aloud. "Or are they just withdrawing to rest up for another punch? Better move while we can. Give her the gun, Barnes."

The Seabee moved from his place by the grenade box back to the controls. Cautiously he spun the motor, and a welcome throb shook them.

"Do we head in, sir?"

"We do." Casey had gone to the bow. "When we get close enough, give them three or four more eggs right up along the shore rocks, just to discourage peeking—"

The LC at her own lumbering pace, half-speed to be on the safe side, went islandward. There was a commotion below, hidden by the ink clouds. Griff guessed that the ravenous feeders of the sea had been drawn to the wounded or dying octopi. He was sure of that as the curved fins of sharks cut in. And where the sea serpent had gone down, there was a whirlpool of activity.

"Okay!" Casey snapped. "This is it! Tickle them up, boys. If there're any of them left along there—"

Therewas a grating noise, and a shudder shook the fell length of the LC.

"We're walking," Barnes informed them needlessly. "Shall I keep her going?"

"After we leave our calling cards. Give it to 'em!"

Casey's signal brought five precise throws. A good section of the sea-slimed ledges before them went down with a rumble into the agitated water. Ink and blood, and floating remnants. The water was a horrible soup.

"Now—! Take her in—all the way! There's a slope—"

"Aye, aye, sir!" For the first time Barnes sounded as if he were enjoying himself.

The LC shook, dipped, and once, for a wild second or

two, slipped on a surface still under water, but her treads caught, and she ground on.

"That's a sub on top there!"

In their preoccupation with the sea battle they had almost forgotten their purpose here. But what Lawrence had pointed out was true. The blunt nose of a sub was slanted into the sky, though most of her lay on the opposite side of the ridge, which formed the backbone of the new land.

"We've gone as far as we can, sir." Barnes switched off the motor.

Ahead the rise was at a sharp angle. If they were to go on, it would be afoot.

Casey was back at the radio, tapping out a call signal.

"International Morse," he explained. "If there's anybody at home and they can answer us—this ought to bring them out of their shell."

They waited a long five minutes by Griff's watch, another five—ten. But there was no sign of life about the bow of the sub.

"Could they have sent that call and then got it—all of them?" wondered Hall.

"Sure. Well," Casey shrugged, "I guess we do it the hard way. You and me, kid," he said to Griff, "we're elected to the mountain-climbing act. They'll cover us from here with the guns, and we don't go out of sight unless there's an extra-good reason. Okay?"

"Good enough." Griff slung two of the grenades at his belt, copying Casey's preparations. They kicked off their island sandals, preferring to make that climb barefooted, not trusting any soles but their own on that weed-slick surface.

There was a strong smell of decay, as things never meant to lie in the open air under a tropic sun disintegrated. Linked together, and to the LC, with lifelines, the two made the first jump from the edge of the bow to a reasonably level ledge.

Had it not been for the rotting vegetable and animal remains the climb would have been relatively easy. But all at once Griff, reaching for a new hold, jerked back his hand. "Look out!"

Casey's head came around. "Some of the snakes after us?"

"No—just watch where you put your hands. See that red stuff—" He pointed to a splotch of crimson, which looked as if it had been hurled against the rock and was slowly slipping from its first point of contact. "That looks to me like the 'plague' weed. And if it is, it may be 'hot'—"

"Oh, yeah?" Casey studied the stain. "Well, there's no use in being a dead hero. What'd'you know, it seems to be rather thick up ahead, doesn't it?"

He was right. The higher reaches of the ledges were dotted with reddish blots, some of which left pink trails where they had struck and then slipped down. Griff recalled his first glimpse of the islet and its besiegers through the binoculars. That arm from the sea hurling something upward—this? But why?

They picked a careful path to avoid the red blobs. Luckily chance had spread most of them up and across walls too steep to climb. With a last spurt Griff reached the top, Casey only seconds behind him. Towering over both of their heads now was the bow of the sub, canting at an angle that fingered it in the direction of the LC.

The surface of the metal was bedaubed with the red weed, which was drying into scabs. It was plain that if the plague stuff *had* been systematically thrown from water level, this had been the target of the attack, and the aim in general had been good.

Though the sub had looked intact from below, what they could see now was a badly crippled ship. Whatever motive power had driven her ashore on the knob of rock had done it with such force as to jam and grind her belly plates, splitting them open as if she were a waterlogged coconut. But all this was inches deep in the red scum. And beyond—downslope so that half its putrescent bulk trailed into the water—was another of the sea serpents, very dead, a ragged hole blasted through its middle.

"They chalked up one hit anyway," Casey observed, "so they must have survived her striking here."

"How can we get down to the hatch?" There was plenty of reason for Griff's demand. The reddened ground was a warning.

"Yeah." Casey pushed back his uniform cap. "Ringing the front door bell is going to be a problem. Ringing the front door bell—" he repeated and then unslung his rifle. "I'm no Daniel Boone, but maybe I can win a cigar on this round. Let's see."

He aimed at the lopsided superstructure of the sub. There was a crack and the answering bong of bullet against metal. Reslinging his weapon, Casey put both hands to his mouth funnelwise and shouted, "Hi! Anybody home?"

There was an answer from the men on the LC, and Griff turned to wave. But Casey's attention was for the sub.

"Give them another shot," Griff suggested when there was movement at last.

In the round entrance to a hatch, a piece of white stuff appeared and was swung back and forth with slow deliberation, proving those within wanted no mistake about their peaceful intentions.

"Hulloooo!" Casey called once more.

"—loooo—" a hollow cry came back. And then framed in the oval hatchway, they saw a figure still waving the parley flag.

"Come on out," Casey urged.

The man on the sub still seemed dubious of his welcome. But he handed his white flag to someone behind him and took in return a swab on a pole. This he pushed before him to clean the sloping deck as he approached a point near the Americans.

"Lieutenant Serge Karkoff!" He introduced himself in understandable, if accented, English and made a stiff little bow. "And this"—he waved his hand over the battered sub—"was the *Volga*. You are—?"

Casey answered for them both. "Lieutenant Bert Casey,

136

United States Navy, C.B., Griffith Gunston. Looks as if you've been having a little trouble—"

The other grimaced.

"Did you come to answer our signal? We could only hope. But where is your ship? Were you not attacked?"

"You didn't hear the battle?" Casey grinned. "Yes, the fish tried to scupper us, but we had their numbers. We're parked on the other side of the island—"

"Parked?" the other repeated dully. "There are but four of us unhurt, Lieutenant. And three with broken bones. We surrender unconditionally. If you can—can get us away from this place—"

Griff saw the Russian's teeth clamp on his lip.

"Leave your arms behind," Casey ordered. "And you'd better bring some ropes, if you have them. There's a stiff climb over here."

"It shall be as you say," Karkoff replied. "We must move with caution. This red stuff—it is deadly. Three of our men had died from it—and those—those *things* keep it all about!"

The rescue of the *Volga*'s crew was a lengthy process. Two of the disabled had to be lowered in slings and then carried to the LC. And those on the amphibian were constantly alert against a renewal of hostilities from the sea.

Now the cockpit quarters were a tighter fit, but the men from the sub were no problem. For the most part they dropped to the deck, staring rather dazedly about them, as if not yet fully realizing that they had been freed from the disabled sub.

"How long have you been here?" Casey asked the Russian commander.

Karkoff shrugged. "Two—three—maybe four days. There was a storm, and we drove into something below which was not on our charts. All compartments but one were flooded. Alexis, Gronmyko, all the rest, they had no chance. We could not tell what was happening. Then—hours later—we were able to cut our way out—and found this. After that—it was a terrible dream. There was the sea beast—we blew it apart with a shell from the deck gun. But the gun burst when we tried to fire a second time. Two men were killed then. Afterwards came the red stuff." With the gesture of a tired and bewildered man, he rubbed his hands across his face, and his cap fell to the deck. "It is very hard to think; you must excuse me. There has so much happened—and all of it strange. There— You are now fighting the war?"

Casey hitched at his rifle strap. "I don't think there's any war left to fight, Lieutenant. We don't know what has happened—"

The Russian was younger than Griff had first reckoned. His broad Slavic face did not register any strong emotion, but his dark eyes held a hurt deep in them. He swayed suddenly, and Griff put out a hand to steady him, pushing him down on the edge of the grenade box.

"It has come then—the big end to everything?" he asked in a low voice.

One of his men reached out and touched the officer's dangling hand, asking a question. Almost impatiently the other answered, and the Russian seaman drew in his breath with a hissing sound.

"Seems so," Casey returned frankly. "But our crowd weathered it well—"

"So I see. You were searching for us?"

"We were out on a mission of our own when we picked up your signal. Now," he spoke to Barnes, "we'd better get on course again. Take her out."

"Aye, aye, sir."

With a throbbing motor the LC reversed and crawled back the way she had come.

"Nickov sent that call before he died," the Russian explained. "We had only a little hope. You are certain that all is gone—?"

"We don't know. No radio broadcasts have been picked up from the north. But just at present we have other things to think about."

"*Da*," Karkoff nodded. "Keeping alive occupies the mind. But if all is gone, why should we struggle to keep alive?"

"One gets in the habit of it," Casey commented dryly.

"And, I, for one, am not going to let any damned fish take over running things!" He spat into the water just as the LC tumbled from her reef footing and became all ship once more.

"Who now is the enemy?" broke out Karkoff. "You and I—or that down there?"

"We haven't settled that yet, sonny boy," was Casey's prompt reply. "But I'm inclined to think that the line-up will be different from this point on—men against fish!"

VI

THE RETURN OF THE *ISLAND QUEEN*

"WE SHOULD BE sighting the Largo Cays about now," Griff observed but without too much certainty. One northern run with the *Island Queen* had been his only introduction to this particular route, and trying to compare the cruising speed of the *Queen* and the lumbering LC added to his confusion.

The vision glass was no help either. Where, by the old charts, it should have shown shallows, it revealed only the darker gloom of depths. But, after they left the island where the *Volga* had made her last port, they saw no more of the octopi. Karkoff was able to add a fact or two to their information concerning the creatures. It was true that this new breed of cephalopods controlled the "sea serpents" and also that they followed an intelligent pattern in their attack on the sub. But why they should be aroused to that attack in the first place still remained a mystery.

"I see nothing—" Karkoff stood in the bow using his own binoculars. "You seek islands—?"

"Not islands—except as guides. We're after a couple of fishing boats loaded with refugees." Casey outlined the story of the end of Santa Maria.

"A whole island sinking!" Again that strained, dazed expression dulled the Russian's eyes. "But why? Why should islands go up and down?"

"I'm no geologist," Casey replied. "But the balance must have been upset. There's a full-sized volcano off San Isadore—as well as the one at Santa Maria. How do we know what all-out bombing would do? The Atlantic may have poured in over part of the States. And in Europe—"

The Russian shook his head. "I think that I do not want to know."

Casey went back to the radio, still hoping for a signal from one of the fishing boats. But as the LC bore on into the sea, there was no sign that any other craft had been there before it. They did not sight the Largo Cays. Perhaps they had sunk. So finally Casey ordered a circling eastward, to head back to San Isadore. Griff felt their failure the more because he assumed the responsibility for it.

"Getting late—" Barnes observed. And they knew what he was thinking.

Night at sea was a double danger. But in the end it was the darkness that brought success to their mission.

An excited exclamation from one of the Russians drew their attention to port. A fiery trail ascended into the sky, bursting in a shower of stars. That was not born of a volcano!

"Head in!"

Barnes obediently altered course once more, and the searchlight on the bow was turned on, sending a broad path of light out ahead. There was a second starry display and a third. The LC pointed at that dead center. Was that the signal of the boats from Santa Maria—or the call of some other castaway?

When their beam caught the boat ahead, they were reasonably sure they had found what they sought. There was no mistaking the blunt lines of an island fishing smack built for durable use rather than for record speed. It wallowed toward them deep in the water, as if overloaded.

Casey climbed up the netting and, cupping his hands, sent a hail across the waves.

"What ship?"

"The *Felice*, Santa Maria— Who are you?" came the faint reply.

"Navy LC out of San Isadore," Casey boomed. "We've been hunting you—"

The *Felice* and her companion, the *Flamingo*, crept with the beat of hard-driven engines, their pace less than the LC's second speed. Faces, white, dusky, dark, were picked up by the searchlight.

"Good Lord!" Hall exploded. "They've packed them in, standing room only!"

"Can you give a tow?" queried someone from the boats.

"This is a pretty tough old girl, sir," Barnes spoke up. "But she can't haul the fleet!"

But that wasn't required. Behind each of the fishing vessels trailed a string of smaller craft. And that underlined their desperate venture. Only a choice of deaths could have sent the pitiful flotilla into the infested sea so poorly protected against the danger now lurking there.

The LC could and did take tows, three from each of the fishing craft. And then, her searchlight still on, she led the way back, southwest to San Isadore. They were forced to creep, laboring at such a pace that a rowboat ably handled could have outdistanced them. And only the merciful fact that the sea remained calm saved them.

All night long they held course, Casey and Barnes alternating at the controls. And the gray light of predawn was easing across the sky when Lawrence switched off the searchlight. By compass they would approach San Isadore from a different direction than they had left and must parallel the coast northward to the base, being now not far from sunken Carterstown.

Once more they swung to avoid the volcanic cone, and Karkoff, standing beside Griff, exclaimed in Russian before switching to English.

"This is one of those new volcanoes?"

"Yes. The night it broke through, San Isadore had several shocks. See that line over there?" He pointed to a double thick horizon. "That's San Isadore."

"Your base?"

"Yes."

"That ship—it is also one of yours?"

"What ship?" Surprised, Griff looked along the line of the other's pointing finger.

Karkoff was right. There was a ship there, a spot of white against the waves.

Before he could ask for the use of Casey's binoculars the other called to him, "Get on the glass, kid. We want to know it if the snakes are preparing a reception party."

Griff went to his post, and the Russian followed him, drawing a deep breath as he shared the vantage point of the glass with the American. The water was changing color; they were in the shallows—those shallows that were always dangerous now. But, though the usual inhabitants of the reef-protected section were there, Griff saw no signs of the enemy.

Again the LC altered course, now paralleling the outline of land. The fishing boats, with their engines driving heavily, sluggishly, copied her maneuver. When Griff dared to glance up, he saw that the strange ship anchored in Frigate Bay was now hidden by a headland. But it must be investigated when they could.

The flotilla was still some distance from the base when the engine on one of the fishing boats gave a final splutter and died.

"That does it!" Barnes exclaimed. "We can't take *her* in tow!"

From a whirlpool of activity on board the boat, her sails arose, cupping some of the trade. At sea it would not have been enough to give her headway; here it at least kept her moving and manageable.

Casey called across, "Can you keep going for a while? We'll be back as a ferry—"

"It's a case of have to," a voice unmistakably American shouted back.

"So far, so good. Any trouble from below?" Casey demanded of Griff.

But save for the usual dwellers of the shore line he saw nothing.

"Give her all you can now," Casey ordered. "We'll have to be back again."

The other fishing boat had passed them. Now the LC caught up and left her astern. Lawerence hailed a shore landmark with a shout of relief. Over a calm sea they headed straight in to crawl up on the beath. The Russians disembarked, as the other fishing boat anchored as close to shore as her crew could bring her. With a hurried explanation to the waiting Murray and a casting off of her earlier tows, the Navy amphibian took to the sea once more, heading back for the disabled refugee carrier.

"Ink!" The battle signal Griff had been watching for billowed. Undersea sentries were alerted. Did it mean attack?

"Lay a couple of eggs as a discouragement," Casey was cool. "Say one ahead and one behind."

The grenades sailed through the air, splashed, and the LC rocked with the force of those twin explosions. There was another sound carrying clearly across the sea—it could only be the crackle of rifle fire.

Barnes got more speed out of the lumbering craft than Griff would have believed possible. Once her treads bit on a sunken reef, but instead of slowing her spurt, that merely added to her impetus. They rounded a rocky point and saw the white sails of the other ship, heard the steady firing. One of the boats she had towed and had not been able to relinquish to the LC floated bottom up on the water, a water now riffled by more than the morning wind.

"Anything below?"

"Ink mostly. It's all screened out."

"Until we see something we can aim at, just plant eggs."

They tossed grenades at regular intervals as they bore down upon the almost helpless ship. Evidence floated to the surface telling them that they had made at least one direct hit on some gathering of attackers. There were wild shrieks as the second and last of the towed boats began to rock vigorously. The LC was close enough for her crew to see those tough ropes of muscle that had tightened about the small skiff. Men slashed with knives. One tentacle was hacked in two—but there were others.

Lawrence depressed the muzzle of the bow gun, fired an experimental burst, which clipped below the surface, and then sent a steady round into the weltering mass. Luck was with him. The tentacles threatening the boat suddenly fell away and sank. By incredible good fortune one of those bullets had reached some vital spot in the enemy.

Barnes cut the throttle, and the men in the small boat hastily took to their oars, brought it alongside the amphibian, and then climbed the netted sides to drop into the cockpit. They were a mixture of native islanders, English-ancestored planters, and two whom Griff recognized as the manager of the Santa Maria airport—an ex-American flyer—and one of the customs officers.

Casey hardly waited until the last was on board before he called to the larger vessel for a towline. And so linked, the LC began the slow crawl back to the base.

The airport manager crouched beside Griff. His eyes were sunken in dark hollows; his wrist was bandaged, and he carried it thrust into the front of his shirt for the want of a sling.

"What's this thing anyway?" he asked. "A seagoing tank?"

"Something like."

"It sure can do the business! Look here—did a plane get through? We sent one off." His forehead wrinkled in a frown. "It must have been the day before yesterday."

"Yes. It came through. Cracked up when it landed, but everybody was all right. That's why we were out hunting you—"

The other sighed. "A little bit of luck. First we've had. My wife was on that plane. They're all safe—you sure of that?"

"I helped bring them down from the salt flat where they landed, so I can say 'yes' for sure."

The other's hand went to his face and shielded his eyes. "Thanks." His voice was a whisper. "Thanks very much."

Griff was back at his post by the glass. The dark cloud

of ink, which had curtained the activities of the attackers, was thinning. Could they hope that the sea things had shot their bolt for this time? Brilliant coral fans, sea plumes bloomed. The unhurried schools of rainbow fish trailed through the drifting threads of weed as they had done for unnumbered years.

"You have any news?" The airport man edged forward. "My people live in Tampa. Any news from the States?"

"No."

The other sank back to stare dully at the flooring of the cockpit.

"Hey!" Lawrence called from the bow. "What's all that red stuff?"

Rippling from wave cap to wave cap, as in more happy days the trails of sargasso weed had moved along the Gulf Stream, was a dull red stain, a splotch that might have been blood draining from some giant wound. But Griff had seen its like before. And he didn't need to sight the fish floating with distended bellies up in the circle of scum to underline its deadliness. The plague!

It had not yet cut across the course held by the LC, but those on board were able to see that it was only the advance part of a vast coat of the stuff, ragged patches of which had split free from the main mass. And from it came the stench of ancient rottenness—of decay fouler than that native to dead sea life.

Insensibly Barnes altered course to avoid those streamers among the waves. But Lawrence's second observation was awed.

"There must be miles of it!"

Yes, they could see that the stain covered the ocean as a blanket. Sea birds dipped, attracted by the dead things floating in its foulness. But then they sheared off suddenly, to rise screaming and baffled. And that which even the birds feared was headed straight for San Isadore. It would be washed ashore all along this end of the island.

They reached the base, and the crippled fishing boat anchored while the LC waddled ashore with her second cargo of refugees. Griff dropped to the sand. It was not until much later that a glimpse of Karkoff talking to Murray reminded him of the ship they had sighted in Frigate Bay, off the now three-quarters submerged Carterstown. Were there survivors aboard her? If so—shouldn't they be helped ashore?

But he couldn't get to Murray. Casey had disappeared. And, although he saw Holmes, he knew better than to try to enlist the aid of the security lieutenant. He had kept the rifle from the LC. Now, after filling a canteen, he went to the caves of the islanders and luckily found Le Marr in the first he entered.

"I think there's a ship anchored in Frigate Bay—near the town. If there's anyone on board her—"

"There be. That has been homin' a long time, many days," Le Marr answered surprisingly. "Yes, we must go to her—"

But he would not explain as they left the settlement and struck southward, with first the cliffs and then the wide beach as their path. The red taint was already leaving its mark on the rocks. He pointed it out to the islander.

"Death," Le Marr said without emotion. "That be death, mon."

The stench of the stuff was thick enough to taste. When they stopped to chew on rations, Griff discovered that, hungry as he had been, he could not stomach food. The odor got between him and every bit he took.

They plodded on into the late afternoon. The mangrove swamp, by some freak of the island displacement, was now higher ground, drained of most of its pools, the mud dried between the knee roots wherever the sun could strike in to suck up moisture. But enough scummy depressions remained to harbor the mosquitoes, which attacked the two so viciously that they had to beat them away, breathing in minute inscets, crushing the larger until their shirts were bloody. However, the reek of the dying swamp cut some of the stench of the plague, and they welcomed the change. Crabs scuttled away from their line of march; lizards moved lightning quick along the branches of the trees. It was a dank green world, and Griff wondered if it were now totally doomed by the draining.

It was close to sundown when they came out on the other side. Had it not been for Le Marr, Griff might have been helplessly lost in the mucky maze. In the old days one could have taken to the sea and splashed around such a barrier. But now that path was closed.

They built a fire of driftwood and ate their rations. Griff tried to scrub the slime of the swamp from him with sand. If he could only strip and wash clean in the sea!

A burrowing owl, devoid of ear tufts so that its head was round, resembling nothing so much as an animated ball of knitting wool, cooed to itself as it appeared in its doorway under the roots of a bush hung with thousands of tiny blossoms. Griff brushed against one of the shrub's outstretched limbs. The owl snapped into cover as a jack-in-the-box. Pollen drifted through the air and with it a strong perfume heavy enough to banish some of the foulness that had clogged his lungs for so long.

They slept there that night, both silent and deep in their own thoughts, the fire at their feet. But the flames died before dawn, and Griff awoke shivering. The red tinge was on the sand here, and the waves brought in the bodies of harmless sea dwellers killed by its poison—lying limp for the tearing claws of the shore crabs, who were not as nice as the birds had been and devoured the dead eagerly.

It must have been close to ten o'clock when they came out on the scrap of road that had once run inland for a half mile or so from Carterstown. The rubble of the dead town lay ahead, three-quarters of it now under water, showing here and there a part of wall or a thatchless roof projecting above the surface.

And there was a ship right enough, swaying at anchor with every rise and fall of the lazy swell, as Griff had seen her so many, many times in the past. The *Island Queen* had come home!

VII

CAPTIVE CARGO

SHE WAS NOT the same trim vessel that had put out from that port more than a week before. Her main mast ended in a splintered nub some feet above deck; her white paint was stained and in places ground from her boards. But there was something else! Fastened to that stub of mast, a colored rag beat out in the pull of the morning wind as might a tattered battle standard. Seeing that, Griff turned to Le Marr.

"There must be someone on board! That's a signal! How are we going to get out to her?"

Between them and that deck rolled the oily water that washed over the ruins of Carterstown. Although the red scum was missing here, the rubble under water provided too many good lurking places for the enemy to invite swimming. Yet Griff *had* to reach the *Queen* some way. A dugout? There had been some in the town, used for fishing within the circle of the reef. Could they locate one of those? Only, such a craft would be as easy to attack as a swimmer!

Le Marr moved off around the edge of the flood, where the new shore line was in the process of establishment. Griff fell in behind, hoping the islander could produce a sensible plan of action.

Under them the ground began to rise. It was part of the old cliff line. Soon they were above the level of the anchored ship, for it *was* anchored. Griff could easily picture Captain Murdock, Rob, or Chris, sick or hurt, pent up in her cabin, waiting for help that was too long in coming.

Under the water from this height they could see the lines of walls, those dark pools that were the interiors of roofless houses. Then a triangular fin cut smoothly through the flood, beyond it another—sharks. Griff slipped the rifle strap from his shoulder. He was aiming at one of those dimly seen killers when another idea occurred to him. The sound of a shot might bring into the open anyone on board the *Queen*.

Pointing the rifle out to sea, Griff fired three times and was amazed himself at the roar of sound. Sea birds wheeled and screamed, and inland there was a wild clatter of hooves, a frightened bray. Some of the island's wild donkeys had survived the storm and were raiding garden patches on the outskirts of the town. But the donkeys were not the only life, as the two on the cliff speedily discovered. They were startled by a shout.

"Oheee—mon—"

Tearing through the thorn scrub came a wild figure, which looked to Griff no more than a skeleton barely concealed in flapping rags. And behind the first came a second, even barer, as its full clothing was a twist of drab stuff about the loins.

"What you do here, mons?" Between panting gasps the words broke, as the first skeleton clawed its way up to them, using hands as well as feet on the ground to keep balance.

"Liz!" Griff almost dropped the rifle. The bony figure, the ravished face, was not the confident woman he had seen in the valley. But this was Liz making her way painfully toward them. He ran forward and tried to help her up.

"Mistuh Gunston!" Her hollow eyes fastened on him with a spark of her old energy. "Then the big storm, it don' take everybody like we think! Oh, there's still mons here—there's still mons!" Tears rolled out of her eyes, and she made no move to wipe them away.

"But, Liz, how did you and—and—" He studied the second figure. The man might have been any age from twenty to fifty, but he moved stiffly, favoring his leg down which ran an angry-looking, puckered slash, and his face was dull, beaten.

"This is my boy, Luce. You 'member Luce, Mistuh Gunston!"

Luce! Griff remembered a young giant he had seen win two wrestling matches, a laughing young man with a fine voice for crooning chants of the island. But that Luce and this were not the same.

"What happened?" he began and then wished that he hadn't. Luce stood with hanging head, the vacant look on his face unchanging. But Liz shivered.

"The storm, that's what happened. We found us a cave— but even there—" She faltered. "You got things better, Mistuh Gunston?"

"Yes, you'll come back with us, Liz, and see for yourself," he was beginning when Luce suddenly came to life. Advancing to the edge of the rise, he pointed out to the *Queen*.

"There's the *Queen*! The *Queen*, she done come home!"

Liz was shaken out of her own concerns. She peered down at the bobbing ship. "That's right! Luce, he call it right," she marveled. "That's the *Queen* come home. But"— she surveyed the sunken town—"that home, they ain't goin' to find it no more."

"You haven't been here before, Liz? No one landed from her?"

Liz shook her head in answer to both questions.

"But someone brought her in and anchored here. There's a signal flag on the mast. Someone may be on board—"

"Why you don't swim out?" Luce asked.

"Too dangerous." Griff wondered if the other could understand. "There are things in the sea—"

Luce's skull jaws split in a grin. "They can't touch you if you got yourself jubee oil—"

Le Marr whirled. But he spoke to Liz and not to the grinning Luce.

"You make that?"

She drew herself up with much of her old commanding air, her hysterical welcome to them forgotten. "I found something," she replied. "You can swim in the sea an' noth-ing—nothing at all touch you."

"You have it here, woman?"

"Done used it all fishin'," she said regretfully. "But we can make us a mess o' it again—do you want it so."

"Do that thing!" Le Marr snapped.

"First we git us a pig. An' they's hard to find now. Luce."
She summoned her son. "Luce, we do want us a pig. How
we git one—?"

The flash of intelligence still lit his face. He put out a
bony hand and drew one finger almost caressingly down the
barrel of Griff's rifle. "With this here, it ain't too hard. I
show where—"

Liz smiled. "You go with Luce, Mistuh Gunston. Git us a
pig, an' we find us what else we be needin'."

"I don't understand," Griff protested, but Le Marr interrupted him.

"It be this way, mon. They's ways the fishermons knows
to poison fishes. Not here on the island—but over there"—
he made a gesture westward—"where is the big land.
Maybeso we find some thing here what will act like that.
There's herbs an' there's bad things—poisons—grown here.
Do we learn to use them right, we's got us something those
sea debbles are goin' to fear. Liz, she knows the plants, better then me she know them 'cause—"

" 'Cause," Liz spoke up proudly, "I do be kin to the old
wise womons as live here for years an' years. There be's
many wise womons in my family, an' they tells to one to the
other all they knows afore they die. Me—" She spread her
hands wide and then tapped her forehead. "I know much-
much. An' this here stuff it work. Luce, he put it on an'
walk right in the water—fish they all go 'way fast. You'll
see. But first you go shoot us that pig."

Somehow a portion of the animal life of San Isadore had
managed to survive the great storm. And Luce led Griff
inland to a gully, where the drift of salty sand deposited
there by the high winds was piled with the earth that had
slipped down in landslides. Luce knew what he was doing,
for the slotted pig tracks ran back and forth in trails.

"You stay here with that there gun." He was almost his
old-time self again as he swung into action he understood.
"I go—git pig—"

Griff stationed himself obediently behind an outcrop of
wall to wait while Luce melted into the patch of scrub

thorn and cacti that had been rooted against the fury of the tempest.

They really should explore the whole of San Isadore soon, he thought. Water might be a problem. Most of the island had depended upon rain tanks for fresh water. He knew that the base had included a conversion unit in its original installations. But whether that apparatus had been salvaged he could not tell. The storms of the past few days had filled emergency tanks as well as all the rock hollows. And under Murray's orders it had been stored and rationed. Water—and food. Much of the arable land was gone. Around Carterstown the sea had taken the majority of the garden strips. There had been a herd of wild cattle, descended from those left by buccaneers to provision their ships, donkeys, some horses, and the pigs. Surely few of those had come through—

A sullen grunting in the brush alerted Griff. He lowered the rifle. Then came an angry squeal. Two rangy sows burst from cover, behind them an ugly-looking boar, who wheeled and turned its head back toward the cover as if to face up to the danger that had flushed it out of hiding.

The pigs of San Isadore were sorry specimens. Most of them would be considered litter runts by any mainland farmer. But the surly tempers and wily animosity of the small herds made them just as dangerous as their cousins that provided sport for hunters elsewhere.

Griff ignored the sows, setting sights on the boar. He fired, and under the impact of the bullet, the hog appeared to rise in the air before it plunged forward, skidding on its head at the foot of a cactus.

Luce skimmed out of nowhere, a brown shadow, his bare body blending into the color of rocks and earth as he went down on his knees to cut the throat of the still feebly kicking animal.

Together they fastened it to a pole for easier carrying. Thin-legged and spine-ridged as the boar looked, it proved to be much heavier than Griff had anticipated. They got it back to the cliff above Carterstown to find there a fire blazing. An iron kettle brought from one of the yet un-submerged houses hung on an improvised tripod over it, while Liz chopped silvery leaves into chaff and Le Marr studied an array of other vegetation he held fanwise in his hand. Two land crabs lay to one side on a palm leaf, and a dead lizard hung by its tail on a nearby bush.

Griff found the preparations so grisly that he wandered over to sit on a rock and watch the *Queen*. Since there had been no response from her in answer to his signal shot, he had given up hope of there now being any life on board. But someone had brought her in, had anchored her, and had left that rag of flag flying. And Griff was determined to explore her.

He had little faith in Liz's concoction protecting a swimmer. On the other hand, the native lore of the islanders was surprising, and such a discovery would be welcomed at the base. He was perfectly willing to play guinea pig himself.

The result of Liz's brewing was set out to cool at last. And they ate strips of stringy pork, fresh broiled, together with Naval rations, while the thick substance with its base of hog grease congealed, Liz testing it from time to time with a finger tip. When she signified it was ready, Le Marr stripped and rubbed it into his skin. After a moment Griff reluctantly threw aside shirt and slacks to follow the islander's example, smearing it first over his skin and then over the trunks he wore. It was smelly and he hated the feel of it, but he trusted Le Marr's faith.

Luce reached out for the rifle Griff had left leaning against the bole of a palm, but the American caught it up. On impulse he tendered it to Liz. She grinned widely with some of her old-time buoyancy of spirit.

"I thinks I'll git me some fresh meats, maybeso. Shark meats—"

Just so he wasn't going to provide fresh meat for some shark in his turn, Griff thought as he padded downslope to the new verge of the bay. Le Marr had waded out along a crumbled, awash wall, water rising from ankle to knee, and then to his waist before he dove to paddle out over what had been the main street of Carterstown. Griff gingerly copied him. Never before, even on that day when he had entered the inland sea pool, had he felt the same reluctance to trust himself to water.

He fell into the effortless strokes of an expert swimmer, heading for the *Queen*'s mooring. The water rolled from his greased flesh. He heard a warning shout and trod water. There was no mistaking the cutting fin coming around in a wide circle. Griff's hand went for the diver's knife.

But there was no need for such defense. The fin sheered off, breaking away in a fury of speed. Griff might have been a sea monster himself. Liz's oil at work?

He had little time for speculation. Le Marr had reached the *Queen*'s anchor line. That must be their means of getting aboard. But the ship was riding unusually low in the water. Perhaps she had shipped a lot of sea in the storm, but from appearances she might have been carrying a full cargo.

Griff clambered up after the islander. The deck was stripped; everything that a high sea could possibly carry away had been torn from its place. There was an odd sucking sound, but otherwise it was very quiet.

The cabin hatch was closed. Griff skidded across the decking, his greased feet slipping. Again Le Marr was before him, prying at that entrance. Under their strength it gave, but Le Marr muttered as he put his shoulder to it, "Locked from the inside—"

With a splintering crash it yielded. Beyond was a thick dusk, too gloomy for their sun-dazzled eyes to pierce at first.

"Anyone there?" Griff called, his heart pounding.

When there was nothing but silence, he climbed over the wreckage of the door to descend the few steps within. There was an evil smell, a sweetish miasma. Le Marr caught at the American's shoulder, checking his advance.

"Wait, mon. There be bad thing here—"

In the murky twilight was a wild state of wreckage. Every object that could be torn loose was piled in a mouldering mess on the cabin floor. And with the gentle rocking of the *Queen,* they could hear the swish of water washing back and forth, trapped in the mass.

"Chris!" Griff could make out the big form sprawled motionless on the stripped bunk. "Chris!"

He stumbled over and through the junk, but he did not reach the mate ahead of Le Marr. The islander pulled at the flaccid body, his hand resting with urgency on the wide chest.

"Chris?" Griff made a question of it this time, looking to Le Marr.

"There still be life. Do we git him out o' here, maybeso we can help—"

Somehow they got the dead weight of the mate's heavy body across the cabin, up those steps, and out into the clean air and sun. Under his dark skin there was an odd greenish pallor, and, in spite of Le Marr, Griff believed that they had brought out a dead man.

"Look for the supplies, mon," Le Marr ordered. "See if you can find food—water. He be not hurt—just sick—"

Griff plunged back into the disordered cabin, digging dog-fashion into the mass on the floor. He found a tin can that appeared intact, though its label was gone, but fresh water was missing.

Back on deck he punctured the can lid with his knife and discovered he had been lucky, as the tart scent of stewed tomatoes came from the battered lid. He passed it to Le Marr and then supported Chris while the other worked pulp and liquid into the unconscious man's slack mouth. As it dribbled out again, Griff's hope sank. They were too late; nothing was going to bring Chris around now.

But some measure of that restorative moisture had helped.

"He swallow!" Le Marr exclaimed excitedly. "This mon not be licked yet. He be tough—"

Griff could see that movement of the throat, too. Yes, some of the watery pulp was getting down. Yet, save for that convulsive swallowing and the very faint rise and fall of his chest, Chris showed no more signs of life than he had when they pulled him from the cabin. And how were they going to transport him to shore?

The contents of the can being at length exhausted, Griff settled Chris gently back on the deck and stood up, studying the disappointing bareness all about. Somehow, somewhere, they must find something on which they could float the unconscious man to land.

"How are we—?" he was beginning when they were both startled by movement in the mate. Chris's eyes opened and passed over Griff as if the American were invisible. His lips, sticky with juice, drew back in a snarl of rage such as Griff had never seen the placid Chris exhibit before. And on his hands and knees he crawled across the decking to the battened-down hatch of the cargo space. There, as if that progress had drained all his energy, he sank down in a heap, but his big hands drummed weakly on the sealed hatch as he collapsed.

"Debble!" His voice was a hissing whisper. "Debble—we done cotched you safe! No more killin' mons. Debble—" His head fell on his beating hands, and they were still.

Griff jumped to help Le Marr pull the mate away from the opening. Then the islander regarded the hatch narrowly.

"I think, mon"—some inner excitement broke his usual calm—"we should look in here. Chris, he goin' be all right. But here—maybeso we find something—"

He was busy at the lashings, and, now that he examined them carefully, Griff saw that the ropes had been wound and tied in a vast network of knots and interweavings—to make very sure that what lay below was safe.

In the end, they had to cut the majority of the ropes in order to clear the opening. And then, together, they pried and tugged until they had the cover up. The same fetid odor so noticeable in the cabin was present to a far greater degree. But there was something else. Water washed below, swinging back and forth with the movements of the *Queen*. But this was no overflow from the storm as it had been in the cabin. Here was water that almost filled the hold, and in it—

"Look out, mon!"

But Griff had seen it too—that coil of living flesh rising with deliberation from below the surface of the dark flood toward the open hatch. As one, the two on the deck moved, sliding back the hatch, fumbling with the fastenings they had cut loose.

"So he did bring back debble," Le Marr observed as they made secure. "This be a good thing, I think."

Griff stared down at Chris with wondering eyes. How had the mate done it and why? But he had. And now the survivors on San Isadore would have the chance they wanted to study the nature of the enemy close at hand.

VIII

MAN IS A STUBBORN ANIMAL

"THE BASE—" Griff paced uneasily across the deck. "If they could send the LC—give us a tow—"

"No other way to go," Le Marr agreed. "Night comes—"

Griff caught the significance of that remark. Darkness had always been a factor in the attacks of the undersea things. Did the prisoner below have any way of summoning its kind? If so, could the *Queen* expect an attack? Was it fear of that which had made Chris lock himself in the cabin?

Le Marr arose to his feet. "I go shoreways. Send Liz to the base. We stay here—"

Before Griff could protest, Le Marr dived from the deck and swam inland. He climbed ashore across some half-awash rubble to the cliff. Griff sat down beside Chris. His imagination was painting a vivid picture for him of that thing below, moving sluggishly about its prison. And the secret of how it had been trapped there intrigued him. Where were Captain Murdock and Rob Fletcher?

Chris was asleep, sprawled out on the deck, every rib underlined beneath his skin. Now and then he muttered, but, though Griff listened closely, he could make no sense out of that gabble.

It was nearing sunset, and he felt naked on this battered deck with no other weapon than a knife, no defense against what might rise from the shallows. If one of those "serpents" were to appear now— They could not hope to face up to that menace.

A splash brought him around in a half-crouch, steel in hand. But no fanged head spiraled up from the water. Instead he saw Le Marr paddling back, pushing before him a crude raft hastily cobbled out of driftwood on which balanced the rifle and the iron pot in which Liz had concocted her brew. From the cut lashings of the hatch cover Griff knotted a line to lift that cargo on board. And when both it and the islander were beside him, he discovered that Le Marr had come prepared for a siege. The pot was full of fresh water, and there were their ration tins and some coconuts, as well as the rifle.

"Liz goes to the base. She will tell the commander what be here. Tell him send crawl boat for us. Maybeso come by mornin'—"

Le Marr roused Chris and gave him some sips of the water, while Griff made good use of the remaining sun time to grub in the wreckage in the cabin, locating and bringing up labelless tins, a fish spear, and a lantern. Le Marr shook his head at the last.

"Light bad thing. Light draw eyes in the night. We be better in dark—"

Griff wanted to protest that, but his common sense agreed. He had not forgotten the night he had dived by the reef and the schools of curious fish that had swum into the path of his torch. Yes, a light might draw to them the very attention they hoped to escape.

They ate and drank sparingly. Griff settled down cross-legged, the rifle resting on his knees. The sea was very calm. Save for the half-submerged ruins of the town, the immediate past might not have been. He was almost drowsing when Le Marr's fingers touched his arm, tightened there in a silent signal of alarm.

Griff, now accustomed to the swing of the derelict *Queen*,

was aware of it also, the slightly different feel of the ship, a displacement of weight that altered her angle in the water.

Le Marr's soft whisper came. "Debble thing restless. It wake—want to be free—"

The American wished he knew more about small sailing craft. The *Queen* was perhaps in danger, riding so low in the water, her motor useless. Could the movements of the imprisoned octopus capsize them?

The effect of that slightest of changes in the *Queen* was electric as far as Chris was concerned. Pricked out of sleep, he sat up, shivering visibly. His wide eyes stared unbelievingly at Griff, went on to Le Marr, and then back to the American. He shook his head and reached out a trembling hand to touch Griff timidly.

"You be there in true, mon?"

"I'm here, Chris—"

Chris again looked from him to Le Marr. The voodoo man's face wore its usual impassive mask until he smiled.

"You be back—back home, mon."

But when Chris looked beyond Le Marr to the altered shore line, he was plainly puzzled.

"This ain't Carterstown—" he said almost plaintively.

"It's what's left of it," Griff answered.

Chris studied the ruins and then, with a sudden dry sob, buried his face in his hands.

"—never no more—" His muffled words trailed mournfully over the waters of the encroaching bay.

"Chris, what happened to the *Queen?*" Griff ventured to ask. "Where's the captain and Rob?"

At first he thought he was not going to get an answer. But at last, in a colorless voice unlike his own, Chris replied.

"The debble things—they came out o' the sea. Rob, he was took—'fore we really see them. Captain—he shoot— the rest—" He shook his head. "It be all mixed up in my head, mon. No more remember. But"—he brought his fist down on the scarred planking under them—"I got this one debble, an' I think I bring him back to the doctuh—to you father. He know what makes fishes do things. Maybeso he can tell why these fish an' bad things come now to git mons. De doctuh can tell us true! You get the doctuh, Griff—"

"I can't. The doctor isn't here now, Chris. I don't—I don't know where he is." But he was thinking that what he had told Casey was still true. As long as one could not see the disaster, one could keep on believing that it had not happened—that some day, maybe tomorrow, word would come that the worst had not happened—that the north was still clean, its cities standing, its lights bright, its people living. He could not believe that Dr. Gunston would never return to San Isadore, that in time life would not be as it had always been.

"He was poisoned by a fish," he continued steadily. "They flew him to the States for treatment."

"Then we keep this here thing 'til he comes back." Chris slapped the deck again. "But the town—what happened to the town?"

"We had a storm, and an earthquake—and there's a volcano out there." Griff pointed seaward. But Le Marr took up the tale at this point.

"There be war, mon, war with the big bombs. The whole world be changed now—"

Griff wondered if Chris had understood, if he could understand—for the *Queen*'s mate sat looking ashore in the thickening dusk, his drawn face a mask of hurt.

"The mons—?"

"They be down island—with the Navy mons—all that be still 'live."

"Everything gone—"

Le Marr nodded briskly. "Everything old be gone. We do other things now. The sea things, they come to fight. We be eaten up 'less we fight back. No more mons fight mons—now they fight other thing—or they don' live no more on this world!"

"Me—" Chris's bowed shoulders straightened—"me, I ain't gonna let no fish thing make trouble for me. I got me one right here. I ain' sayin' fish be smarter nor me!"

Le Marr was only a black blot now in the three-quarters

dark. But his soft chuckle held the approbation they could not see. "There's other mons think that too, Chris. These Navy mons, they ain't shakin' the head and cryin' out 'oh, my, oh, my!' You has done a big thing, bringin' this debble back to San Isadore. We gits it to the Navy mons, an' they makes their own voodoo wi' it. *If* we gits it to the Navy mons!"

"Whyfor you say 'if'?"

"This here debble thing ain't happy. He make his own voodoo. Now he move—"

Le Marr was right. Griff felt the tremor in the *Queen*. Could that creature burst out? Had the ship's sides or bottom been weakened to the point of giving away if the prisoner applied intelligence to the business of winning its freedom?"

"Let him move! He be put in the *Queen* like beef in the can." Chris sounded almost cheerful. "Beef, he don't git out 'til mon takes him. Neither do this—"

"Do he bring help, we have us some things to think 'bout."

"There be debbles here?"

"They be everywhere. They got 'em a sub, didn't they, Griff?"

"Well, maybe they didn't wreck it in the first place, but they sure kept it tied down afterwards!" agreed the American. He spoke almost absently, trying to be alert to every sound about the *Queen*, tense and conscious of that remitting tremor. Could that very faint pulsation carry through the water to summon—?

"There are two kind debbles," Chris remarked thoughtfully. "There are the long necks and the octopi. The long necks, they stay mostly in the water. These kind"—they heard his hand beat the deck—"can come out a little way. But we gotta teach 'em they better stay in!"

"So we try," Le Marr agreed. "Now we eat ourselves something. Nobody can do everything in one day." He portioned out rations brought from the base and cans hacked open.

Griff ate cold baked beans with his fingers and ended by sucking a square of dark chocolate. He had been watching the incoming waves, and now he pointed out a phenomenon to the others.

"What's that glow—there—along the water?"

He was familiar with the phosphorescence of the southern waters—had seen it fly in foam from the cutting bow of the *Queen* in happier days. But this was different. It appeared to move under the water, not on the surface, and in lines. Then material he had read in the now vanished library of the lab flashed to mind and brought him to his feet in alarm.

The greater octopi from the depths were spangled with bright sparks of luminescence!

"They comin'?" Le Marr sounded neither surprised nor disturbed.

"Maybe—" He had been a fool not to bring some of the greandes, though explosions so near to the crippled *Queen* might have torn the derelict apart.

He was sure his guess was correct. Those odd trails of light were not just slipping along the waves in the aimless fashion of phosphorescence; they were converging on the ship. And her deck was now hardly four feet above the water level. Any of the octopi he had seen about the islet where the *Volga* rested, or which he had watched attack and try to overturn the boats of the refugees, could reach the planking on which the three were huddled. He spoke to Le Marr.

"I think they must have spotted us. And we've got to have the lantern now, for if we don't keep the deck clear—" But how could they do that with only one rifle, a pair of knives, and a fishing spear?

There was a rasping, scraping sound. Griff instinctively moved back from the edge of the deck. It would be only too easy to seize him from below and whirl him over before he could make a defensive move.

A yellow glow cut the thick dark. The three drew together by the cargo hatch. Chris levered himself up on his hands, peering wide-eyed into the dark. Griff nursed the rifle, facing the direction from which that ominous sound had come. Le Marr finished lashing the lantern tight with cord to the hatch cover and then picked up the spear.

If they only had one of the atomic flood lamps from the base, Griff thought, and then forced a twisted grin. As long as he was wishing for tools, he might as well make it a box of grenades or one of the LC's rapid-fire guns. There was a flicker of movement just within the farthest reaches of the lantern's beam, and he tensed.

"They come—" Le Marr straightened.

"An' he know it, too!" The faint tremor of movement below was increasing to a definite shaking, which rocked the *Queen.* Chris's prisoner was either seeking communication with its kind or striving to break out of confinement.

"Can they turn us over?" Griff appealed to his more seawise companions, hoping for an emphatic denial.

But there was no answer except a shrug from Le Marr. Chris continued to stare at the dark. There was a thumping underneath now, regular pounding blows making the planking of the ship ring.

Then Griff saw a brown snake-whip wave above the edge of the deck, as if in blind search for a victim. Would bullets be able to rip that? Anyway he couldn't trust his marksmanship in this light. With a machine gun set to spray, they would have a better chance.

Le Marr was busy, his hands flying as he bound bits of raveled cord about the point of the fish spear. Having provided a wadding that suited him, he pried open the lid of a flat can of sardines, one of the supply cans Griff had found in the cabin. Carefully he smeared the oily fish back and forth across the wadding, working in the greasy liquid.

The battering of the prisoner now shook the deck. With a smack, the rope arm waved through the shadows to the planking. It might be seeking either prey or a secure hold.

Le Marr went into action. He ran his greasy torch into the lantern flame. Fire burst in a sputter of sparks. With the precision of a careful workman he reached out and applied the blaze to the tentacle. For a second or two there was no response. Then Le Marr jerked away his improvised weapon as the arm loosed its hold upon the wood, writhed up, and beat down on the deck with a force that rocked the *Queen*.

The islander stood his ground, and as the arm came to a momentary rest, he was ready to touch it again. Once more the length of stringy muscle and ropy flesh flashed up until they saw the suckers dislike on its length. Then it snapped back into the dark and was gone. In the lantern light Griff saw that Le Marr was laughing silently. And Chris grinned.

"That thing—he don't like the fire."

Le Marr chuckled. "The things of the night, never do they like fire. Fire belong to mons. An' mons, they don't give up fightin' easy. We show these debble things that!"

If they had fought off for the moment the assailant that had attempted to get a hold on deck, they had not settled the captive below. And now Chris showed concern.

"The *Queen*—maybe she can't take this poundin'. Nothing we can do 'bout that one down there?" he appealed to Le Marr.

But the other was forced to reply in the negative. Griff could hear rasping sounds, feel even through the pounding of the prisoner a sucking pull against the sides of the *Queen*. Although no more arms appeared within the circle of light, he could not rid himself of the idea that a net of sorts was being woven about the ship, that the sea things were working with patience and intelligence to overturn the *Queen* as they had overturned with far less effort the tow boat of the refugee ship.

And that was borne out by action as the *Queen* slowly, minute by dragging minute, developed a list to port. There was no more movement in the cargo hold. Perhaps the captive recognized the work of its kind and was content to wait for an opportunity before wasting its strength.

"A little more of this," Griff said between his teeth, "and we'll slide over." It was one of his worst nightmares coming true, and he could do nothing to halt the inevitable. Surely there must be a whole school of the monsters down there lending their weight to the project. The ancient horror stories of mariners were coming true. Here were the kraken who could and would drag down a ship to be plundered at their leisure in the deeps.

"Hellooooo!"

Griff had been so intent upon the immediate scene of action that he had forgotten the shore, the dark waters that washed in upon the deserted town. A band of light, which completely blotted out the feeble gleam of the lantern, caught and pinned the *Queen*.

"Stand by to secure line—"

Griff caught the shout as Le Marr stuck the smoldering spear butt down on the hatch to free his hands and Chris struggled up on his knees.

The line flew in from the dark to fall on the deck. Its weighted end had scarcely landed before Chris had it. Then Le Marr jumped forward, and with fumbling help from Griff they made it fast about the stump of the splintered mast.

But the list of the deck was increasing. They held onto the hatch lashings to keep their balance. Then Chris muttered, caught the diver's knife from Griff's sheath, and with that between his teeth inched his way to the stern.

The anchor! Griff had forgotten about that. Chris sawed at the rope as Le Marr covered him by thrusting the torch-spear into the dark. The tie gave, and the *Queen* bobbed. Perhaps Le Marr had disconcerted the attackers, for the list righted a bit, enough to allow the two to crawl back in safety to the hatch.

Now the line to the shore grew taut. Slowly the *Queen* answered that pull, began to move inland. Once her side grated against a wall, but for the most part they followed along the line of the main street, and, while the roofs of buildings were black blots above the water, they managed not to strike any of them.

For a space the listing continued, even grew. But as the *Queen* took her slow course inland, she began to rise in the water. The attackers were loosing their holds, falling away. At last the bow smashed against a wall with a shock that might have tossed her passengers overboard had they not had a firm grip on the hatch. There was a horrible grating as the pull from the shore continued. Then the line went limp, and they were hailed.

"Can you make it now?"

Griff scrambled to his feet. The wall on which the *Queen* hung canted her up. But within easy leaping distance was a rise of dry land. Yes, they could make it. And with assistance to bring Chris ashore, they did.

Murray and Casey were there—and the smaller towing machine from the base. Karkoff was standing beside that, watching the stranded *Queen* with keen interest.

"How did you—? Did Liz—?" Griff sputtered.

"We heard about this ship from Karkoff and started overland to see her. Met your Liz about an hour ago and heard about your find," Murray explained. Then he spoke to Chris. "So you've one of those things shut up inside that hulk have you?"

"In the *Queen*," Chris corrected sharply. "He sure is, Cap'n."

Murray gazed into the dark bay. "All his little playmates were coming to the rescue, weren't they?"

"They certainly were!" Griff tried to see if those trails of light had disappeared from the waters. He could distinguish none—the enemy must have withdrawn.

"This is round three, and it's still our decision," Murray observed with obvious satisfaction. "If they want to go a full ten, we'll meet them all the way!"

IX

THE LONG ROAD BACK

GRIFF SQUATTED on the edge of a salt-water pool and stared intently into its depths. Save for its size, it might have been the one he had once ruled over near the laboratory—only no one was going to swim lazily in the sun-warmed water cupped there.

Eyes, which were blank saucers without any readable

expression, yet which somehow conveyed the impression of implacable hatred, met his. There was no means of communication between the brain behind those eyes and his. More experienced and better trained minds than Griff's had tried to find some common ground of understanding. Here was intelligence to a high degree; they recognized that. But it was a form of intelligence so alien to the human ways of thought that there was probably an unpierceable barrier between.

The Octopus-Sapiens endured captivity. It ate the food supplied; it sank into the same semiconscious state during the brighter hours of the day as had the small cephalopod Griff planted in the spray pool. There were several features about the prisoner, however, that set it apart from the octopi already known. Without dissection they could only guess and deduce from photographs and observation. But it was apparent that the brain had evolved to a higher degree, and two of the great arms had developed at their tips smaller, off-shoot tentacles, which the creature was able to use, if clumsily, with some of the advantage of human fingers.

Whether it was a species old to their world but hitherto dwelling unsuspected in the deeps until roused out by the recent disturbances—by explosions during atomic bomb tests —or whether it was a mutant whose evolution had been forced by radiation from those same tests, was still a matter for dispute.

Islander, refugee, Seabee, sooner or later every present inhabitant of San Isadore spent some time by the pool watching with a fearful fascination the captive brought back in the *Queen*. Hughes hung over it, studying it for hours, raging at times because he could not summon to share his vigil other authorities in his field. Sheer frustration made him blow up in irritated outbursts, which were far removed from his one-time self-satisfied complacency. He pestered Chris with demands as to how the creature had been captured, hoping to add another to their bag. But the mate had replied over and over again that he could not honestly remember—that the horrors of the *Queen*'s last voyage did not remain in his memory except as a faint dream. Examination by the base doctor had shown that the island sailor suffered from exposure to mild radiation and that he was lucky to survive at all.

But the captive in the pool was not the only problem. The waves had deposited a thick harvest of the red scum along three-fourths of the island's shore line. And there Hughes had been successful, for his suggestion of using fire to cleanse the beaches and rocks paid off. Ignited, the stuff had burned with a choking oily reek, which set them all to painful coughing but did clear the land.

What was left was a black ash with a sour, nasty smell. This was shoveled and pushed into pits by the base machines, only to prove a disguised blessing—for some of the ash blown into pockets of sheltered earth provided a rich fertilizer never before seen. The pits were then reopened so that this strange sea bounty could be disinterred and put to work increasing the productivity of the garden patches, a move that might mean the difference between life and death in the future as the store supplies dwindled.

It was still not entirely safe to fish—though there were few fish that had escaped the poisonous scum. Thanks to Liz's concoction—which the base doctor analyzed to the last disagreeable drop—small boats well smeared dared venture out along the shore—but there was always the danger of running into one of the "serpents."

"If we could only get into this fellow's think-tank"—Casey came up to the pool behind Griff—"we'd have answers to a lot of questions. You know"—he teetered back and forth, his eyes narrowed speculatively as he studied the captive octopus—"I used to read stories about fellas going to the stars and meeting up with alien life forms. There was a lot of clever mish-mash in some of them about how they established communication. They usually started off with numbers. You know—the old two-and-two-make-four routine. But how are you going to talk to something that probably doesn't give a hoot whether two and two make four or six? Didn't you say once that these things signaled to each other with their ink sacks? Then how are we going to palaver back? With a bunch of paint cans ready to pour?"

"That's already been tried—" Griff pointed out.

Hughes had tried it. The chemical make-up of the ink exuded by the cephalopod clan in moments of emotional disturbance was a matter of record. They had been able to reproduce it in the base medical lab, and it had been introduced in small quantities into the pool—arousing no discernible reaction in the then quiescent captive.

"Sure—Doc's stuff. I saw them try that. But what about some of those native goos—like that stuff your friend Liz cooks up on demand? Did that voodoo doc ever get a chance to try some of his bright ideas?"

Griff had to answer no to that. The island population of San Isadore, or what remained of it, had withdrawn to their own new settlement, spreading away from the base, where the off-islanders, both Naval and refugee, were inclined to remain. In the press of establishing a going concern, everyone was so occupied that even Griff had rather lost track of Le Marr and the others. Casey might just have an idea worth following up. Griff got to his feet. Those black saucer eyes below watched him indifferently.

It was a fine day. In fact, since the great storm, the weather had continued almost uniformly good. Griff watched a flight of birds make a half circle about the new radio tower. Radio tower—perhaps that was the most useless piece of construction they had done since the start of the rebuilding. Yet no one had protested its erection—they all still hoped for news, to learn that some portion of the old life still existed. And among the Naval personnel no one clung more to that installation than did Holmes. He spent most of his time hunched in the hut with the operator, a dogeared wad of messages in his hand, ready to push them through for transmission as soon as contact with the States was once more established. In his way, Griff decided, the security officer was as hopeful in a hopeless position as was Hughes—though it might be easier to awake a response from the pool captive than it would be for Holmes to treat with his superiors in the dim and vanished offices of the United States Navy.

Casey might have been reading Griff's thoughts, for he laughed. "Poor old Holmes, he'd like to do the dirty on the skipper, only he can't get through to the Big Brass. D'you know, maybe Murray's the biggest brass left right now. Only Holmes won't accept that. He's had fourteen fits since we brought the Russkis in here."

"They got it just as hard as we did."

"Sure, kid. And these have turned to and worked like the rest of us. I'm not calling names. And if they plastered us—they got it back as hot and heavy—maybe worse. It isn't going to help matters to shoot Karkoff and his boys—they didn't give the word to start firing. Though you know," he added shrewdly, "if they hadn't been found by us—but by survivors of a bombing—they wouldn't have lasted. We got our bad punches not from the Russkis, but from the sea, the quakes, the storm. If we'd had them from a bomb, we wouldn't feel the same way. As it is now, we're closing ranks—man against nature. If you're human, you're on our side. So they were lucky, darn lucky to end up in our section of the world."

"How about the plane? Any chance of getting it up for a look-see?"

The Navy plane had gone during the great storm, but they held hopes of being able to restore the transport that had brought the cargo of refugees from Santa Maria. Like the mast of the radio station, this plane served as a defiance, a hope. If they could take to the air on an exploring trip—even venture out in a radius of a hundred miles or so and chart the changes—

"Well, Hooker's steamed up about what they were able to do last night. We have a couple of mechanics who can build anything if they have scrap enough. They're trying to fit her with an atomic motor from a wrecked crawler we located. If they can ready her to take off, Hooker's game to fly her."

They had come upslope from the octopus pool and now stood on the crest of one of the heights that had been born during the quakes, giving San Isadore respectable hills for the first time in her existence. The settlement was a ragged circle below—the coral-block, thatched buildings, rather like blocks spilled from some giant child's play box, the half-cave, half-house section of the base, and the islanders' huts, where trickles of smoke arose from cooking fires. It had a hastily slapped-together look but at the same time a vitality that had never been seen in Carterstown.

"There's your voodoo man down there now—taking it easy." Casey pointed to Le Marr seated on the trunk of a dead palm.

The islander was not lazing though. His slender hands moved skillfully as he wove dried fronds into one of the wide-brimmed hats that were the island protection against the sun. And he glanced up with a welcoming smile as Griff and Casey slid down the bank into what was the backyard of his private domain. A cock, tethered by its leg to the other end of the palm log, stopped pecking in the earth and offered crowing challenge.

"Be a good day, mons. Sit you down an' rest your feet." He gave the traditional island greeting. "There's cocomilk for the drinkin'. Shut your big mouth, you crazy bird!" he bade the cock, and astonishingly enough its clamor subsided at once.

"I wish you could do that with the devil." Unconsciously Griff gave the pool captive the name conferred on it by the islanders. "Talk to it, I mean."

Le Marr's swiftly flying fingers paused. "Whyfor you wants to talk with that thing?"

"Not talk exactly. But it is intelligent. If we could find some way of communication, maybe we could—"

"Make peace 'tween ocean an' land? Listen, mon. This here"—he held up a piece of the dried leaf he was using—"is one kinda thing. Once it live, it grow, maybeso it had knowledge. Not like the knowledge in mon's head, but knowledge what was for it. But can you talk with this? All right, all right. This debble, he think good—better nor dog, better nor donkey, more like mons. But not the same way as mons. He don't want the same thing as mons wants—"

"He wants to live, doesn't he?" cut in Casey. "Everything wants to live. Maybe we could get that idea across."

"How you be sure he wants to live more then he wants other things? Mon wants that—but do debble?"

Griff pulled the conversation back from the philosophical to the immediate problem. "But is there any way we could communicate with the thing, Le Marr? That grease of Liz's keeps the things away—or seems to. Is there anything which will attract them?"

Le Marr shrugged. "How do I know? I don't want to talk to this thing. Better we would be if this thing be gone away an' we spend no more time with it. Sea an' land, they never mix. An' they ain't goin' to—You mons, you make the big bombs, you make the plane, the rocket to carry those bombs. Then—" He made an erasing gesture with his hands, and the half-finished hat fell to the ground. "Then you use them! An' what be left? Trouble—death! Mons don't use things right. Maybeso this world be tired o' mons. Now you want more kinda knowledge, you want to start all over again. I say no!" One of his hands came down in a chopping motion as if he were beheading something. "Let mons live quiet, do no thing to learn what will start more bad things—"

Casey clasped his hands about his knee, leaned back.

"Brother," he announced, "you've got a good point there. It's one which has been stated before by a lot of earnest souls. There's only one thing about it—it won't work!"

"An' why not?"

"Because, as a species, we're bitten by a queer bug. We've *got* to find out what lies beyond the next range of hills, and not only geographically. Our curiosity is bred into our bones. I'll bet there were those in the cavemen days who deplored the use of this new-fangled fire, who didn't see why tying a stone onto a shaft and making an ax out of it was the right thing to do. You could kill a horse or a deer better that way, sure, but it also was a mighty nasty war weapon. That knowledge which made the bombs gave us the atomic motors which have kept this base going since the bust-up. You can't withdraw from living, Le Marr—unless you want to commit suicide. And we're so constructed that mass suicide does not appeal. There's a long road back stretching ahead of us now. And we have to take it. Perhaps half our globe is uninhabitable. For all we know it is. We haven't yet faced the horrors of a fall-out, of radiation sickness. We may be doomed right now. Don't you suppose that every man over there at the base hasn't thought of that? But have you seen anyone stop work and sit around waiting for the end to catch up with him?

"What are you doing here?" He scooped up the half-made hat. "You're weaving a hat—a mighty neat job of it, too. But why do it? Tomorrow you may be dead—we may all be dead. Who'll be left to wear it—that thing over in the pool, one of your donkeys? There's that woman over there scraping up earth to make a garden. She's planting seeds; will she live to see them sprout? She thinks so—or she wouldn't be doing it. You see, Le Marr, inside we all believe that we're going to keep on breathing and walking around. We accept that the more because we *have* already survived some pretty tough treatment. And if we accept that we have to be practical.

"There's the problem of food and clothing. It was lucky for San Isadore that the Navy supply dump was here. We have supplies for several years. But this island is not going to support her present population without some help. And the refugees from Santa Maria may not be the last to reach us, which means we eventually will have to spread out—or import from other surviving communities. And we *have* to have mastery of the sea for that. It's either sit down and die, or it's get up and fight! If we can learn anything useful from that eight-armed thing over in that pool, we have to do it—the sooner the better. It may be a matter of *our* survival, and that is enough to build a fire under any man. You may not agree, but that is the truth as I see it."

For the second time since Griff had known him, Le Marr

answered with the speech of an educated off-island man. "You make a good case for your side of the argument, Lieutenant. As you say—this is the truth from your point of view. And for your race it is. We are a mongrel lot, we islanders, and we have certain traits of our own. To our way of thinking, nature has turned against us, and that is a belief rooted in the supernatural. You do not know it in your portion of the town, but some of us have reverted to very dark practices." For a moment his face had the same look of strain it had worn during their weird battle on the *Queen*. "I have some influence with these, my people. I am trying hard to hold that influence—to prevent their falling into the savagery from which they climbed painfully long ago. If once more they turn to certain rites and sacrifices—" He stopped abruptly, his lips thinned as if he tightened them against dangerous admissions. "I can do this only because I do share some of their beliefs and appear to share others. Should I now change in my attitude, should I—as they would see it—attempt to traffic with the devil they fear, I might lose all the control I still possess. Then, Lieutenant, we might have yet another danger to contend with, a situation which might end, once and for all, all your bright plans of a world rebuilt."

"Do they still think that we are responsible for the trouble?" Griff thought of the destruction of the laboratory, of his father's work.

"Some of them do. Others can be readily influenced to join them. Your strange machines, the lights you use, the larger percentage of your belongings"—he was speaking now to Casey—"are sheer magic to my people. It is only since Dr. Gunston and you Naval people have come to San Isadore that our world has changed. We were a century behind history— Now we may have caught up with it, to find the transition not only bewildering but for us—fearful. You believe that you have nothing to fear from us but—"

Griff had a flash of understanding. "You have your own ways of force, of dealing with an enemy—the ways you know, Liz knows—"

Le Marr gave a slow, assenting nod. At the same time he took the hat from Casey and began his work again. "Yes, there are ways my people may make their displeasure felt—if they are pushed too far."

"We have to work together—we *have* to!" Casey brought his fist down on the trunk of the palm. Shreds of dried bark drifted on the wind to the ground.

"Some of us already realize that; the rest must be brought to such an understanding. During the days of the storm we took refuge together. But now you go your own road. You are busy on foreign concerns, and it may appear to you that we have nothing to offer in support of your labors. My people hope that you will go and leave us in peace—that you will repair the plane, ready your seagoing LC's—and that after you are gone, the old world will return. That is what they wait for. If it does not come then—"

"They may take steps to hasten it?" prompted Griff. They had taken steps about the laboratory after it had become suspect—drastic ones.

"We shall hope not."

"Then"—Casey hunched forward on the tree trunk—"can't you use that for an excuse in coming to our help now. We would never leave with the sea closed to us. The plane, if we are ever able to get it off the ground, couldn't carry more than a pilot and a few observers. But if we can free the seas—"

Le Marr made a meticulous business of braiding, of fitting small rough ends into smoothness. To all appearances he was concerned only with that. But a moment later he said, without looking up, "It might be done."

"Can you ask the others to help? Would such a project bring us closer together?"

"That also might be done. But you do not intend to leave—"

"How can we? Maybe not for years," Casey admitted. "We have no idea what's waiting for us out there. Maybe you are right—at your gloomiest—maybe we are washed up, maybe man is no longer top dog. But we won't accept that

175

decision without a fight. I don't think, if it comes right to the point, your people will either. And it's up to you, Le Marr, to see that they fight the right way—on our side, with their minds and their hands—and not their superstitions and their emotions!"

"You are of one kind, my people of another," warned the islander. "Don't try to drive us too hard or too fast. We are like our donkeys—sometimes we may be driven, but other times we must be coaxed, and always we must have our minds and desires considered. Very well, I shall do what I can. If the first step toward cooperation is the study of devils, then I shall undertake the study of devils." He smiled his slow, shadow smile.

The sea wind was rising, beating through the leaves of the standing palms as if the trees applauded him with clapping fronds. Casey stretched.

"Oh, we'll make it back." His confidence was such as drew belief. "I'm not saying 'uncle' to any fish. Just give us time— say a hundred years or so—and you won't know the bloomin' world, you won't for a fact."

"I hope so—with all my heart I trust that that may be true." Le Marr spoke with conviction.

Griff stood up; the wind pushed against him with its old demanding force. Without being conscious of movement, he turned to face north. To him the long road back must always point that way. Would *he* ever tread it openly?

TWO AGAINST THE JUNGLE PLANET

Rees Naper and his uncle Milo had never seen eye to eye about the Ishkurians. Milo felt that these reptile-men had been wronged by the Terrans and could be won over by brotherly love. But Rees knew the Ishkurians well, knew that the "crocs," as they were nicknamed, were filled with hate for all Terrans and could never be trusted.

The Terran authorities had now decided to withdraw from Ishkur and allow self-government. Rees Naper's worst fears were realized when the crocs went on a killing rampage. Now they were searching for Rees' own scalp.

Cut off from civilization, Rees saw that his only chance for survival was to outwit the cunning Ishkurians. To do this he would have to learn to think like a croc, to feel like a croc, and see through the eye of the monster!

Turn this book over for second complete novel

EYE OF THE MONSTER

by

ANDRE NORTON

ACE BOOKS, INC.
1120 Avenue of the Americas
New York 36, N.Y.

I

Rees Naper opened his eyes. He had come into almost instant consciousness from the night's sleep as he always did. But there was something about his awakening this time, and he lay without any other movement save the raising of eyelids, trying to hear, to sense, to think what was different this morning.

A faint breeze shifted through the sonic net across the window to stir the rustling inner drapery within touching distance. That was it! The sounds, or rather the lack of the right ones for this place and hour. Those he had awakened to hear about the mission for months were missing this morning.

Rees moved swiftly, his hand burrowing into the chink between the foam plasta mattress and the bunk frame, reaching for what he had put there last night after hearing the last urgent warning on the com. Leather, satin smooth and silk supple, curled about his fingers as he pulled out the blaster belt with its holstered weapon. He clasped it to his chest as he rolled off the bunk and went to look through the sonic designed to keep out jungle insect life.

The courtyard of the mission lay open in Ishkur's greenish sunlight. A hoobra hen pecked at a bug, then made a run-

ning leap to capture the escaping victim before it took wing. Otherwise that space between the buildings was empty, save for the small creatures that lived in the ornamental flower beds and circular pool.

Rees hurriedly pulled on shirt and the breeches with their attached jungle boots. He was chilled in spite of the day's warmth. You could smell it, sniff it up as surely as if it were the perfume of the violet tipped toofaa reeds out there in the water garden. Trouble—bad! Uncle Milo was wrong, and they were going to have to face up to the result of that error in judgment, that ingrained stubbornness on the part of the head of the mission.

Now with the blaster riding on his hip, Rees glanced over his other emergency preparations; the trail bag he had packed last night. It was too late to hope to get away with more than a survival kit. Again, because of Uncle Milo and his refusal to face facts as they were and not as he decreed them to be.

Rees slapped his palm on the hand lock by the corridor door. In the hall he paused for a long moment, his back against the wall, to listen and smell. Six months as Duggan Vickery's hunting assistant had given him some training with which to face this crisis.

No sound of any of the Ishkurians about nor any trace of the distinctive body odor of the natives, so easy to detect when their emotions were aroused. Instead the beckoning scent of Terran coffee. Rees followed that quickly. No Ishkurian would drink coffee. The off-world beverage was rank poison as far as they were concerned and even to smell it upset their insides. Which meant the natives must have cleared out of the mission completely or Dr. Naper would not be brewing a pot now.

Rees sped past three rooms to the door at the end of the hall. The man seated at the table in the room beyond glanced up from the recorder-reader, a faint trace of frown automatically lining the space between his deep-set eyes.

"Good morning, Rees." His tone was precise and, as always, disapproving. Milo Naper and the nephew who shared his

6

quarters shared very little else, neither ideas, emotions nor interests.

"What's going on?" Rees halted by the table. The com unit stood in the corner but its message screen was dark. It was not even turned on. He hurried to flick the button, only to be greeted by a din of static. A mountain storm must be in progress, blanketing out any call from the port at Nagassara.

"We can certainly do without that," Dr. Naper snapped. "Turn it off at once. I do not care to hear any more of this foolish blithering about trouble with the tribes. The utter stupidity of those chair warmers at the port leads one to completely despair of the Forces. If those officers would leave their comfortable quarters once in a while to get out and really learn something about this planet and its people, we'd have no more of this howling about trouble to come when the Patrol pulls out. Trouble to come—faugh! I've been on Ishkur for twenty years, and the tribes have always been peaceful and very grateful for what we have been able to do for them."

"What about what happened at Aklanba?" Rees curbed his impatience and exasperation. "And the Patrol's always been here to keep order."

"It has always been my experience that off-world traders cause disturbances. Their greedy grasping for profit can start any number of minor outbreaks, even on peaceful worlds. Aklanba should never have been established that close to the Places of the Old Forest. To permit that was just another typical ill-judged decision of the government, a perfect affront to the High Trees. And doubtless the garbled report we heard about the disturbance there was greatly exaggerated. This fear of an Ishkurian uprising when the Patrol leaves is an evil thing.

"I told Jawin yesterday when he chose to take himself and his family to Nagassara—the Fermals also—that neither of them need look for any further employment here after they discover how foolish their panic was. In fact, I have dictated to the recorder my condemnation of their desertion

at this time. Fifteen years of labor and aid to these jungle tribes can not be cancelled out merely because a few troops are going off-world—as they should have done long since. The Council is only coming to their collective senses at last in breaking up such autocratic bounds of control. I have the highest confidence in the assurances of tranquility given by the High Trees. To send away the Patrol is the first step in righting the wrongs of colonialism."

"There was a burning a month ago, and Ishback, Ishgar and Ishwan, all High Trees, directed it." Rees held tightly to his self control. Uncle Milo accepted wholeheartedly the mission line when it came to administration policies.

Dr. Naper's thin cheeks showed a stain of red. "I will not have such falsehoods repeated in my house! That vicious propaganda of the military is enough to foul the mouth of any man who repeats it. I know Ishgar, he has been educated in our schools at Nagassara. To resort to those vile superstitious practices would be utterly foreign to both his training and his nature. If you cannot forget that asinine indoctrination you had at the academy then please do not attempt to spew out such stuff in public here!"

"Then you will continue to stay, in spite of the warning last night?"

"Stay? Of course I'm staying."

"Did the 'copter return yet?"

"I don't know, nor do I care."

Rees held to his temper with a maximum of control. "What about the Beltz family? And that Salarika trader, Sakfor?" he persisted.

"I am glad to say that Gideon Beltz has not been carried away by this irresponsible hysteria with which we have been deluged for the past few weeks. And what the Salariki do is no concern of the mission."

"None of the natives are here this morning."

"Certainly. And I do not expect to see any for at least three days. This is the First Fast of the Leaves. Which only underlines the crass moronity of those officers in Nagassara. The tribes will be fully occupied with planting rituals for

the next ten days. And it would be impossible for Ishkurians to make any hostile moves now, which they surely don't wish to, as you will see. This, Rees, is all the result of that infernal meddling on the part of Survey and the other Services. All this clamor concerning trends and precognition reports—the fiasco will simply discredit such twaddle. You will thank me in years to come, boy, that I was able to make the necessary decision on your behalf before you became a real part of their justly disliked and mistrusted employment."

Rees' lips were a thin line, pressed hard against his teeth. He had learned to swallow a lot in the past three years, but this morning he knew he would have to get away from Uncle Milo in a hurry or he'd say the unforgivable and unforgettable. While he had nothing in common with Dr. Naper, and they did much better apart than together, still he had not been able to leave last night with the Jawins. That would have been standing by with a holstered blaster while his uncle, unarmed, faced the charge of a kaga bull.

He did not share Dr. Naper's belief in the good will of the tribes and their continuing friendship once the Patrol's pacifying strength was removed. And somehow he must get his uncle to see the truth and clear out in time. But he could not do it if they quarreled.

"Where are you going now?" Dr. Naper demanded. "You haven't eaten any breakfast."

"I still have a job, if Vickery didn't pull out," Rees said over his shoulder. "By the looks, I'm late at camp already."

The younger man hurried on into the courtyard. It was true that the First Fast could have drawn the mission people back to their villages. But the feeling of danger, which Rees had had weighing on him since his awakening, quieted his tread now, set his eyes to watching bushes, the shadows in doors and windows.

"Rees!"

He whirled in a half crouch, blaster out and ready. Then with the same speed he thumbed the weapon back in the holster.

9

"Hey, Rees, you're sure a quick draw!" Gordy Beltz materialized from under the low hanging branches of a buppu bush, his face liberally smeared golden with the juice of buppu berries. "You going to the animal camp? Take me 'long, please, Rees! There's nobody to play with and I'm lonesome."

Rees hesitated. Gordy could be a pest at times. But at the moment his small form in the oval of the courtyard did have an oddly forlorn appearance. And it certainly wasn't wise for the small boy to be wandering about by himself today.

"Where's your mother, Gordy?"

"She's got lither fever. Dad gave her a shot and told her to stay in bed. And Ishbi and Ishky never came this morning. Dad gave me a py-ri-ration out of the can for breakfast. Please, Rees, can't I go with you? I want to see all the animals again 'fore Captain Vickery ships them out."

Rees stood with his feet slightly apart, his hands on his hips. "And if I take you—what's the order?"

"Don't touch, don't touch anything. I promise, Rees." Gordy pulled a narrow leaf from the buppu bush, spit into its middle, twisted it into a knot which he threw into the pool. "By the Tree Blood I promise."

Kids picked up things and got them surprisingly right, Rees thought fleetingly. Gordy made that oath with the same gestures and intonation a Guardian would use. Sure, kids picked things up, they remembered well, too. Why, he himself could still do the fish dance of the Salariki and he was a year less than Gordy in age when they lifted off that world. But then he'd had special training from the time he was old enough to notice anything, intended to make him absorb points of alien culture. As the son of a Survey officer he was supposed to follow his father into that service.

If only Commander Naper had come back safely from the Volsper run. But he had not and Uncle Milo Naper had turned up relentlessly at the cadet school and jerked Rees out. Well, in spite of his efforts, Uncle Milo hadn't made a mission man out of his nephew, only left him dissatisfied

and rootless, unhappy, a constant irritation, in a way, to the dedicated people of an antagonistic way of life.

"All right," he told Gordy now. "Come on." He knew what being lonesome meant, to a greater degree than he hoped Gordy would ever realize.

"You aren't going by the main path, Rees?"

"I want to look at the 'copter park."

"The 'copter isn't there. It didn't come back yet. Rees, what does a red alert mean? They were sending that on the com when Dad shut it off."

"Some trouble—maybe in Nagassara."

" 'Cause the Patrol is leaving? Why'd the Patrol leave, Rees?"

One thing Rees had learned from his father's training; straight answers and truthful ones were due children. He tried to simplify this one.

"Ishkur has been a part of the South Sector Empire. That means a collection of different worlds under one government. Two years ago the Council decided that frontier planets, such as this one, should be allowed to set up their own ruling states. So they ordered the Patrol to withdraw by a certain date. And all off-worlders who thought they might need the protection of the Patrol were to go then also."

"But the Empire was bad, wasn't it, Rees? Dad says it was bad. The off-worlders shouldn't rule Ishkurians."

"Some things were bad. In every form of government we've used so far, Gordy, there are bad things. But on some worlds our ways were better than the rule the natives had for themselves before we came."

"Not here, though, Dad says that." Gordy grasped Rees's hand and varied the trot he maintained to match the young man's strides with a series of skipping hops.

"Perhaps—" Rees had reached the landing area. Gordy's report was correct, there was no sign of the 'copter. Yet neither Jawin nor Permal would have left the flyer on robo-control when they disembarked with their families at Nagassara. And so it should have ridden back the guide beam for a

11

landing hours ago. Rees' fingers tightened on Gordy's hand until the boy gave a yelp and tried to pull free.

Vickery had a 'copter, one really larger than the mission's, since he had to transport the caged animals in it. They could pack in the Beltz three, and the two Napers easily in one trip. And perhaps the Captain could argue Uncle Milo into seeing some sense. To Dr. Naper, Rees was a boy, stubbornly wrong-headed, but Uncle Milo would be forced to admit Vickery knew the Ishkurians very well and his advice would mean something.

"What's the matter, Rees? How come we have to hurry so fast?"

Rees had quickened pace until Gordy was running.

"I'm late, and if the guides and hunters have left, the Captain will need me to help feed the animals."

At first the clearing down by the river appeared normal. Except no Ishkurians squatted about checking on capture nets, or charring torkum leaves over the fire before they chewed them. The cages ready for transport were arranged around three sides of a hollow square, with the river to the west. But at second glance Rees saw that those cages doors were now swinging wide open, their occupants had all been loosed.

He ran to the plasta bubble of Vickery's tent, pulled open the zip-close. The owner, his guns, his jump bag were all missing. Vickery had cleared out and in a hurry.

Rees fairly leaped past the line of cages to the clearing of the 'copter. Pulled to one side was the jungle roller car, but the flyer was gone.

"Rees," Gordy had followed him into the tent, now he came running with a folded paper in his hand. "This has your name on it. Where's Captain Vickery and all the animals?"

"Gone away." He grabbed the paper from Gordy.

"Notice from the port." the words were hurriedly scrawled. "No ship-off possible for the animals. Red alert, I have to answer militia call. Can't find Kassa, when she turns up, keep her for me, bring her in with you."

Rees swallowed. Kassa! Vickery had not delayed to hunt Kassa! He felt cold all through his middle, sick and cold. Kassa, the Spician hound, was Vickery's prized tracker. The hunter would not have left her except to obey the most urgent order. The off-world militia must have been called up to answer some trouble at the port.

"Gordy!" he called harshly to the boy who had wandered toward the river, "come here!"

"Rees—I can hear something! Please—come and listen!"

But Rees could hear it also, a low throb of whimper, a noise which added to the sick feeling inside him. Suppose—suppose Vickery had not lifted with the 'copter after all? Suppose what had happened at Aklanba had also chanced here? Rees swallowed down growing sick panic.

He caught Gordy's shoulder, propelled the boy to the jungle roller. Pushing him into the seat Rees climbed in also to make a check. Vickery had not even waited to dismantle the sonic screen or dismount the flamer.

"Sit still now!" Rees ordered, caught a glimpse of growing fright on the small face turned toward him. He set his boot heel down on the floor button and the machine came to life.

They smashed straight through a corner of the cage compound, moving to parallel the river. But they did not have far to go. At first Rees was so overjoyed to discover that he had not found Vickery, that he actually drew a deep breath of relief. Until Gordy's cry of horror aroused him to action and he used the blaster on the tortured creature still feebly struggling. That could not have been there long. If it had been in place before Vickery pulled out the Captain would have flamed the whole jungle apart to get even with Kassa's tormentors. Was it meant to be a warning or was it a signal of victory over one off-worlder, and that one a long-time friend?

Gordy was crying now, noisily as might an ordinary small Terran boy, but with dreadful sobs which shook his body. Both of his fists were locked on the fabric of Rees' shirt.

"It's all right!" Rees flung one arm about that shivering

13

body, pulled the child closer. "It's all right now, Gordy." But it was not all right and nothing could make it so. Not now. He shouldn't have brought the child here, but neither could he have left him alone. Somewhere, out in the jungle, eyes watched, Rees was sure of that.

He kicked the roller into action again. Uncle Milo would have to listen to reason now. They could dismount the flamer from this machine, turn the main building of the mission into a fort, appeal by com for rescue. Rees' mind skipped feverishly from one part of a workable plan to the next.

Captain Vickery had stood very well, to all outward show, with the natives. He had drunk leaf beer with two local chiefs and witnessed the Felling Dances. You could not say that barbarity was visited on Kassa for any sin of her master. This was no matter of a trading station set up on the border of forbidden territory. This was here and now, an icy warning to every off-worlder in the immediate countryside.

What about the Salariki? Dr. Naper knew nothing about them. Had they been able to go last night? With the machine still turning around at his guidance, Rees hesitated. To cut down by their post would take more time. On the other hand, to leave the Salariki there unwarned was unthinkable.

Their felinoid ancestry did not make them any less "men" at a time such as this and he knew that Sakfor had women and children of his species with him. Rees made a full turn and jammed the speed of the roller up the scale. It took to the air in one of the ground covering bounds which exhausted far too much of its fuel charge but which cut minutes to seconds. The Salariki station and then the mission—and he could only pray that time would not run out for them all!

II

As were the buildings of the mission, the trading post was constructed of glegg stone blocks, cut, while the substance was still workable, in an excavation on the river bank, put then together to harden under wind and rain into metallic toughness. Short of a force flash such walls could not be razed. But that oily yellow smoke curling up into the sky, the throat catching scent of burning oganna, told Rees now that Sakfor's fort had not been a refuge. His season's gatherings were afire.

Rees slammed the lever on the controls. With a toothrocking force the roller halted behind a screen of bush through which the Terran could see the post set in a curve of river bank. There was activity there. Rees' hand flailed out, knocking Gordy off the seat of the machine, down where the boy could no longer view what was happening. For a moment the young man's fingers rested on the firing trigger of the flamer. But they were too far away to catch the looters in its beam. And to betray his own presence there would no longer help the Salariki.

The Terran kicked the reverse, glad that the purr of the sonic screen drowned out most the sounds. The reality of the massacre now ending there was worse than any description broadcast by com. Rees fought the revolt of his stomach as he edged the roller away from that hell which had been a peaceful trading post.

Something flashed away from the forward thrust of the machine as they turned about. Tawny yellow. That was no animal! Rees' jungle trained eyes registered its difference and he pulled up quickly, thumbed off the sonic.

But there was no chance of hailing what he believed he had seen. The terrible cries from the post, muffled as they were, still rang. And his own call might bring lurking Ish-

15

kurian scouts down upon them. There was a low bush shaking to the right, the fugitive might be sheltering under it. Rees drew Gordy up to face him.

"Listen," he looked directly into the boy's eyes, "this is important, Gordy. Over there, under that bush, I think one of the Salariki children is hiding. If I go over I may frighten it into running. Do you think you can crawl in and bring it out?"

"Rees, what's happening? Rees, that noise—" Gordy shivered in the young man's grasp, his small face registering shock and fright.

"Gordy, that bush over there." Rees shook the boy gently. They could not leave any survivor of the post. And for him to beat the bushes would only drive the terrorized alien child deeper into hiding. Gordy was the only way to locate the Salariki cubling.

Gently Rees turned the boy around, pointed to the bush. Then he shook Gordy again, thankful to see a measure of comprehension dawn in the child's face. With drawn blaster in one hand and the other on Gordy's shoulder, Rees eased them both out of the roller and towards the bush. Still some feet away from the objective he released his hold on the boy, gave him a push in the right direction. Mercifully that yammering screaming had stopped. What they heard now was only the blatting of the natives.

Gordy went to his hands and knees, crawled under the dropping branches of the shrub. There was an agitated shaking and Gordy's plump buttocks, his scuffed boots reappeared. He was retreating backwards, tugging at some recalcitrant captive, both hands clasped about two small wrists while fingers with claw nails writhed for freedom.

Rees made a swift swoop, felt the rake of those nails, cruel and sharp across his cheek and chin as he gathered a spitting, wildly threshing small body up in his arms. Gordy, without being told, was already streaking back to the safety of the roller. And Rees followed, to put his fright-maddened captive down in the seat between them. He fended those raking nails with his forearm while he activated the sonic

and set the roller on its way again. Only then, when they were in motion, did he take a closer look at the rescued.

She crouched all together, her point-tip ears flattened against her rounded skull, her mouth half open as she hissed silently in the heritage of her long ago feline ancestors. The fine, plushy, fur-hair on her head and along her backbone and outer arms was roughened and standing erect. Her orange-red eyes, set aslant in her broad face, were slitted and wild.

Rees had no way of determining Salariki ages. She might have been younger than Gordy or older. Her torn garment was a short kilt held about her waist by a jeweled belt from which still hung a few scent bags suspended on beautifully patterned ribbons. The ribbons for others were torn and fluttering free. So, by her dress, she was still a young child, and a favored one, probably one of Sakfor's daughters. Salariki females did not circulate freely except among their own people, and Rees had no idea of the number or ages of those composing Sakfor's late household. The Terran did know that a man of influence living off the Salariki home planet was allowed more than one wife, usually marrying two or three sisters from the same family clan.

The Salarika's head turned slowly as she surveyed Gordy, Rees, and the interior of the roller. A red, sharply pointed tongue licked out across her face and flipped in between her teeth again.

"She's got fur on her." Gordy put out an investigating finger but he did not quite touch the soft golden down covering the outer side of the arm next to him. "She sure smells nice, doesn't she?" His nose wrinkled as the heavy scents from those waist bags grew stronger in the machine. Apparently he was so interested in the newcomer he had forgotten the sights and sounds of the immediate past. Rees nodded.

"Salariki people love perfumes, Gordy. Those are their principal trade items." He could have bitten out his tongue at that slip but Gordy had not apparently noticed.

"What's her name, Rees?" the boy continued.

17

"I don't know," the young man was more occupied with finding a way through the mass ahead. To keep the machine to any open path was to invite immediate discovery. And what had happened at the mission? Had his decision been the wrong one? Had he thrown away the lives of three Terrans when he had chosen to go fruitlessly to the post? Sweat beaded Rees' face, rolled in glistening drops down to salt his lips and drip from his chin.

"What's your name?" Gordy asked in Basic. "I'm Gordy Beltz. I live at the mission."

The Salarika licked her face again and then raised one hand. Blood oozed from between two of her fingers. She applied her tongue there also.

"Rees, she's hurt! Her fingers're all bloody!"

Rees glanced sidewise. "A bad scratch, Gordy. But it's stopped bleeding. I'll see to it as soon as I can." He hoped that the Salariki followed the usual off-world custom and innoculated their kind against alien diseases. But he must reach the mission, he must.

"We're almost home," Gordy announced a short time later. "I see the big crook-tree. Mom, she'll give you something for your finger," he assured the Salarika. "Does it hurt much?"

Those almost noiseless hisses no longer issued from the alien. Her examination of her companions continued, but her hair was no longer standing erect and she appeared to be settling down. Rees doubted if she understood Basic. But he believed she had sensed the good will of the Terrans and their difference from those devils back at the post.

"Rees, what are you stopping here for? Why don't you drive down the road?" Gordy's questions were strung together. His face was paling once more as the young man pulled the machine to a stop well away from the mission buildings.

Rees dared not drive in until he knew conditions ahead. It would be better to avoid the usual approach and take a more concealed way from the copse of farb trees. Those would screen any scouting expedition clear to the laboratory building.

18

"Rees, Dad's going to be awful mad at you, running this roller across a planted field, he had doman seeds put in here last week." Gordy's hands clenched on the edge of the instrument board. "Please, Rees, what's the matter?" His momentary interest in the Salarika forgotten, he was beginning to shiver once more.

"Gordy, be quiet!" Rees maneuvered the roller along, trying to keep it screened from any enemy that might lurk about the mission. He thought he could get the machine well in unseen. Of course, so far he had seen no sign that the natives had been here. But they might well infest the jungle, be closing in about the clearing ready for an attack.

Rees brought the jungle car to a halt and turned in the seat to face both children.

"Now listen, Gordy, this is very important. We have to get your Dad, your mother, and my Uncle Milo, take them away from here or else gather them in one place where we can fight. Do you understand that?"

Gordy's hands were knuckle-white in that grip on the edge of the panel. But his nod told the young man that he was taking this all in.

"You are to stay here, in the roller with the Salarika. She's afraid and if she's left alone she may try to run away again. Then we might lose here in the jungle. So I'm trusting you to see she stays here, Gordy."

"While you go to get Mom and Dad, Rees?"

"Yes. And if there are native hiding around here they mustn't see us so don't leave this machine!"

"You can send a message on the com, then the Patrol will come and take us away," Gordy's hold on the panel eased.

"Yes, we'll do something like that. But you stay right here with the Salarika, Gordy. I'll be back as soon as I can. Now see this button? It controls the sonic. I have to turn that off when I get out. You press it down to put the curtain back up again. And keep it up all the time I'm gone."

Gordy nodded solemnly. Rees hoped he would follow orders. With that sonic up the children had a measure of

protection. It reacted against Ishkurian ears in a painful manner—but that was scanty enough.

"I'm going now. And Gordy, even if Ishbi or Ishky come—don't go to them." Rees had no way of knowing if the mission natives were among the raiders, but he dared take no chances that they were still friendly.

"Yes, Rees."

The young man got out, watched Gordy thumb on the sonic, and then sprinted for the side of the nearest building. The cloying scent which had filled the interior of the roller, rising from the Salarika's clothing, began to clear from his nostrils. He stood braced against the rough wall for a long moment, using both ears and nose to give him warning of trouble.

Only the chirrup of insects, the bubbling call of the hoobra hens, the sigh of breeze through shrubbery, all peaceful sounds. But no welcoming hum from the laboratory—the a-motor was not running. And Rees tensed. He slipped along the wall, no windows broke its surface here, he would have to go around to the courtyard side before he could really see anything of the mission's interior.

At this hour Beltz should be in the lab, and Rees' uncle either there or in the house. Gordy said his mother was sleeping off one of the fever attacks. Three people to locate and warn. Mrs. Beltz first? Or the men in the lab? But they would have screens up there; a small protection but still enough to give them warning. The woman was alone; Again Rees must choose.

He was still against the wall, masked by one of the bushes. As far as he could see from here there had been no change in the garden courtyard since he had crossed it more than three hours ago.

Then the warning hit him full force, carried by a puff of wind ruffling the long spikes of leaves about him; the reek of native body odor, musky, nauseatingly strong. That was the smell of a Croc who was heated, excited. Croc—a forbidden epithet here, but one Rees knew. Croc stink here, and strong!

20

The Terran studied the peaceful scene, trying to guess at the source of that stench. It could be that one of those horny bodies crouched very close to him now. Or the smell could be only a lingering reminder of the recent visit of an Ishkurian aroused to the fever pitch of some strong emotion.

To reach the Beltz cottage, he would have to keep between hedge and lab wall, past the storeroom, hidden most of the way. Crouching low Rees began the ordeal of that venture. So far his nose could not pin the Croc smell to any one section. And he had seen no disturbance in the courtyard. His training in hunting craft, all he had learned during those months with Vickery, would now be put to the test.

Rees scuttled from one clump of lace-thong to the next. Then his hand went to the sill of the window which must open on the Beltz sleeping room. To go around to the door meant advancing into plain sight. And he could endure the pain of passing through a sonic long enough to get in. Cara Beltz should still be sleeping after that shot. He would have to rouse her.

He was head and shoulders over the sill and then he lurched back. The Croc reek was a deadly miasma in that room. He did not need more than one sickened glance at the bed to know what had had happened. Stomach heaving, Rees crouched back into the bushes, using the control he had been taught at the academy to master his body so it would not betray him by sounds of retching. At least she must have been still asleep when they got to her and probably never knew. He could cling to that hope.

There was no reason to try the lab now. The absence of motor hum was only too well explained. What about the com? Could he summon help by that? But that warning last night had been firm and final. You had to reach the port by 'copter then—and on your own. No rescue missions to be flown. And their 'copter had not returned. As for the one at the trading post, the Crocs would have destroyed that, they weren't stupid.

However, in the house were other things which could mean life for fugitives. His own trail bag and its contents—

he must make a try for that. Rees mastered the involuntary shaking of his body, studied the courtyard once more while he mapped out his next movements.

He did not make those until he had decided just what and where he must go. Then he went into action with swift sureness to reach another window, that of his own room.

Crocs had been here all right. Rees' took in the incredible confusion of the looted room, the paw marks and scratches where they had tried to force palm locks of the cupboards. But Ishkurian body heat was radically different from Terran. They had not been able to activate those controls. Short of chopping down the walls the storage cupboards were safe.

Rees pressed his hand over one of those smears, his flesh shrinking from even such a remote contact with the murderers. From the now open cupboard he snatched the bag he had packed so carefully and he gathered up three spider silk blankets too, as well as the long bladed dagger which had been one of his father's gifts. Good as dura-steel was, it could not penetrate Croc hide, but there was other life besides the natives to be met in the jungle. And the jungle would have to be their refuge.

Opening one of the blankets Rees dumped all his gatherings into that and knotted the whole into an unwieldy bag which he hurled out of the window. Outside again he stood above his loot to listen and sniff.

Why the Crocs had struck and then gone so soon puzzled him. There had been no fires here, no evidence that they had amused themselves after the beastly fashion they had at the post. A quick kill of the Terrans, then a fade away. Why?

Sakfor's post had been a relatively primitive structure, his storehouses easily raided. The mission was a more complex system of lab, warehouse, living quarters. Had the Ishkurians perhaps been afraid of the lab and its equipment? Or did they intend to return at their leisure for a more prolonged looting?

The natives working at the mission whom Dr. Naper

had promoted to tasks about the lab did have some elemental technical training. Those three at least knew the value and the use of much of the equipment. And there were things in the lab which could be turned into far more formidable weapons than the dart guns and throw ropes of the jungle people.

Rees did not know why he thought about that now. But it stuck tight in his mind, a kind of "hunch". And in the Academy hadn't they always stressed the value of examining the basis of such a hunch? Somebody might have wanted the mission left intact, somebody might be able to turn off-world machines, off-world ideas against the off-worlders who had imported them. He must remember that, and be prepared to face just such a problem.

But there was nothing he could do here to wreck the installations. In fact, the two Ishkurian technicians knew more about what was in the lab than Rees did. And he had to get back to the roller before it attracted any attention.

Gordy saw him coming and snapped off sonic. Slinging his bundle back into the storage space. Rees settled himself once more behind the controls.

"Where's Mom?"

Rees flinched as much from that question as from the touch of Gordy's hand on his arm.

"She's gone, Gordy, so has your Dad, and Dr. Naper."

"Where? But Mom wouldn't go without me!" Gordy's protest was sharp, fear-filled.

"She was sick, remember, Gordy. She must have been sleeping when they left. We're going on to the big plantation by the mountains, maybe we'll meet the 'copter and them there."

Rees could not bring himself to tell Gordy the truth, not there and then with Gordy's own memories of Kassa and the trading post still raw and horrible. And he had to think ahead further than just a few minutes, or an hour. The post, Vickery's hunting camp where he had been gathering the animals sold to off-world zoos, the mission; as far as

23

Rees knew those were the only off-world holdings this far west.

The proxlite mines had closed down two months ago when the first broadcast had suggested off-world withdrawal. But between them now and the mountains, the range which sealed away the plain and the Nagassara space port, there were two plantations. One of them, Wrexul's, was large enough to maintain its own private police force. If the fugitives could reach that and the off-world staff had not already left— A black collection of "ifs" but that was all Rees had to hold to.

The immediate problem was to find some place to hole up until dark came. In the night he would dare to use hopping power and really make speed. To keep to the jungle floor was to leave a trail a half-blind, jungle-foolish tourist could follow. And to hop in daylight was as revealing. Yes, a hiding hole for now; and after dark run east for Wrexul's!

III

THE ROLLER WAS concealed between two points of rocks, crouching as might a spurred yandu in a tree den. Rees had driven back along that camp trail which numerous hunting expeditions had beated down, and then lifted the machine by one carefully timed hop into this pocket. Lace thongs made a protecting gray-green curtain about them when he had pulled those elastic branches into position, following a pattern which Vickery had early taught him during their trapping. He plunged in the sense alarm making them safe from any surprise attack. And, with a stone wall behind them, the flamer facing the only entrance way, they were in the best fort he could improvise.

Rees looked at his watch. Four hours and a little more

since he had left Uncle Milo at the breakfast table. Four hours, enough time to end a world.

"Rees, I'm thirsty." Gordy tugged at his sleeve.

Water? Food? There were always survival rations stored in the roller. But how was the water? To check the tank had been one of the first morning jobs, he had had other things to think about today.

Rees knelt on the seat to read the gauge. About half full, which meant they must use that supply sparingly. But there were other ways of obtaining water in the jungle and they should keep the contents of the tank for emergencies.

"I want a drink!" Gordy persisted.

"I'll get you one. You stay here, turn on the sonic again after I get out but stay inside, understand?"

The young man worked one of the plastic canteens out of its hold hook and tucked the jungle knife into his belt. Both the Salarika and Gordy watched his preparations with round-eyed interest.

He slid out of the roller, wiggled between two of the lace thongs, and then paused, to listen and sniff. What he sought should be found not too far away. Rees rounded one of the protecting rock piers and plunged into the misty, gray-green of the jungle world, his boots sinking inches deep into the powdery earth.

A ghost-wing fluttered by, its pale, almost completely transparent wings making it seem the shadow of the living creature which no Terran had yet been able to classify either as a bird or an over-large insect. Rees stood statue still to check that flight. And he was rewarded when the ghost-wing settled on a bulbaceous growth swelling a loop of vine about the rough trunk of a thorn-rump.

That would be on a thorn-rump, Rees thought ruefully, measuring the distance between the ground and the vine by eye and guess. Luckily the tree was old and so there was a goodly stretch of open space between the dark purple thorns. He could climb, though it was a chance he would not ordinarily take. Setting the knife blade between his

teeth and thrusting the canteen into the front of his shirt, Rees gingerly took finger hold on the threatening thorns, pulled himself up until he could hook one hand over the vine near that promising swelling.

Seen this close the growth was not a part of the vine, but a parasite rooted on it, globular, with a fantastic spread of hairlike purple foliage sprouting from its lower end. The ghost-wing emerged from among those waving fronds, fluttering out in panic. Rees made a one hand stab with the knife into the side of the globe. The purple filaments writhed up and about his wrist. But he had braced himself in advance for their scratching and he knew he was immune to the particular poison they dug into his skin.

Restoring his knife to teeth grip again, Rees now pressed the mouth of the canteen tight to the hole he had made in the globe, boring in with all the strength he could exert. The bulb shrank under that pressure and the purple threads hung limp about an emptied husk, the liquid contents of which now splashed in the canteen. Rees dropped back to the floor of the jungle, a good supply of drinkable water now in hand.

His return was a backward crawl, for as he went he erased with a branch the marks of his boots. Luckily the powdery soil was easily smoothed. Then he was again in the roller with the eager children. As he let them drink the Terran wondered about the Salarika's immunity. Gordy was safe against jungle virus and the results of most insect bites. But was this small alien also protected by some form of inoculation or mutant control? They would have to chance it that she was.

She drank thirstily enough and he tried again to talk to her in Basic. Though she watched him with close attention, she did not answer, and he thought that if she did understand his words perhaps she could not speak that common stellar tongue.

However she allowed Rees to examine her torn hand. The blood had been licked away and the scratch looked clean. When the Terran tried to cover it with a plastic band, she

shook her head violently and pulled away, licking at it again with her tongue in a methodical up and down fashion. Rees guessed she was following her own species' way of dealing with such hurts. It was better for him not to intefere, what served one people did not always aid another.

"Why are we staying here, Rees?" Gordy demanded. "If Mom and Dad are waiting with the 'copter by the mountains I want to go on now!"

"We can't go until dark," Rees returned, summoning patience. To stay cooped up in the roller for the rest of the day would be hard on Gordy, probably on the Salarika child, too. But they dared not leave its safety. How frank could he be with the boy? Rees' own father had treated him as an adult, but then he had been Survey.

When his mother had died Rees had been only a little older than Gordy was now, but already the veteran of two prelim settlements on newly discovered planets. And he had continued to accompany his father as a matter of course, that life was a part of Survey training, until, at the age of twelve, he had mustered in at the Academy.

Specialization in service families had reached the point that children were born into their fathers' and mothers' occupations. That was why the wrench had come as a major break for Rees when Dr. Naper had taken him from the Academy and tried to refit him into the mission pattern of life. He could not subscribe to Uncle Milo's abhorrence of Survey's basic tenets. Just as he could not and would not agree that Survey's opening of new planets only tended to increase the colonial rule of the Empire and perpetuate what Dr. Naper and those of his association considered the most pernicious aspect of Terran galactic expansion.

But Gordy was of a mission family and relatively far less tough and less prepared for just what had happened today. Was he still young enough to be elastic, or would memory re-hab be his lot if and when they escaped?

"If we move now the Crocs might find us." Rees tried to explain.

"You mustn't call them 'Crocs'," Gordy corrected him. "That's a degrade name."

A degrade name! There it was, mission conditioning. Rees frowned impatiently. He'd like to force the mission high echelon personnel to sit through a tape film of what had happened here three hours ago. Sure, any one with a fraction of good sense did not intentionally degrade any intelligent alien race. But neither was it right to disregard the fact that in dealing with aliens, Terran, or even humanoid standards could not remain the measuring sticks of judgement. On the side of the mission there had been such a determined indoctrination away from normal human wariness in dealing with X-tees that to question any "native" motives was close to a venial sin. Rees supposed that what had just happened here would be explained and excused by those policy makers in a way to satisfy everyone but the dead, the tortured dead.

"The natives," Rees corrected. "Gordy, this is important—the natives don't like us any more. If they see us—they'll kill."

"Like what the Patrol officer said on the com?"

"Just as he said on the com," Rees confirmed.

"I want Mom and Dad!" Gordy's lower lip protruded stubbornly, now it quivered.

"Well, they aren't here!" Rees' exasperation grew. He knew that this had been a day of shocks for the boy, but the mere fact that they were still alive meant something. Though, he corrected himself silently, Gordy had no way of recognizing that.

"Tonight we'll turn on the hopper, head for Wrexul's plantation. Now let me switch on the hummer and you and the Salarika curl up back there and see if you can sleep."

"Travel at night," Gordy considered the possibilities that offered. "Stay up all night and maybe see an air dragon, Rees?"

"Truly. But you won't be able to see any air dragon unless you get sleep enough so you *can* stay awake tonight." Rees accepted the diversion gratefully.

He spread out two of the blankets on the floor of the storage compartment, gave each of the children another drink, set the small hummer, once used to quiet newly captured animals, to lull them to sleep, pleased that the girl seemed content to follow Gordy's example. Then Rees settled himself down in a corner of the driver's seat, on his knee the recorder which was one remainder from the good life with his father.

Commander Tait Naper had never been on Ishkur. But he had had training in handling widely varied alien beings. And his private note tapes, left behind when he had taken off on that last voyage, were a rich inheritance for his son. They held distilled experience hints from his successful career. Rees thumbed the button now, thought the key words for his own need: jungle, hostiles, escape, and waited for the re-run beam to reach his mind.

Fifteen minutes later he snapped off the recorder. None of the specific information the beam had planted in his mind was closely applicable to the here and now. But a general idea or two . . .

"Eye of the spider," he repeated softly aloud. " 'If you would fight a spider, you must attempt to see through its eyes, think with its mental equipment, foresee its attack as it would make one. ' "

The spiders in this case were the Crocs and Rees would have to strive to think Croc in order to out-think Croc, a a rather confused estimate of the task, but a correct one.

What did he know about the Crocs, the educated ones at the mission, the servile class that did the heavy labor, the guides and hunters with whom he had worked in Vickery's camp? These were three types, reacting in three separate ways. You could tongue-click and clapper Croc speech, the audible speech. But no off-worlder could mind-touch as it was certified that Crocs did with one another.

Yes, you could learn something of the outward forms of Croc life: the fisherfolk of the sea shore, the hunters of the jungle, the handful of those who had chosen to learn something of off-world education and galactic civilization.

29

But you did not really know what went on in those sloping, reptilian skulls. To use the eye of the spider here—the task was close to impossible. But Survey never accepted the term impossible.

Rees closed his eyes, tried to evaluate as he had been taught; if he had only had more training! He was in the position of a man ordered to build a spacer, with a full list of materials to draw upon, and only a beginner's knowledge of engineering. His concentration became close to physical pain as he forced himself to study the problems of getting under a rough, armor plated skin, seeing through the "eye of the spider," trying to foresee the moves of the Crocs against the fugitives.

Again it was the absence of sound which alerted Rees, as it had when he had awakened hours earlier that morning. The sonic! His hand was already reaching for the proper button on the control panel. Could the roller power unit be failing?

But as his finger rammed home on the button, that faint vibration began again. No power failure, a turn-off. Gordy! Rees hunched around to peer into the storage compartment behind the driver's seat. But Gordy was there, stretched out full length, short arms and legs flung wide. Gordy was there—the Salarika child was gone!

How had she known? But then she'd watched Gordy turn the sonic on and off. Why had she gone; after food, water? Rees had fed the children, and the half full canteen was within easy reach. No, the canteen was gone, as was a fish spear which had lain along the back of the storage space—water, a weapon of sorts. Their fugitive from the post must be following some definite course of action. Was she going back, trying to find others of her family? That was far more probable than the idea a child would strike into the jungle for any other reason.

Rees rubbed his hands across his forehead. She couldn't have been gone very long. The breaking of the sonic had alerted him. How much of a homing instinct had her feline ancestors bequeathed her? Enough to guide her through

the miles of jungle to the post? Not that she could make such a journey. The jungle was safe only when traveled by a hunter; any off-worlder must go in a machine equipped with the ingenious multitude of detective and protective devices this one possessed.

But how could he hunt down a small Salarika who probably was determined against being found, with a thousand good hiding places to hand? There was only one answer, and it was a danger for all of them—the roller must be used. The sense detector in it could be used to nose out any living thing with intelligence about a set quotient. Rees had it connected now as a Croc warning but it could as easily put him on the trail of the Salarika.

He leaned forward to study the dial. That was set to register at the mark Vickery had put there months previously, reporting on Croc mental radiations, meant to keep track of foot hunters on a drive. What would Salariki thought beams be? Closer to human, Rees guessed. The Crocs were a reptilian species; Salariki were mammals, warm-blooded and off-world. He moved the pointer with infinite care and then his heart beat faster with excitement. A tiny spark of answer. He could use the tracer though that meant hunting with the machine.

Rees activated the motor, his eyes moving quickly from what lay ahead to the tracer dial. The spark fluttered faster, then settled to a steady dot of fire. He was on course. The path weaved away from the rock pillars, heading on the slight down slope. That was a direct route back for the post. If they only had a common language and he had been able to explain the danger. He could now believe that the cubling was certain she had been virtually kidnapped, taken by force from her own kind. Perhaps, as a female, she had had so little contact with off-worlders of other species that she associated Rees and Gordy with the raiding Crocs!

Now that the Terran was sure of the direction of her trail he could try something else. Rees set the prowler to hop, cleared a large patch of vegetation and settled down

31

in the midst of a stream where water circled about the treads. They were ahead of the fugitive now, instead of trailing. And she would come to them.

Only she did not. Rees' frown grew. The spark on the dial remained constant. The Salarika was making no move. Had she witnessed their hop, was she remaining hidden to wait out the hunt? Well, he dared not waste the time in such games. This called again for Gordy's aid. Rees snapped off the hummer, reached back to shake the boy awake.

It required a moment or two to make Gordy understand. And when he did, he stared up the slope where the bush was thick and shook his head dubiously.

"I don't see, Rees, how we can find her there. There are so many places she can hide."

"Our noses will have to do it for us." Rees stepped out of the roller, almost knee deep into the water, and then swung Gordy from the machine to the up slope bank. "She's still wearing those perfume bags. Here, sniff this!" He had dosed himself with the inhaling powder which made him sneeze and had an even more violent effect on the boy.

"That hurts!" Gordy complained, rubbing his nose vigorously with the back of a grimy hand.

"Only for a minute," Rees assured him. "Take some deep breaths, Gordy." The inhalant had only a temporary effect and it could not be used again for hours. But the perfume of the Salariki clothing should be easy to pick up when their sense of smell was so intensified.

They started up the slope together, Gordy still rubbing his smarting nose. Suddenly he looked up at his tall companion. "I can smell, lots of things—different things!"

The sense of smell, so blunted in his species during their evolvement on their own world, was probably not yet as keen as that of an average animal, but it was far more effective than usual. And they were favored because the breeze was towards them—down hill. That wind must pass over wherever their quarry was in hiding.

"Over here!" Gordy jumped to the right, skidded down on one knee and scrambled up again. Rees moved to join him.

The boy was right. That scent which had hung about them so heavily in the roller was on the down breeze. They could not be too far away. But there was something else, a reek that was no perfume. *Croc!* grabbed for Gordy.

He held the boy fast as he drew a deep questing breath. Salariki and Croc all right. But the Croc stench was old, certainly nothing as strong as the taint left at the mission. An excited Croc had been there, but was no longer lurking nearby. Rees released Gordy but the boy did not move away.

"I smell . . ." he began and Rees nodded.

"Yes, but it's old, maybe since yesterday. Come on."

Rees broke through a stand of bushes, to face a dark hole in the ground. He cried out and threw himself flat, to wriggle forward and look down into a trail trap dug for one of the large beasts the jungle natives considered the best of eating.

The pit was dark, only a small portion of its covering had broken under the slight weight of the Salarika girl. Rees wondered if she had jumped from above to the seemingly secure surface of this place and her landing had snapped the roofing of the trap.

She was inside right enough, on her feet, her back against the wall, her forearm streaming blood where the flesh had scraped a upward pointing stake set to impale a captive. Mercifully she had escaped with only that hurt. Her yellow eyes were alight in the dark as she looked up at him, voicing a faint wordless plaint.

"Gordy!" Rees turned his head as he edged back from that danger section. The Crocs always undermined the edges of such a pit against any escape efforts. His own weight here might bring about another slip which would entrap them all, hold them prisoners for the Croc hunter. Gordy would have to act as his tool now.

"Is she down there?"

Rees nodded as he slashed and dug at the roots of the bushes about that hole. Those were long and tough, pulled

up fairly easy when the fastening tendrils were loosened. They would make a rope of sorts and Gordy must do the rest under Rees' direction.

IV

REES WORKED FAST. With the root lengths freed from the soil, he jerked and tore off the smaller side tendrils until he had a length of reasonably supple line, tough enough to stand the strain of Gordy's weight. He explained carefully to the boy what must be done, made him tie by himself twice over the necessary knots. To Rees' relief, Gordy was an apt pupil, appeared to understand just what he must do and why.

Then, with one end of the root rope tied about his middle, Gordy crawled out to the break and dropped into the pit. As Rees had feared the saw action of the root cord on the brink of that drop sent another portion of the concealing covering cascading down into the pit below. But Gordy swung free well above the danger of the stakes.

Rees looped the rope about a sapling, lowered it hand over hand until Gordy hailed that he had reached the bottom. The rope went slack, Gordy was unfastening it. Then there was a jerk, a series of them as the boy knotted it in turn about the Salarika.

"Take your time," Rees called softly. "Test the knot, Gordy."

"I will," the promise arose out of the ground where dust motes still danced upward. "Ready!" Gordy's pipe was echoed by a pull on the rope. Rees began to haul it. At least that second cave in seemed to have taken all the loosened earch with it. Though the rope still sawed the lip of the pit, no more of the soil gave way. A small hand waved suddenly above the surface and the claw nails of

the Salarika dug into the ground as the child helped to pull herself over and out.

Rees drew her to him, loosened the knot Gordy had tied, and threw the rope back. The Salarika crouched against his legs, tonguing the gash in her arm, shivering throughout her small body. But Rees had to get the boy out before he could make a closer examination of her hurt. When Gordy was back on firm ground once again Rees knelt beside the little alien, gently drew her hurt arm across his knee—and then froze as he saw those pricks in the grayish skin, pricks already marked a brownish tinge.

"Ka thorns!" Rees whispered. One of the most devilish devices in a Croc hunter's armory. And one for which there was just one antidote. Rees bit hard on his lower lip. He had an aid kit in the roller, but he could inventory its contents too easily, just as he could also visualize that shelf back in the lab where stood a slender container of green fluid, the one outstanding achievement of Dr. Naper's Ishkurian research; an answer to the poison of Ka thorns, as well as to several other usually fatal jungle-fostered deaths. The Salarika in his arms was going to die, almost as painfully and horribly as had the rest of her family back at the post. And there was nothing he could do about it, nothing but think of that container and its contents, which might be as far away as Terra itself now.

Gordy must have heard that whisper. Now he laid his hand on Rees' shoulder, his eyes big and wide. "The medicine, Rees, that's good. You can give her that, make her well. Dad said it always works!"

They had all been so proud at the mission of that discovery. But it was lost now, along with the men who had made it. Just as the child who now lay across his knees was lost. If her only had the container out of the lab!

To return would be the wildest folly. They had only one hope for escape, to head quickly for the eastern mountains and the plantations at their feet. The charge in the roller motor, Rees could not be sure it would last that far. To

go back to the mission where even now the Crocs could be crawling . . .

A hand with golden fur across its back raised towards his face. Again sounded that pleading whimper he had heard from the pit. Rees got to his feet, cradling the slight, soft body against his shoulder. He was a fool, a mad fool, but he was going back. The roller was, in its way, a small moving fort, and he knew the territory about the mission as well as if every portion of its expansion was imprinted on his brain.

Back in the machine Rees settled the Salarika on the blankets once again and then started the motor. The stream in which the jungle car rested angled slightly to the right, its course must run in the general direction of the mission. Rees squinted at the position of sun and shadow about him. He had about an hour, he judged, until the onset of twilight. If he could conceal the roller, visit the mission at dusk—

"Where are we going, Rees?" Gordy wanted to know.

"Back for the medicine," the young man replied, his plans crystalizing. Hide out the roller, so leave the children in a measure of safety, he knew where to do that. He would make the rest of the way on foot. His blaster carried a full charge and he would be prepared for an attack. Which the victims of the morning Massacre had not. If the lab had not been looted . . .

The Salarika was moaning pitifully three quarters of an hour later as the Terran stopped the car under the overhang of bushes he had planned as a base. He forced her to drink from the canteen, getting as much of the liquid down her as he could. Then he gave Gordy his orders. No leaving the roller, the sonic curtain kept on, and to stay out of the driver's seat, back on the blankets with the girl. There was a chance that even if the Crocs sighted the jungle car they might think it deserted and leave it alone. Crocs did not like machines, none of the hunters and guides had ever chosen to ride in it when they went hunting with Vickery. And Rees knew that part of the feeling against

off-worlders was rooted in the importation of such travel devices.

Rees slipped into the brush, watched Gordy lock on the sonic, and then made his way to the blocks of the mission buildings. He circumvented the 'copter park, sniffing. Croc stink, yes, but already fading. The Terran began to believe that the raiders of the morning had not returned. The beaker would be on the lock shelf under a force shield, in his uncle's lab office. And the force shield, as were the cupboards in the living quarters, was sealed to a palm lock. Luckily Dr. Naper had taken the precaution a month earlier of setting that lock to the pattern of every adult Terran living there, otherwise Rees' errand would have been fruitless.

The lab door was in full sight of the courtyard. Any scout from a Croc band would be able to sight the Terran before he got in from that direction. But there was another entrance, one only desperate measures would force on him. Rees crept behind the living quarters, got down on his hands and knees, running his left hand over the ground while he still grasped his blaster in the right. His fingers found the grip under the sliding gravel and he jerked up the trap door giving on the water tanks. Smells, none of them too pleasant, arose from below, but they were not Croc.

He found the ladder, edged down into moist dark, holstering his weapon so he could feel along the wall with one hand as he clung to his support with the other. A lever to be pulled back, answered by a round opening on the cramped repair tunnel to serve the pump system. Rees scrambled into that, wriggling along on his belly, fighting down the almost panicky fear he always had of tight, dark quarters. If he had not given Permal a hand down here, much against his will, last month, he would not even have known of the existance of this under-the-floor slit which ran the full length of the lab building.

"Two, three . . ." His shoulders scraped from wall to wall, his hair brushed the roof over him. He was counting in a whisper the outlets. "Four!" This was it. He would

come out in the lab, then he had only to get around the corner into the office.

The exit seal was stiff. Rees beat against it with his doubled fist, his impatience becoming fear as the outlet stubbornly refused to yield. He could retreat to the third opening. There, it was giving!

Light lanced in at him. No hum of motor, but the wall lights were on. And Croc stink, also other smells, the reek of chemicals, of burnt stuff.

Rees knew that the exit was under one of the stationary sinks which would afford him partial cover as he crawled out. And as soon as he was free of the repair tunnel his blaster was back in his hand.

Though his view of the room was greatly foreshortened, The Terran could seen the wreck of the lab. Broken tubes and containers, smears of chemicals, covered the floor.

Avoiding crushed glass, Rees crawled free of the sink, crouched to listen. Three strides would take him to the door of the office. He stood up. Several yards away was a huddle of stained rags. Rees averted his eyes. No use to investigate that closer.

On the office threshold was a wide sear of brown fluid. Croc smell strong enough to churn Rees' already queasy stomach. One of the raiders had fallen there. In the last few moments of his life Dr. Naper had accounted for one of his murderers, made such an impression on the enemy that the body pinned by darts to the desk inside was headless. The Terran's skull would be as preserved as that of an enemy warrior dead in battle. After one sickened glance Rees kept his attention strictly on what had brought him there. The beaker was still intact, the brilliant emerald of its contents seeming to glow. He inserted his forefinger in the waiting hole below that shelf, twisted right and then left, to brush the sensitive spot within its core with his flesh.

A ghostly shimmer of light as the force field flashed off. Rees caught up the tube and then the record tape box by it. Uncle Milo and the mission might never have any other monument but that discovery, and to take this with him

would be his last gesture for the project of which he had been so unwilling a part.

Back down the tunnel, holding the tube in his mouth for safe keeping, the tape box digging into his chest as he inched his way along. Luck seemed to be his and that gave him a prick of doubt, it was too easy. The "hunch," that odd form of awareness which could not be defined but which was inbred in his kind, fostered by his early education, was delivering a warning which became stronger as he emerged from the tunnel into the tank. The blackness in there was complete and again fear bit at him. What if he could not raise the trap door again, was trapped in here? He could always go back through the lab. Yet his sensitive inner alarms told him that something had gone wrong, that he was now in a pinch of danger. He did not know what or why threatened. Go back or on? Try to leave the lab through the courtyard, or raise the door here—perhaps to find himself facing a ring of waiting Crocs.

Rees climbed the ladder, braced himself under the door, put his palm to that barrier and tensed. Then he sent the door hurtling up and out with all the strength he could put into one vigorous shove. It slammed down on the ground, showering sand and gravel. His blaster was out and ready, but he was facing nothing at all save the creeping shadows.

Up and out, a heave and a roll, bringing him free of the tank and under a fringe of bushes where he lay, trying to control his hurried breathing, listening, smelling.

Neither ear nor nose added anything concrete to back that inner warning bell. If the Crocs were on the hunt, they were not yet near enough to betray themselves after the usual manner. Rees got to his knees and then his feet. He put the tube under his shirt with the tape, to give an ever present notice of their presense against his stomach muscles.

Too easy, far too easy. He was thinking that as he went, just before he stumbled, even as he fell forward, that he had been tripped up by a skillfully aimed throw stick. With a writhing which wrenched his back painfully, Rees

turned just as he his the ground, brought his blaster up to fire.

A split second, that was all he had to deflect the beam of his weapon. For the body lunging at him, a short hand axe swinging up, was not the brown scaled monstrosity of a tribesman, but a lithe, furred, silvery creature. He smelled the aroma of Salarika perfume as his attacker half fell on him, the axe coming down.

Pain, and dark, soft slur of words. Rees lay in a torment hardly aware of himself save as a focal point for pain.

"Come, come . . ." Flashes of more pain as his body was shaken. He blinked at a world which tilted about him crazily, and then was able to see those slanted green-blue eyes staring into his, as if by the very intensity of that demanding glare they could arouse him to coherent understanding.

Nails which were closer to claws pricked the skin on his shoulders as the hands of the Salarika supported him in a sitting position. The scent of the alien was familiar. Rees blinked again. No, this was not the cubling he had left curled sick and in pain back in the roller. Golden fur was blue-silver here. And the newcomer was an adult, equaling him in height if not in body structure. For the stranger was also a female, delicately made. However, her grasp was steel strong and she seemed well able to hold up his limp body.

The fine fabric of her upper robe was fringed into rags from her gemmed waist belt down and only three of the encircling wealth of scent bags still dangled from frayed ribbons.

"Zannah, where is Zannah?" Her voice was a low purr which arose from the depths of her throat, her eyes cold slits.

Rees tried to collect his thoughts in spite of the pain in his head.

"Zannah!" the Salarika woman repeated sharply, a hint of hiss in her Basic.

"Little, little girl?" Rees asked groggily.

40

"Yiss." This hiss was more strident. "Where isss sheee?"

"Roller—back in the roller," the Terran managed to answer.

She was already on her feet, her nostrils expanded, her head turning slowly as she sniffed, until she faced the direction from which he had originally come. Then she took two or three springy steps before she turned, impatience expressed in every line of her body, to look at him. Rees tried to stand, swayed wildly. She darted back to catch him. The Salarika might have given the impression of delicacy, but her strength as she lent it to his support was all he could have asked of a Terran male.

Just how they did make their way back to the roller Rees was never quite sure. His companion retraced the path he had taken, towing him with her, and the Terran was sure she found the way by scent. The first thing he was truly conscious of, was landing on the seat of the machine while his companion crowded over and past him to the children in the storage compartment. He caught at her plush-furred arm.

"Ka thorns'—" Rees had difficulty in finding the right words. "Take some of this, moisten cloth, lay it on the wound, quickly!"

Clawed fingers caught the tube and he leaned forward to rest his head on the arms he had crossed on the control half-wheel. Rees had to rest so for a long moment until the weaving world about him settled into stability and he could fumble at the aid kit. The Terran mouthed the tablets he had sought dry, swallowing convulsively to force them down. Then his headache dulled into a bearable throb, and his vision cleared. A delicate explosion by finger tip told him that over his left ear the scalp was broken, but the blood there was already congealing. Either his own efforts at escape or a belated realization of his identity on the part of the Salarika had saved him from a cleft skull.

"Rees, you are hurt!" Gordy leaned over his shoulder, inspected the damage with wounded, surprised eyes.

"Not too bad. Look in the stores, Gordy, get four Viv-ra-packs and open them."

Rees continued to sit and let the tablets work while the boy brought out the small tins. One Rees left in Gordy's hands, one he put on the seat beside him. The other two he offered to the Salarika woman. The child lay in her arms, a cloth with bright green splashes on it wrapped around the injured arm. Rees indicated the pressure point on the ration pack.

"Press, it heats and then opens," he told her. She nodded.

"Where do you go?" she asked as she put one can to Zannah's lips.

"Without a 'copter our only chance will be one of the big plantation, probably Wrexul's."

"This machine can take us there?"

"I don't know, we can only try. Tell me," he must have an answer to his question, "Why this? You could see I wasn't a Croc." He raised his hand to his head well away from the tender area about the wound.

"I did not see until just before I struck. I scented—Zannah." One of the nails flicked a scent bag at the child's girdle. "I knew that one of the children was gone, might have been taken by the snake-ones. There was their stink about also, very strong."

"So you thought I was a Croc that had taken her? Anyone else escape from the trading post?"

She shook her head. "I am Isiga, second-companion in the house of Lord Sakfor. The snake-beasts, they came to trade as usual, and their stink, it made me sick, for I have only been on Ishkur for two moons. So I went into the far part of the garden until they would go. Then I heard the screams and there was burning between me and the house, they had set fire to the oganna bales waiting there for shipping. So I hid in a tree place. Afterwards . . ." Her ears were skull flat, her fur-hair roughened and partly erect. "They hunted but they did not find me. Then I crossed Zannah's trail also and knew that she had run from that evil.

42

"But with her were others scents, those of you people. So I hoped that she had been found and was at the mission. But when I came here I found again that the snake-beasts had struck. I think by then," her tongue swept across her lips, "I was not clear in my mind. All I could see was the snake-beasts and what they had done and could do again to the little one. So when I caught her scent, if only faintly, and gave the rally cry to which she did not answer, then I believed I was to avenge one already dead—"

"Anyway you didn't carry that through all the way," Rees commented wryly. "It's getting dark. As soon as I think we can get by without being sighted, I'm going to set this car on hop and head for the mountains. If we continue in luck we ought to be able to raise Wrexul's by dawn."

"That is well," she gave prompt assent to his plan.

V

As Rees guided the roller toward the eastern heights his thoughts continued to play with the wonder as to why they had not met the Crocs once more. The natives had struck the mission and post with vicious ruthlessness. Then, they had seemingly, vanished into thin air—or the jungle. Croc hunters were expert trackers, tireless on any trail. How had the fugitive off-worlder been able to avoid them so far? Rees' efforts at concealment would have been easy for them to spot. And he did not believe that the natives had been so sated with bloodshed that they would willingly allow the escape of aliens.

Maybe time had something to do with this lull which made him so uneasy. The First Fasts: normally this was the season of native withdrawal to the inner sanctuaries of the High Trees, a district of which the off-worlders had heard but where no non-Ishkurian had ever penetrated. Because

this was a period of intense Ishkurian preoccupation with their own affairs had been the very reason the withdrawal of the last Patrol policing force had been scheduled for this date, when most of the natives would be out of contact. Had the massacre on the fringes of stellar civilization been only an isolated gesture before the Crocs began their annual pilgrimage? Rees hoped so, but he could not be sure.

There was a stir beside him. Isiga slid fluidly across the barrier between the driver's seat and the storage space to join the Terran.

"The children sleep," she reported, "Also, it is well with Zannah."

"Why didn't you traders leave when the red alert came from Nagassara?" Rees asked. Mission and trading post had had little contact. But he knew something of the Salariki temperament. Sakfor's stubborn remaining past a warning was a puzzle; the aliens of the trader's species were noted for prudence and wariness.

A small sound came through the dark a hiss of feline anger. "Lord Sakfor was made a promise from the lips of the High Tree Ishgil. Traders were needed, so it was said. There would be nothing for us to fear."

"Apparently that was not true." Rees kept his eyes on the dials before him. In the dark he had to depend much upon the auto-pilot.

"So someone shall learn the result of such split tongue talk!" The cold confidence in that was a threat, or rather another kind of promise. Salariki civilization was based on a feudal organization. Such a tragedy as this which had struck down Sakfor's household would, on the trader's home world, instigate a blood-feud to be taken up by his kinsmen of all degrees. But there would be none to answer such a rallying on Ishkur.

"You think," she was indeed reading his thoughts now, "that one female of a household can not draw a knife and call for the rightful deaths of the enemy. For the moment, no. But the time will come. I am now Name-Head."

She was right! Rees was startled. Under certain con-

ditions, which seldom materialize except in extreme instances such as this, the living adult survivor of a family, whether male or female, became the Name-Head of the victim clan. It was within providence that the woman beside him could demand vengeance from the Truce Court of her own planet and even so set an inter-world war ablaze.

"First," Rees pointed out, "we, ourselves, will have to be safely out of this."

"You believe that these Wrexul people will still be at the plantation?"

"If they haven't voluntarily withdrawn, and there was no hint of their doing that the last I heard, they would be in better shape to meet an attack than any other off-world holding this side of the mountains. They fortified their headquarters buildings last season and have a private force of off-world police."

In the reflected light of the instrument panel he caught a shimmer as she moved and the silvery fur-hair on her arms gleamed.

"And if the Wrexul staff are gone?" she asked.

"Lady," Rees gave her the proper form of address," you had better pray to what God or Spirits of Power you own that they *are* there. We have an energy change in this machine which, with luck, will last to lift us that far. After that, well, there is no way of crossing the mountains in a roller. And I do not think such a journey is possible on foot."

"I thank you that you speak plainly with me," she said after a short pause. "But tell me this also, you have much experience of jungle ways, you are certain we could not travel on foot?"

"Not with the children. I am not even certain a trained Survey Scout could get through, with the Crocs out hunting."

"Our future lies then on the edge of a knife blade, and if the blade cuts . . ." Again that shimmer of silver, she had given a very Terran shrug. "Listen now, Lord Rees . . ." He was startled at that formal title. Though she had just assumed the head-ship of her own clan, she was granting him equality

on the terms of her own world, a rare concession for one of the aloof Salariki. "If such a failure is upon us I would wish this, that we go as best we can into the high places, for I have heard that the snake-beasts do not favor the cold and snow in the peaks. Then, should there be no chance of any future for us, we take the warriors' way, going so Behind the Seas, our bodies undefiled. Or do you of Terra not believe that such a course is right and proper?"

"To me that sounds proper," he assented, "if it must be done. We of Terra believe that much; that children and women should not be allowed to fall into the hands of such as the Crocs while men still live."

"Yet there was a woman of your breed at the mission," Isiga pointed out. "And she died so."

"There were divided minds at the mission. Some believed that because they had lived here for many years and treated the Crocs with kindness and fairly, they had nothing to fear."

"Kindness! Fairly!" Her head went up, she made a hissing accusation of each word. "What is kindness, fair treatment, for aliens? To the Salariki kindness is first for his companions-of-the-inner-court and the cublings he fathers there, then to his clansmen. He does not waste good will lightly on strangers without the courtyards. Fairness, yes, that he practices with all, as long as the Peace Flag flies and no man arms for war. Kindness, fairness—to the Salariki those words have one meaning—to Terrans another—to the snake-beasts yet a third. We walk in the patterns set by our ancestors, how can we change to other trails and expect to discover no pitfalls in them? Those who believed the snake-beasts thought the same thoughts, they were fools!"

"Well, they have paid for their folly," Rees said heavily.

"Yet I do not think you were of a like mind. Why did you stay?"

"Because Dr. Naper, the head of the mission, was my chief-of-clan." He put into Salariki idiom the relationship with his uncle. "I was a warrior of the household."

"Then it was fitting that you stayed," she agreed instantly.

"Yet you were not one of them in thought, for they were not a people going armed and ready for war."

"You seem to know a great deal about them." Rees was rather puzzled. Dr. Naper and the rest of the mission personnel had certainly not fraternized with the post. And he himself had been so much of the time off in the jungle with Vickery, trying to escape an atmosphere where too often his beliefs gave offense, that he had not had much contact with the post either, having seen Sakfor only twice since the Salariki party arrived six months previously.

A sound which might equal a Terran chuckle came from his seat companion. "In this place if a pat-gru flower blooms a sun before its time there is talk of such a wonder for half a moon. Do you not think that curiosity led us to speculate concerning the only other off-worlders within reach? We knew what food you ate, what beds you rested upon, what clothing you wore, and what thoughts you held or, at least, how you expressed those thoughts in deeds and words. Thus we knew well that those of the mission did not believe in walking a road of warriors. Thus, how easily fighters were able to gobble them up!"

Rees was stung. Isiga only repeated what he thought to be the truth. Terran could critcize Terran but to hear that scorn in an alien voice made him begin a retort he choked off in mid-word.

"But the Salariki al—"

"The Salariki also were victims? You speak that which is right. So we may see that both of our peoples have been fools, each in our own fashion," she replied. "Now we can only prepare not to fail again. Ah!"

A silver finger tip beckoned his attention, pointing to the right. They had taken to the course of the river as soon as the sky had darkened into night, using the faintly phosphorescent water, cascading from a source somewhere in the eastern mountains, for a guide to ground the roller's touching between soaring leaps. The jungle vegetation, discovering no rooting room on the rocky verges of the stream, was a black mass well to either side of the water's

path. Here and there sparkled a lamp-bush, eerily green-blue, drawing to its deadly trap by that light the night flying things it fed upon.

But the color in the night to which Isiga pointed was no lamp-bush. This was a leaping burst of flame, flame consuming some highly combustible fuel, such as the energy blocks necessary to power a roller or 'copter.

Rees hazarded a guess as to the sourse, one which shook him in spite of the bleak forecasts he had forced earlier on himself. "Ffalow's!"

"The relay station for the Patrol flights over mountain," she added to that identification. "But would there have been any supplies left there to burn? I thought they had closed that down two weeks ago."

"They might have left a cache, as an aid to the mission, or to your post. Uncle Milo didn't say anything about such. But he was so opposed to the idea of withdrawal for the mission that he wouldn't have done so, even if the District Officer had notified him."

"The blocks would have been carefully stored and protected."

"Exactly!" The Terran snapped agreement. "The Crocs are moving east. That fire couldn't have been set more than a few moments ago."

"They go to Wrexul's to raid everything off-world this side of the mountains." It was as if she thought aloud.

"I'd say that's it," Rees agreed. "They know, or think they know, that there won't be any force sent out this way from Nagassara. They probably plan to clean up quickly and then go on their pilgrimages."

This could well explain where the Crocs had gone. Suppose the natives had put only a limited force of jungle fighters into the field? The raiders had begun with the mission, then jumped the post, were now moving purposefully eastward. If so the roller now had to pass a Croc task force, pass through or over natives who were firm in their design to wipe out all off-worlders this side of the mountains.

"So we must pass them." Again Isiga's mind matched his.

"Yes."

Eye of the Spider, see through your enemy's organ of vision. Needful, yes—but possible? Rees shook his head against a surge of fear. He *couldn't* insert himself inside a sloping, armorplated Croc skull, see through a pair of those slit-pupiled eyes. He didn't even know if the murderous forces moving east were jungle aborigines, or those who had had enough contact with off-worlders to have garnered a paper-thin patina of stellar civilization, enough of it to have their mental processes slightly twisted into more recognizable patterns of plan and follow-through.

Rees' knowledge was speedily augmented. Above the roller, but a little ahead, a cleaver of white light cut the night, sliced towards them as might a headsman's knife.

Completely blinded Rees gripped the control wheel fiercely as the roller bucked, rode up to an almost verticle position on the back wave of the force flash. He feared that they would flop over upside down. Then that buck became a sideslip to the left, carrying the machine away from the river towards the jungle. Rees fought to level out, to bring the roller out of that erractic and broken hop to ground safety.

Roller treads bit on a solid surface. Then they bounced into the air again, slammed sidewise against a whip of vegetation which gave under the blow, so the machine slewed into the mat of growth. Behind him Rees heard the screams of the frightened children. Then he realized another pair of hands had joined his on the control wheel, that Isiga was lending her strength to his in an effort to ground them.

Somehow they hit the level once more, or approximate level. Still unable to see more than the fiery flash before his eyes, Rees judged that the nose of the roller was higher than its stern, for their bodies were jammed hard against the back of the seat.

"A force beam!" Isiga's cry made sense. The Terran felt her fur-hair brush against his arm and shoulder as she

turned to the children. Then her voice was a soothing purr as she spoke to them.

Rees cupped his hands over his eyes. For a moment of icy panic he was shaken. Was he really blind? Or had the flash only dazzled him temporarily? A force beam! Some one of the Croc mop-up squad had the knowhow to use, and the possession of, a Patrol weapon. Had the Ffalow's station still been manned—and over-whelmed in a native rush, so the off-world weapons had fallen into Croc claws? Force beams were strictly security limited weapons. How *could* the Crocs have them?

But *how* natives had gotten that piece of armament was certainly no problem of the fugitives; what they did with it was. Rees groped out, caught at a furred arm.

"Listen!" he demanded urgently. "We did come down on the left bank of the river, didn't we?"

"That makes a difference?" she asked quickly.

"I'm sure that beam was grounded on the right bank. If so we have the water between us and them now."

"We did move to the left. What is the matter with you?" Her voice rose a note or two.

"Eyes—that flash—I can't see yet."

A sharp hiss of breath. Then her arm moved. Rees felt a faint touch of air against his lips, guessed she was passing her hand back and forth across his face.

"Temporary." He hoped that was true. How had she escaped similiar blinding? Perhaps her head had been turned so that she had not looked directly at the flash.

"How are we fixed?" he asked in the next breath.

Isiga moved about in the seat, once leaning across him as if to see what might lie on the far side of the roller. When she spoke her voice was even, giving a concise report.

"We rest on flattened brush. But there is a tree of some size leaning from the front part of the machine so we are not level."

"Behind us?"

"More brush."

"No trees?" Salariki eyesight at night was far better than

Terran, as he knew. She must be able to see in greater detail.

"None of any size."

Rees moved one hand in a sweep over the instrument panel. If the roller itself just had suffered no harm from their rough landing . . .

"I am going to try backing," he told her. "But you'll have to watch and guide me."

He fumbled for the right button, pressed it down. The roller lurched from side to side, shook in a way which told him that much of the surface of both treads must be supported on broken bushes above the ground level. Now the machine rocked back and forth, but it was also creeping in retreat, the tree support in front holding them less high. There was a crackling of brush all around. How long did they have before the Crocs swam the river to bag their victims?

And how badly was the roller damaged by the backwash of the beam? Rees clung to one small hope—that the attackers might have seen that erratic crash landing and that it appeared, from a distance, worse than it really was. The natives might now believe they were firmly grounded. If that were true the Crocs would take their own time about following them, sure of their own ability to track down and take any survivors.

The jungle car rested on an even beam now, its treads getting a grip on something solid through a mush of leaves, twigs and splintered branches. Also the brilliant pinwheels before Rees' eyes were fading.

"Now," the Terran appealed again to his companion, "any clear sky around except straight up?" The roller was no 'copter, it could not be jumped from a stand into a vertical rise.

"Not here."

To go out of the jungle to the open of the river bank was to offer themselves as an easy sitting target for the beam operator. They could plow ahead, waiting to find a clearing big enough to afford them the necessary hop run.

51

"Where's the most open ground path?"

Again he felt her move on the seat, guessed she was making a careful survey of their surroundings.

"Trees ahead and to the right. Only brush to the left but that way will return us to the river bank."

"Behind?" The roller was responding sluggishly.

"Yes, it is better that way."

They began a painful retreat, the machine swiped and beaten by branches and vines. Rees became aware that the sonic curtains had failed and a pounding on its button aroused no answering hum. Insect life— Rees flinched as a pin-point of fire lanced the side of his neck just above the shoulder meeting. But this was no time to worry about such minor matters.

"Wait!" Isiga's hand clamped down on his forearm, until her nails cut his skin. "A little, just a little more and you can turn. No trees there, just bushes and many vines."

No trees maybe, but vines could be worse in their way. However, he could only try. Rees waited for her cry of "Now!" and swung the control wheel. The roller obeyed awkwardly and they crackled on, beating a path through the resisting jungle wall.

VI

"GET YOUR HEAD down, keep the children back there, well under cover!" Rees ordered and crouched lower on the seat. The whipping lashes of brush and broken vine swept across the top of the roller as they crunched a path onward. The young man blinked frantically. Shadows against shadows, a faint difference in the quality of light, the pin-wheels fading. He gave a sigh of relief; the blindness was only temporary as he had hoped.

"The dials, to the left, second on the panel on your

side," he got out breathlessly, his words shaken from his lips by the jolts of the roller. "Any change of the indicator?"

"The bar points straight up."

"Bang on it with your hand!" Rees rapped out, afraid to accept that without a test.

"Now the bar swings," she reported a moment later, "but it returns to the same position."

"Then it's still working—and we aren't followed yet."

But why not, Rees thought. Unless, unless their over-the-river crack-up had looked much worse than it was to any Crocs watching. The enemy might deem them grounded; either dead or else easy meat for more leisurely follow-up, to be picked up later after they had wiped out the last off-world pockets in this section. He said as much to Isiga.

"Since I, too, thought we were finished," she observed, "perhaps they are not to be blamed in judging our descent fatal. How long now to Wrexul's?"

"I don't know. If we could appeal for a com cast we could ride a finder beam in. As it is we'll have to depend on the spy-scout, and make sure it doesn't guide us to a Croc raiding party. But Crocs with a force beam! They can break . . ." He stopped short, aware at last of what that fact could mean.

"A force beam," Isiga finished for him a greater calm then he believed he could summon at the moment, "could also burn a path through the Wrexul defenses, is that not so?"

"Yes. But if our people knew that the Crocs were so armed, they could do something."

"What?" she asked bleakly.

What indeed? A well defended post such as Nagassara port itself, that could stand up to a force beam, put up a counter-force cast which would send the power of the attacking beam back, to burn out the caster and those who sighted it. But not even Wrexul's would possess protection of that type here. The defenders would not be expecting to front one of the top Patrol weapons in the hands of jungle fighters. Also, primitive jungle hunters would not know how to use it, certainly not with the accuracy which

had downed the roller. Someone in that band had had training in modern off-world weapons.

"Wrexul's is our only chance," Rees said dully. "We can't lift over the mountains in this machine." He was beginning to doubt if they were going to roll any distance further here either. The roller was handling in a way which could not be explained by the rough terrain through which they were boring a path. The sonic was out. What about its other protective measures?

"Wait!" Isiga's voice was sharp. "That dial, the bar on it moves now!"

Rees gripped the half-wheel tighter. "In what direction, to what degree?" To him the faint glimmer of the instrument panel was too blurred to read.

"It swings right . . . ten points . . . now more . . ."

"That means the Crocs are across the river What's ahead of us?"

Her hand was on his shoulder to steady herself as she stood up in the rocking machine, using her better-than-Terran night sight on the path before them.

"Ahh! Pull up—quick!"

Rees obeyed, and the roller lurched as he applied the cut-off, slewed around in the crushed brush. The flamer! If he could use the flamer! He fully expected to front a Croc attack out of the dark.

"We are near to the edge of a drop," Isiga reported. "How deep a one I do not know, but it is wide. Can we hop it?"

Rees' fingers went to that other button, thrust hard. The machine spurted, but there was no answering surge strong enough to raise it from the mass of vegetation where it rested. He was right, more than the sonic had suffered back there in the crash.

"The hop power is out," he said. What to do now? Try to swing around so he could rake the brush with the flamer? All he had been trying to remember this nightmare day and night about the spider's eye was at last beginning to pay off. He'd be taking the biggest gamble of his life, a

bigger one perhaps than he should have. But it could be their only chance.

"Get this," he spoke incisively having made his decision. "I'm going to turn, with my back to the drop. You empty the storage compartments, fill the canteens from the tank, take all the rations—you can pack it all into those blankets—get the children ready. As soon as we stop, take them and the supply packs out of here. Head to the right, along the edge of the drop. Wait . . ." he unfastened the blaster belt with its comfortably filled holster. "Do you know how to use one of these? Three pressures of the firing button gives you maximum, and you'll need that to burn through Croc belly armor."

"And you?" She took the weapon from him.

"I'm going out in a blaze of fire power as far as the Crocs are concerned. It's the pattern they follow when they are cornered in battle. They'll come up, get the flamer in the face. And then the roller will buck back into the drop and blow up. If any of them survive that toasting, they'll think we all went up with the machine. I'll join you as soon as I can."

"This machine is too disabled to aid us farther?" Her cool acceptance of their danger was a steadying support.

"Yes. It might conk out completely at any moment. Now get moving!"

He helped her gather the canteens, the packs of rations, the aid kit, two bush knives. Then he handed Zannah out into her waiting arms, saw Gordy stumble after, the small boy manfully lugging the second blanket bundle. They were gone and Rees was alone, grimly hoping his choice was the right one. With any luck he should be able to make their pursuers believe that they were all trapped in the disabled roller.

Gingerly he maneuvered the jungle car about, and his suspicions concerning the future were amply proven by the stiff, limited responses to its controls. Once the motor cut out entirely and Rees thought it was gone, unil it answered haltingly to his frantic coaxing. He was turned

around now, his back to the gulf masked in the darkness, the flamer facing the way the Crocs must come. Luckily his eyes had recovered to the point where he could read the spy-scout dial. Its pointer had swung well past the half-way mark. The Crocs were coming, fast now.

They couldn't carry a beamer, not over this broken ground, unless they had it mounted on a lift platform. And if they also had one of those . . . Rees smiled, a stretch of thin lips which did not in the least denote humor. That would have to come straight along the swath the roller had cleared. The flamer would take it, the beam it transported, and any firing crew riding it, dead center.

The Terran made two other preparations and sat quietly to wait. He regretted the loss of the sonic. The under-growth flattened in the passage of the jungle car must have been the valued home of countless insects. All Rees could do was trust in the strength of the repellent he had smeared on his skin moments earlier, but that did not guard him against all stings, bites, and the crawling exploration of creeping things he could not see (and did not want to anyway). Waiting; that bit, too, worse than any insect. He began to count mentally, try thus to estimate how far Isiga and the children could have traveled since they left the roller.

Rees' eyes adjusted, and not a moment too soon! Not even Crocs, jungle wise as they were, could mask that object hanging well above the road of the roller, appearing as a blotch against the sky. It swung on and the diffused radiance of a half crushed lamp-bush gave Rees an idea of its outline. So they *were* bringing in the beam on a lift!

The Terran pushed the flamer button. A tongue of raw red fire licked out. It must have caught the lift platform and its burden square on. But Rees did not wait to make sure. His arm shielding his eyes from the glare, he spun out of the seat, clung to the door with one hand, just long enough to kick at the starter. Then he hit the ground and squirmed to his knees, scuttled over a rocky surface which bruised the skin on his plams.

Roller treads grated on the rock as the car groveled backwards. Fires were blazing around as the flamer slewed back and forth, tonguing out in a fan-shaped sweep before the retreating machine. Then that spear of fire pointed skywards as the car teetered on the brink of the drop. Rees, yards away now, dared pause to glance back.

Down it went, toppling back into the gulf. And some of the enemy had survived. The rasping, coughing screeches of the Crocs made a harsh clamor. The Terran took to his heels, hoping that they would congregate on the edge, even start down towards the wreckage. He had hit them hard and they would be swept out of prudence, wanting to take his head. The skull of a valiant enemy was a far better trophy for the High Tree of a clan than that of a victim cut down in a massacre.

Rees gasped as a pain caught him under the ribs. Now he must depend not only on his own speed and agility, but on Isiga's night sight. If the Salarika kept to the edge of the gully as he had ordered, he should catch up with the fugitives before too long. But as he scuttled faster to put as much distance between him and the crash as he could, Rees still waited for the finale he had planned.

That came with more force than he had deemed possible. A crackle of light fiercer than the native sun lit up the Ishkurian landscape, even though its source was at the bottom of the drop. Rees stumbled on, a sound rising from his lips, not quite a laugh. Any headhunters caught in that explosion of a heated motor fed a full stream of energy would no longer be interested in skulls—not even their own!

The leaders of that Croc party must have been operating the force beam on the lift. And Rees could probably count on their having been killed by the flamer. Now if there had been any survivors of the roller explosion they would not be out to track off-worlders. Rees had copied the pattern of their own people when facing overwhelming odds; get the enemy and end one's own life into the bargain.

Only, now he was beginning to worry about Isiga and the children. Surely they could not have gone any farther than

this. He slackened pace, trying to see more than the splotches of lamp-bush. Then another light brought Rees to an abrupt stop.

Well overhead, but coasting down on a flight track which would connect with the ground just ahead of him, was a red line, or rather a pinpricked outline of a monstrous head, jaws agape and every fang a small pulsating coal.

In the roller or even in the open with a blaster, Rees would have been able to face that menace with the confidence of the superior armed. But his knife was no protection against an air dragon in the thing's own territory. This was a creature of the Ishkurian night, using its light celled head to dazzle and terrify its prey into helplessness. And it was on the hunt now but Rees realized he was not the quarry.

The others! All the jungle had come into terrified wakefulness at the noise of the battle. Screams of disturbed flying things, of the small dwellers in the mass of vegetation were a loud uproar, through which the Terran could not hear the ominous flap of those wide skin-and-rib-boned wings. He could only watch that wicked, red-outlined head as the thing approached in a purposeful glide.

Isiga had the blaster, and he knew her sight was excellent. But if she used that weapon to finish off her attacker, she would also advertise to any Croc that the fugitives were still alive. Their sacrifice of the roller would mean nothing and they would be easy prey for trackers.

Rees' feet continued to carry him forward, though he had no glimmering of idea as to what he was going to do with two bare hands against those red coals of teeth and the tearing foretalons which hung below the too-well-defined head.

The air dragon was at tree-top level now, the smaller trees which rimmed the gully, not the towering giants of the true jungle. Those jaws snapped with cruel visibility. The hunter must have caught some flying creature bewildered into flight. But the morsel was too small to satisfy it. Now it hovered, perhaps some ten feet above the ground, the red outline of its head jerking back and forth. Rees gave a gasp

of relief, his left hand pressing his aching ribs. What the air dragon sought was under cover.

Unfortunately these things did have some intelligence, that and a habit of stubbornly settling upon one prey and that alone in a night's hunting. The air dragon would continue to patrol above, waiting for its intended meal to break from the protecting cover. And its very presence there, especially in a jungle already awakened and alert, would be a signal to summon others, the ground beasts, those that feasted on the remains after the flier had sated his more fastidious appetite and was gone.

The skull-rats, the progies; those would gather. And a pack of either would flush the dragon's game into the open. Rees had heard Vickery's stories of such combined hunts and knew that the animal collector did not exaggerate in the least. To stay was death of one kind; to move was death of another.

He estimated the circling course of the dragon. It flapped back and forth leisurely, not in the least concerned over the eventual outcome of the action. Rees was as certain as if he could see them clearly that the prey it sought was Isiga and the children. They must be—Rees studied the swing of the red tipped head above—under some bush or thick branched tree, a little to the left and even nearer to the edge of the drop. Perhaps the Salarika had been trying to reach that when the dragon had swooped too near for her to longer expose them to its pounce.

Rees took to cover. Belly flat he wormed a way towards the spot he had fixed upon as the core of the dragon's interest. He must move quickly, before the skull-rats or the progies came!

Then he was flattened under a thin curtain of cover, aware that that red pitted outline of a head swung about, was not pointing towards him! If he were only close enough! There was one action they could combine upon. Or if Isiga could use the blaster with an expert's ease and a narrow beam. With Vickery he would have tried such a move at once but now he must be sure.

Something thudded out into the patch of open cut so invitingly and menacingly on the very lip of the gully. It winked with the reflection of pale light on metal as a spark in the bush from which it had been flung fastened on it in an off and on beam no stronger than the body light of some night insect. The blaster! Isiga must have seen his arrival and was now signalling to him the position of the weapon.

Rees swept out his hands to either side of his body, raking in the muck of old leaves and twigs, hunting for a fallen branch he might use to reach the blaster. There was nothing to be found save some wood so rotted it crumbled to evil-smelling powder in his grasp.

The blaster was there in the open, the air dragon alert and ready overhead. Its circle was tight above the clearing. The longer Rees waited the less he would be able to nerve himself to what he had to do now. The Terran set his teeth, tensed his body.

He did not really leap, rather he threw himself low, as he might have done in tackling a runner, concentrating on that weapon. As his hand fell upon it, he flopped over on his back, swinging the blaster up so that it pointed skyward from his chest. And he stared wildly up into pure nightmare.

The monstrous head was not just a red outline now. All its horror bloomed in the sudden beam of a handlight. And that ray dazzled it for just the second Rees must have to thumb the blaster to narrow beam and fire. He saw the pencil of energy leap at the gaping mouth and then kicked into a roll which carried him on toward the bush from which the hand light had come.

A clawed foot raked, scraping along the Terran's side, tearing clothing from his body. But the strength of that stroke flung him on and away. Rees heard a scream of terrifying volume as he came up hard against fur and flesh and lay gasping for air.

Somehow he squirmed up into a sitting position, the blaster again ready. But there was nothing out there to aim at, neither in the air or on the ground.

"What? he began.

"It went over and down." Fingers fastened on his shoulder. "You are hurt?"

Went over where? Rees tried to make sense of that as the hands swept down his arm to his scraped side, touched some scratch there to stinging life. Into the gully! That's what she meant; the air dragon must have been so severely wounded it had fallen into the gully!

"You shot a dragon!" Gordy's voice was a breathy cry of triumph. "It's head went all smash! That's just what it did!"

"And you have taken no great harm." Her hands were busy applying some substance to his side in swift, competent strokes.

"We've got to get out of here," Rees assembled his wits to the point where common sense was again in command. He still did not quite believe that this had really happened, that he had pulled off their second wild gamble of the night.

"Down the gully," Isiga told him, "there is a sheltered way. I had just found it when the dragon came. And there are signs of a path, we can not be too far from the plantation."

"Then let's get going!" Rees urged.

VII

"No SIGNS of life." Rees lay flat, his chin supported on an arm stretched across before him. A screen of scarlet-tipped grass stood between him and the sharply sloping drop toward a barrier which caught and reflected the greenish sunlight. He could not be wrong; the sentry towers at the four corners of that enclosure, the size and substantial structures the wall protected, said this was Wrexul's. But nothing moved from one of those buildings to the next, the place had a deserted look.

"The 'copter park," Isiga was beside him, her silver fur-hair and grey skin blending better than the Terran's torn clothing and pink-tan hide with the color of Ishkurian soil and grass roots, "there is nothing there."

Rees had already noted that disappointing fact. The off-world staff could have sealed their headquarters, taken off in the 'copters, trusting to luck that the trouble would be settled and they could return. From what Rees could sight every building was closed, the gates shut. And he imagined that persona-locks were on. A barrier tuned to Terran body heat would permit his entrance and Gordy's—but he was dubious about the Salariki. He said as much to his companion.

"We should go there, even if your people have left?"

"They didn't take the com with them. And that must be on direct beam with the port. If I could make contact with the authorities a 'copter could be sent be on robo-control."

She nodded. "But what if the snake-beasts behind us have another force beam?"

Yes, what if their brush back by the gully in the night had not knocked out the full enemy force? The rest of the Ish-kurians could be ringed around down there, just waiting for a chance to get into the plantation stronghold. There was a wide swath cleared of all vegetation, fire burnt to the soil, about the four sides of the barrier. That had clearly been done since the last full rain, the black ash was still to be noticed. Someone had ordered that destruction as a reasonable pre-caution against any creep attack. In order to get to the gates Rees must cross that open. And only the gates, one of those two, would pass him as soon as his body heat activa-ted their controls. Then, once in, he must locate the con-trol room, clear the persona-locks for Isiga and Zannah. Or else head directly for the com, send his message and return here to await the arrival of a rescue 'copter. Rees outlined the alternative plans to the Salarika.

"You believe that this 'lock' is set against us, that neither I nor Zannah could pass it?"

"Wrexul's had a straight Terran staff. Your people seldom sign wage contracts with Terran firms."

"That is true, Is it now a matter of time?"

"Not too closely, I hope. And down there, with that barrier in working order, the Crocs couldn't get at us. Not unless they do have another force beam."

"So many guesses, and so easy to make the wrong one," Isiga commented. "But for this I am willing to throw the quass sticks and take what count of red Fortune offers. To be within walls which hold off snake-beasts, that would make one's heart beat less fast, smooth one's hair sleek again."

"Then stay right here, all of you," Rees cautioned. "When you see me return to the gate, then make a run for it. I will cover you with the blaster."

He shouldered the larger pack of their supplies and began to run. Under his boots the slope seemed to stretch itself, making a longer dash through the open than he had estimated when under cover above. Rees skidded against the surface of the barrier, his shoulder meeting it with force enough to jar painfully along his tender side.

Was the gate on persona-lock? The Terran waited breathlessly, clinging to that hope. Certainly the staff would not have set the combination to any but a general Terran body heat. There was too much chance that any one individual might not return. But at least Rees had not been burnt to a crisp at contact, or given a brain washing sonic blast. And he was sure the Wrexul people must have left some warm and fierce welcome for any Crocs daring to nose around.

There was a click, hardly louder than the sounds made by some grass insects. A portion of the wider gateway to his left slid back. One-man heat, one-man door, that figured. Rees leaped through and the panel went back into place behind him.

The control room, which should hold the com also—which —where? Rees surveyed the buildings and tried to guess their uses. Finally he chose one which was attached by a short corridor to the living quarters. Its outer door must also

have been set on persona-lock because when he was still a foot or so away it folded into the frame.

This was a power room right enough. And one showing signs of hurried abandonment. A cup stained with dregs of Terran coffee sat on a shelf beside an instrument panel, a scarf trailed from the back of a built-in seat. Rees made a hurried examination of the board beside the coffee cup. While the mission had never used a persona-lock, in fact Uncle Milo had dismantled part of it three months ago to take out the pack motor for the repair of a lift beam, Rees knew what he was searching for. And that dial with its attendant row of buttons was easy to find.

One second to press full release, then he was running back to the outer gate. He waved his hand high over his head.

Gordy came down the slope first, carrying the other bundle. The boy stumbled once, went to a scratched knee, and, when he got up, smeared the back of his hand across his dirty face. Isiga, carrying Zannah, padded light-footedly up behind the child, the encouraging words she used to spur him on reaching Rees merely as a sing-song purr. The Terran sprinted out as they neared, swept up Gordy, in spite of the boy's indignation, and somehow hustled them all inside the barrier. It was necessary now to close the gate by hand. He slammed it and ran to re-set the lock.

"Food," Isiga pattered along after him. "That's what we need. And have you found the com?"

"Not yet. I'll look for it now." But as Rees went slowly about the room his steps dragged. He staggered once, steadied himself with a hand against the wall. That last spurt through the gate lugging Gordy—it was as if that effort had used up all the reserve of strength on which he had been drawing so heavily since they had left the mission. How long had it had been since he had dared to relax, to rest? More than one Ishkurian day. And even now he dared not think of sleep.

"You sick, Rees?" Gordy blinked at him owlishly.

"Just a little tired. Don't you want to go with the Lady Isiga and find something to eat?"

"Where's Mom, Rees, and Dad? You said they'd be here with the 'copter. And I haven't seen them. There's no one here but us. I want my Mom."

For a moment Rees was unable to understand that; his fatigue was like a mental fog. Then he recalled dimly the excuse he had used to cover the tragedy for Gordy yesterday morning.

"They must have gone on again, Gordy." He knew he was fumbling, not handling this well. But he was too tired to be very imaginative. "We'll call a 'copter and go on to Nagassara."

"I don't believe you!" The boy stated, frankly hostile. "I want my Mom and I want her now!"

Rees lurched over to sit down in the chair from which the scarf trailed. The whisp of soft material fluttered to the ground and Gordy pounced upon it.

"This isn't Mom's," he told Rees accusingly. "She hasn't never been here. I'm going home right now, I'm going home!"

"You can't!" Rees' control was on the ragged edge of breaking. He could not deal with a frightened, stubborn child on top of everything else, not now. "Isiga!" He shouted, knowing that he did not have either the will power or the energy to leave the seat and hunt out the Salarika in person.

"You can't make me stay here." Gordy backed toward the door, his face a sullen scowl as he wrung the soft scarf between his scratched and dirty hands. "You can lock me up, but I won't stay! I'm going back to Mom and Dad. Dad's going to get you, Rees Naper, for bringing me away. He said I wasn't to go around with you. You're a bad man, you fight."

"So I fight," Rees repeated grimly. "Well, it's a good thing I know how, whether I like it or not. Listen here, Gordy, you're just tired and hungry and I know you want your mother. But we must get to Nagassara. The Crocs. . . ."

"Dad said 'Crocs' is a bad word!" Gordy's voice was shrill. "You say bad words and you tell lies and I'm not going to stay here!"

He whirled and dashed out of the doorway. Rees got to his feet and stumbled after. The persona-locks—Gordy could pass by them—leave either gate without interference. Rees must reach the child, keep him from leaving the plantation fort.

"You, you let me alone! I'm going home right now!" Gordy struggled in Isiga's grip, hitting and kicking, his voice now a scream of pure hysteria. But, as Rees had discovered earlier, the Salarika's hold was strong. And she not only continued to restrain the boy but bent over him with a soothing croon.

Her eyes met Rees' and he read reassurance in them. This was now woman's business and the Terran trusted the Salarika to handle the rebel. He must go back and hunt for the com.

He had located the unit and was seated before the call mike when she slipped in to join him.

"Gordy?"

"He has eaten, now he sleeps. Also I have put a catch on the door. But his purpose is firm. We shall have to watch him. He does not know that those of his inner court are dead?"

"No, how can you tell a child a thing like that?" Rees appealed. "I had to keep him in the roller, away from the mission. So I told him his mother and father had gone, that we would catch up with them later."

"Such evasions always lead to complications," she pointed out. "But, yes, I can understand how you found it too hard to speak the truth to a little one. Perhaps, when he wakes and is quieter, I may be able to tell him something. He is now too angry and frightened to listen."

"I suppose so. The sooner we can raise Nagassara the better!"

"There are those there who are his kin?"

"No." For the first time Rees considered Gordy's future. "No, there's no one and I don't think he even has any close kin off-world. He'll be the responsibility of the mission foundation."

"And you, you have other kin?"

"No. My father was a Survey Scout. He did not return from Rim run. Dr. Naper was my uncle."

Her green-blue eyes regarded his thoughtfully. "We heard that you sought animals in the jungle with the tamer of beasts. You did not work at the mission?"

"Hardly!" His old bitterness was sour and heavy. "Uncle Milo took me away from the Survey Academy, he was strongly opposed to the Service. But he could not make his ideas mine. So now I am neither one thing, nor another!"

"And what will you do when we reach Nagassara?"

Rees shrugged. "I don't know. Join the militia maybe. Hunt up Captain Vickery anyway. We have to get there first."

She flexed her slender fingers, casing and uncasing her claw nails, and there was a spark centering each slit pupiled eyes.

"Yes, that is true, we must reach Nagassara before we can earn a future. But, Lord Rees, keep this in your mind; I am now Name-Head of a clan, a trade clan. In Nagassara you may have more than one chance. Are not Free Traders explorers too?"

Rees blinked, not really taking in the meaning of her words. Nagassara was the width of a mountain range and more away. What did any future beyond the immediate one of trying to reach there mean now?

He pressed the key of the com. The call light sparked on the board. Wrexul's personal call symbols he did not know, so he resorted to those of the mission. And such coming in on the Wrexul beam length would alert any operator at the port to the fact that this was a distress call.

Tip-tap-tock. Rees beat out the pattern. But the plate to receive remained obstantly blank. The com was alive, sending. Why no answer? Cold squeezed Rees' middle, added to the leaden weight fatigue had hung on his arms and shoulders. Was—was Nagassara already abandoned, had the last spacer lifted? Or had the Crocs erupted all over the planet and crushed the stronghold of the off-world government?

"No answer!" Isiga's fingers hooked, claws fully out, as if she would tear the symbols out of the plate by force. He could hear her heavy breathing through the beat of the key.

"Could—could they have gone?" She put one of his fears into words as desperate moments lengthened into minutes—two—four—six . . .

"I don't see how." Rees bore down the sending key. "There may be a mountain storm, those cut the beams at times. It must be that, it has to!"

He stared at the blank mirror face of the receiver as if by the demands of will alone he could bring a responsive flash to it. *Tip—tap—tock.*

"Identify!" Imperious, demanding, that single signal on the key. Two Terrans, he gave their names and place of origin; two Salariki, cut off without transportation at Wrexul's, an appeal for a robo-copter. He reeled that off, began to repeat the message with the same ragged speed.

"Naper—give name of X-Tee instructor, Survey Academy five years ago."

Rees stared blankly at the symbols on the mirror, wondering for a dread filled second or two if he had cracked under the strain, as that message had no earthly, or galactic, connection with the S.O.S. he had broadcasted. But the symbols remained there without alteration when he asked for the reason.

"This is no time to play games!" The Terran burst out, banging his fist on the edge of the panel.

"Not games, I think," Isiga said. "There is some need for them to be sure that you are who you say you are. Can it be that the snake-beasts are using coms to call out either would-be rescuers or to gain transportation into Nagassara?"

Rees relaxed. That made some sense. But Crocs using the com units that way? Only they had been armed with a force beam, too, he had to remember that. They were not just up against primitive jungle runners after all.

"X-Tee instructor—Zorkal." Luckily they had asked him to name Zorkal and not, say, the astro-math man. But Zorkal

had given Rees extra instruction when he had discovered how keen the young Terran was on X-Tee.

"Set your field guide beam on C-2-59 over Y," the mirror told him, apparently satisfied now that he was Rees Naper in the flesh. "You will have to wait. There is a flash storm in Nass Pass and we can not send the Robo until that clears."

"A storm!" Isiga's voice was close to a sigh. And Rees could have echoed that sound of frustration in a far more vigorous outburst if his weariness was not so complete.

The Nass Pass could be storm blocked for minutes, hours or days. And it was very true that a robo could not fight the winds there and get through with only a ride-beam to bring it in. Rees set the guide as directed and then let his hands fall into his lap. He was literally too worn out to move. Then Isiga's warm clasp on his bowed shoulders roused him a little.

"Come eat, sleep," she purred close to his ear. "You will have time if there is a storm."

"You need rest also," Rees suggested. But he was standing up under her surprisingly strong pull, staggering to the door where she steered him.

She had found supplies left by the plantation staff, produced a meal Rees ate his way through, hardly aware of what he chewed and swallowed, or why, while she sat opposite him at the table drinking some liquid of her own choosing in delicate sips from a cup she held in both hands.

He was in the jungle clearing of Vickery's camp, facing the three walls of cages. And in each cage crouched a Croc, their snouts high, their teeth bared. The horrible stink of their hatred and anger choked him. Now the cage controls were weakening. Rees knew that without actually seeing the give of the latches. And there were no weapons at his belt, nothing but his two bare hands with which to face their charge.

To escape—to escape he must get into one of those plated bodies, see through those red eyes. But how? How did one become a Croc? Yet he must, he must!

Rees was sitting up, gasping, his heart pounding heavily

within the wall of his chest. He flailed out with an arm, grazed a body which dodged that blow. Then his gaze steadied on Isiga. He must have been dreaming!

"The robo—it's here!" He got up from the bunk, ready to go.

Rees wavered. Her tone, eyes—the expression in them brought him into full wakefulness. He drew a deep breath and the air seemed to catch in his throat. That smell, that couldn't be any hazy hold over from his dream! Less heavy than the stench of his nightmare, but unmistakable for what it was. Rees whirled to face the window open above the bunk. The breeze pushed in through the sonic unchecked. It was the cool wind of early evening and the gray shadows of dusk fogged out there.

"They've come," he said in a half whisper.

Croc stink; he would never forget it as long as he was able to breathe.

"Have they shown themselves yet?" Rees' head swung back to Isiga.

"No. But that is plain that they are there." She waved a hand at the window and the wind.

"And there must be a lot of them."

"Gordy is gone."

Rees didn't take that in at once. He had been too busy listening, thinking about the force which must now ring in around the plantation fort.

"Gordy . . ." The Terran repeated absently and then the meaning of her report sank in. "How long?" he snapped.

"Zannah says only a half hour perhaps. We searched the rooms first."

Rees ran, heading for the gate, that gate through which only a Terran could pass, which should have meant their safety and escape. But which to Gordy could mean . . . No, not that—please, not that!

VIII

"GORDY!" Rees yelled with the full force of his lungs. There was a faint echo resounding from the higher land, but no other answer. And the gate was closed.

Rees pulled up. "He could be hiding," he said to Isiga who had run along behind him. She shook her silvery head.

"We searched as I told you. Zannah also says he went to look for his mother."

The boy could be anywhere in that wall of vegetation beyond the burned strip. And with the Croc smell this strong. To try to track a missing child in the jungle which was the enemies' own hunting ground was the rankest folly.

Eye of the Spider! Rees froze. He knew, now he knew what was going to happen as clearly as if his brain did occupy one of those armored, saurian skulls, look through the red alien eyes. Gordy was a key, a key to be used to open Wrexul's.

Perhaps the Crocs had already tried to cross the barrier, found the persona-locks past their breaking. Some scout, left on sentry at one of the high points cupping in the stronghold, could have witnessed the fugitives' entrance, marked the ease with which the Terrans had passed the gate. The Ishkurians might have been just waiting for some such chance, and Gordy had given it to them!

Rees turned, began to walk back to the buildings at a slower pace.

"What is it?" Isiga matched her steps to his. "What is it that you have thought of?"

"Gordy, they won't harm him yet. Because he's their key to the gate!"

"The lock!" Again her voice was a hiss of anger. "They will use him to open the gate for them."

"So they must bring him back to us," Rees held to that fact which was the only one holding a fraction of hope.

71

"And what do we do?" she wanted to know.

"You and Zannah must wait at the 'copter park, ready if and when it comes. Maybe we can find weapons."

"No, for those I have already looked. There are none left."

"Maybe no apparent ones but I want to see what is in those store rooms." Rees headed purposefully for the windowless building he had marked down as the warehouse.

"That is time locked, I think. I could not open it."

"A lock can be shorted," he snapped.

The dusk was deepening. Night came fast here in the foothills and the darkness would provide cover for the Crocs using Gordy. Lights, they needed floods to cover the whole inner area. Wrexul possessed a flood system, the standards and lamps were in sight.

Rees set about preparing for the attack he knew was on the way. Even if the robo arrived now, they could not leave. Or he could send Isiga and Zannah. But he would have to remain until the natives moved in with Gordy. The robo could be sent back again.

The control room gave him the power of turning on the floods and Rees made a glittering day within the perimeter of the stronghold. He tried to keep his mind on what he must do, tried to forget what could happen to Gordy. But the tightness in him was a physical pain by now.

Now the store rooms! Rees, carrying tools, went to work, making the necessary adjustments to wiring, watched the portal open. Bales, boxes that were the last crop ready to be shipped, supplies from off-world. He tore open boxes, read labels with feverish haste. In the end he brought out his selected loot, rolling two bales into the open before he tore at the sacking bagging their contents.

"Oganna!" Isiga came to him. "What is it that you would do?"

"This." Rees pulled the closely packed leaves apart, the oily drops gathered on their surfaces pasting them together so that separating them was a task. "Spread these around to wall in the 'copter park. Pile them thick."

"Yes," her eyes held the feral spark of a hunting cat's. "Yes!" She snatched up an armload of the stuff and sped away. Zannah pattered out of the shadows, her injured arm in a sling. But in the other hand, she, too, picked up a bundle of the oganna and hurried after Isiga.

The flood lights which made day about the barrier were dimmed here by building shadows. Rees did not believe any Croc watchers could be sure what the activity of the off-worlders meant. Croc eyes did not adjust well to bright light. The enemy must now be considering days and means of putting out the floods.

He went on with his leaves, piling them up, watching Isiga and Zannah working to outline the square on their side. Only directly facing the space before the outer gate did Rees leave a break in that low wall of odorous vegetable material.

"That is the last." Isiga came to him, brushing one hand vainly against the other in a useless try to rub away the sticky oil. She saw the gap and glanced from it to Rees with sudden understanding.

"Do you dare?"

"It is that I must," he told her bleakly.

Her fingers arose to her lips and then she jerked her hand away before they touched her mouth. But those wide feline eyes narrowed.

"Come!" She beckoned him back to the living quarters. There she caught up one of the spider silk blankets. To tear one of those was, Rees had thought, close to impossible. But somehow the Salarika achieved that task, using a knife and her claw nails. She coiled the strips across the table and brought out a basin. Water splashed from the wall tap into that container. Then she knelt before the aid kit, chose tubes and boxes whose contents she had sniffed. Powder and liquid went into the waiting water and was mixed thoroughly by sloshing the bowl back and forth. That done she turned to Rees.

"Your clothing," she indicated the remains of his shirt,

the scuffed boot-breeches, "off. I do not know how well this will protect you but it will be better than nothing at all."

He stripped quickly as she soaked the parts of blankets in the basin. Then she went to work deftly to wind the sopping material about him from foot to neck, leaving the binding of his head, with only a narrow opening for eyes, nose and mouth, to the last. The liquid had turned a bright purple-blue and Rees guessed that he must now present a weird appearance, perhaps startling enough to actually work in his favor as a momentary surprise for the Crocs when he had to face them at the breakthrough. He flexed shoulder muscles, had Isiga loosen the bindings about the upper part of his body, ready for any action he must take.

At a trilling cry from the outside, Isiga looked around.

"They come, Zannah says."

But Rees did not need the small Salarika's warning. The smell was enough—sickeningly heavy. Yes, Crocs were on the march.

"Get to the robo landing, keep under cover!" He gave her the blaster and picked up his own weapon, if one could call a sleek coil of hagger hide rope a weapon.

Isiga dodged out the door, caught Zannah's hand and ran. But Rees' path led him towards the gate. He had earlier marked down his post there and he reached it now after a zig-zag route. So he crouched at last between two of the supporters of the flood nearest the barrier. Crocs would head for that, to douse the light, as soon as they were through the gate.

Hooting—harsh barking. The Ishkurians were certainly making no effort to hide their presence outside, attempting no sneak attack. They must know how few and weak their quarry were. And here they came!

A brown plated head, revealed in detail in the light, raised a snout pointing at the gate as might a hound what had treed a quarry. And, riding on the Ishkurian's shoulders, Gordy! Rees' heart gave a lurch of relief. The child was still unharmed!

The Croc's scaled hands went up, he stopped a trifle to

allow Gordy to slide from his plate ridged back. Rees'
breath came out in a hiss close to Isiga's expression of anger.
That was Ishbi from the mission. No wonder Gordy had
accepted such an escort readily. The native whom the boy
had known as a friend for at least half of his short life, Ishbi
who was a link with his home and family, Ishbi whom Gordy
would now trust sooner than he might Rees himself.

Gordy walked forward confidently. He paused by the
gate to look back and Rees saw Ishbi's head jerk in a movement approximating a Terran nod of encouragement. Other
Crocs emerged into the open behind Ishbi, a wedge of them
carrying some burden. Gordy was to open the gate and they
would insert a prop to keep it so until they could all pour
in. Simple, neat, and it would work. Ishbi had enough familiarity with the mission installations to head straight for the
power and shut off all controls there.

The door in the larger barrier opened and Gordy walked
boldly through. A concentrated rush from the wedge of
hovering Crocs sent a log crashing into that opening. Now
Ishbi, holding two giant slabs of taluc bark on either arm,
took a running leap, skimmed along the log. The taluc bark
smoked and the native threw them from him as he hit the
inner side of the fortress wall. There were others coming the
same path with their temporary shields covering them for
that instant when they must pass the portal and cut the protecting ray operating there.

With the log providing them passage over the ground
wire and the improvised shields, swift and daring runners
could make the passage. However, they were not all to be
so lucky as Ishbi and his first follower. The third native to
make that jump gave a snorting cry as a convulsive leap took
him through, only to lie writhing on the ground. There was
a halt in the advance. Ishbi barked an order and turned to
Gordy.

But the child was staring wide-eyed at the dying Croc.
With a cry he began to back away. Ishbi made a grab for
him and Gordy, looking up, must have seen something in the
saurian countenance looming above him which was utterly

disillusioning. He backed farther, his hands raised as if to fend off the big Ishkurian.

Rees went into action. The rope snaked out in a loop which encircled Gordy and pulled tight. Rees jerked, the distance between them was short enough so that the boy would not be hurt and it was the only way to get him quickly out of Croc clutches.

Gordy screamed, high and shrill, and Rees hauled him in. He held Gordy, rope and all, before the surprised natives were fully aware the Terran boy was out of reach. Gordy, his arms still pinned to his sides by the loop, fought and kicked in Rees' hold, but he was too hampered to break loose.

This was the worst, the dart and dash the Terran must make into the shadow of the nearest building, with two Crocs loose and perhaps more ready to attempt crossing the log bridge now that they were inflamed by seeing their prey directly in view.

Rees cringed within the wrapping bandages as he sped, expecting at any moment as he held to that zig-zag path to feel the bite of an Ishkurian dart in his back. Perhaps it was his weird appearance in that purple covering which gave him a few seconds grace when the Crocs sighted him. If they were expecting a Terran or Salarika to show, then a purple thing of totally alien species would be momentarily startling. And the majority of Crocs were not quick thinkers.

Even so Rees was hardly able to believe he had actually made his first run without opposition when he crouched in the door of the com unit building, Gordy still wriggling and screaming wildly in his hold.

"Gordy!" The young man put his face closer to the boy's, hoping that the sound of a familiar voice, a chance to see his features through that opening in the head bandages would prove his identity. "Gordy, it's Rees, Rees Naper!"

But Gordy had past the point where reason could appeal to his mind, he was completely hysterical. Holding him tight, Rees steadied for another rush. Ishbi leading that in-

vading party was bad luck. The Ishkurian could recognize the guide beam, turn it off and ground the robo. Yet Rees could make no stand here, not with Gordy so wild and without a weapon.

He reached around, pressing the struggling child tight to his chest, and caught up the waiting blanket he had left there. That was also wringing wet with Isiga's preparation. Gordy gave a gasp as Rees wrapped the clammy folds about him, then subsided into a limp weight. Once more Rees broke into the open.

There was a crack behind him and the flood by the gate went out, shattered by some well flung dart. But the ensuing dark was an aid to the Terran now, not a danger. He ran for the 'copter park. Fire, a green-yellow fire ran along the ground there, stiffened into a four walled square of odorous flame. Rees marked the narrow gap before him, knew he must risk the tongues licking out on either side. He measured the distance ahead, put his face down against the bundle which was Gordy, and ran at the best speed he could muster for that slit passage to safety.

Heat scorched his hands, face. Rees raised his head. Isiga crouched in the square, the blaster barrel steadied on her forearm laid across her knee. Rees dropped Gordy, grabbed for the weapon.

"Have—to—get—back," he told her in labored gasps, "must —smash—beam—control."

Her ears were flattened, her lips curled in a cat's snarl of spitting rage. He caught the blaster as she released it. Already the flames from the oganna leaves were fifteen or more feet high, their heat spreading inward. With his palm Rees pushed the Salarika away from him toward the middle of the square. She pulled at Gordy and obeyed Rees' gesture, while the Terran turned again to face the gap, hardly sure now where the opening was.

One arm over his face, the other holding the blaster as tightly as he had Gordy, Rees set himself for another dash. The three would huddle down in the open, covered by wet blankets, hope that the robo would come in before the fire

died. If he could reach the beam and render it safe from intereference, a danger she should have foreseen.

Rees leaped, cried out as he met fire. Then was beyond its breath. His bandages were no longer so wet. A charred strip fluttered free from his waist as he ran.

There ahead a shape moved, shadow against shadow. Rees fired with the blaster ray set on a wide fan, was answered by a hoarse croaking cry. Now he was in the control room, the light on as he had left it. But a brown serrated back, a snouted head, were between him and the panel. Once again the Terran fired, saw flame crisp across the Ishkurian, go on to cut the panel in two. The light in the room crackled and went out. Only the flickering dance of the burning oganna leaves gave any radiance. He had finished the main power set.

But the robo guide beam was equipped with a secondary impulse. And it would continue on that emergency change-over for at least an hour. Time and the duration of the storm would battle for their future. Rees had done all he could to safeguard their one slender hope. It remained for him now to try to save himself. With all controls off the Crocs would stream through the gate unchallenged. But they could not cross that flame wall, not until it smoldered into ashes. And oganna had a long burning period.

Rees slipped away from the control room. The smell of the burning leaves was heavy and aromatic, removing one of his safeguards, the ability to scent the enemy. Croc cries were harsh in the night and then, as if by command, they were suddenly stilled. He thought the natives were combing the buildings, circling that core of flame, attempting to herd their prey inward.

But the Terran still held one advantage, the ability to cross the fire wall, or so he hoped. Hurriedly Rees ran his hand down his body. Those protecting bandages had dried, but they still covered him. And he had no choice, he had to pass the gap for the third time. Death that way, painful as it was, would be better than any the Crocs would deal out to a prisoner.

Now to locate the gap once again. These waves of flame were confusing, and the slit had been a narrow one even in the beginning. To choose the wrong place meant complete disaster.

Behind Rees there was a noise, a guttural grunt. He fired at the sound and ran. Once more he flung his arm up to shield his face as he took off in a leap designed to carry him through the spot he believed was the thinnest in that wall of fire.

Then he was rolling over and over, his bandages smoldering in half a dozen places. When he was really aware of anything beyond the pain and heat, he knew that he was lying flat, most of his body bare as Isiga worked feverishly to tear those charred strips from him. Burns smarted, but he must have been luckly, very lucky.

"Can you move?" The Salarika bent over him to ask. "We must get back out of range."

Rees turned his head and saw what she meant. Darts were arching through the flames, catching fire in the process, to rain down on the pavement of the park. He rolled over and tried to creep out of range, but the pain in his hands, under the pressure of his weight, was too great for him to stand. Somehow Rees got to his feet, leaned heavily on Isiga as she towed him to the blanket heap which was the children. There she pushed him down and held a canteen to his lips while he drang greedily.

"Listen!" Her head went up, ears aprick. Now he could hear it too, the warning landing whistle of the Robo coming in to set down. They caught the green wink of its lights as the flyer made its verticle descent. Rees stood blinking as the tripod feet of the cabin touched the pavement. He wavered forward with an outstretched hand, and then moaned with pain as his seared fingers proved that that vision was indeed real, that they had beaten the nightmare after all.

Seconds later he waved Isiga into the pilot's seat, saw the children huddled behind her.

"They'll have her on robo-beam in reverse," he said. "Use

the lift button, and then the all-clear so the beam can pick us up."

Rees pointed out the proper controls, his hands so painful with the slightest movement that he had to grit his teeth against crying out. But in spite of that torment he smiled weakly as they rose straight out of the hollow of flame into the clean, cool air of the night. The spider had woven webs and caught victims, but not all, not all!

There was going to be a future in Nagassara or off world for them after all. Isiga's hands dropped from the controls as the robo pilot took over smoothly. She leaned toward the Terran, concern in her cats' eyes. But Rees continued to smile as they rode out on the beam lifting to the mountain pass where the day and the future were arriving close upon one another.